Praise for

D0456318

RT Book Reviews Career Achievement Award
Affaire de Coeur Hall of Fame
RT Book Reviews Pioneer Award

"Rosanne Bittner proves time and time again that she is a master at her craft! Highest praise should go to Rosanne Bittner for creating characters that are unforgettable!"

—*Literary Times*

"Rosanne Bittner's stories are powerful because she creates memorable characters who enlighten readers as they rekindle the magical spark that belonged to the first people to love this land."

—*RT Book Reviews*

"Western-romance readers will thoroughly enjoy this."

—*Library Journal* on *Thunder on the Plains*

"Extraordinary for the depth of emotion...Bittner is one of those writers whose talent has grown over the years; that talent truly blossoms in *Wildest Dreams*."

—*Publishers Weekly*

"Excellent, a wonderful, absorbing read, with characters capture the heart and the imagination...belongs on that cial 'keeper' shelf; it's a romance not to be missed."

—Heather Graham on *Outlaw Hearts*

"Rosanne Bittner retains her title as a premier Indian romance writer... Poignant and startling."

—*RT Book Reviews* on *Mystic Visions*

"Filled with suspense and high emotion, quests and visions, this compelling love story is sure to please Bittner's fans and to win over new converts."

—*Booklist* on *Mystic Dreamers*

"A beautiful, spellbinding book; historical fiction at its best... [Bittner is] a true artist at blending historical detail, excitement, and drama."

—*The Lebanon Reporter* on *Mystic Dreamers*

"Powerful, mystical, and eloquent... Historical fiction at its very, very best."

—*RT Book Reviews* on *Song of the Wolf*

ROSANNE
BITTNER

Copyright © 2013 by Rosanne Bittner
Cover and internal design © 2013 by Sourcebooks, Inc.
Cover Design by Gregg Gulbronson

Sourcebooks and the colophon are registered trademarks of Sourcebooks, Inc.

All rights reserved. No part of this book may be reproduced in any form or by any electronic or mechanical means including information storage and retrieval systems—except in the case of brief quotations embodied in critical articles or reviews—without permission in writing from its publisher, Sourcebooks, Inc.

The characters and events portrayed in this book are fictitious or are used fictitiously. Any similarity to real persons, living or dead, is purely coincidental and not intended by the author.

Published by Sourcebooks Casablanca, an imprint of Sourcebooks, Inc.
P.O. Box 4410, Naperville, Illinois 60567-4410
(630) 961-3900
Fax: (630) 961-2168
www.sourcebooks.com

Printed and bound in Canada.
WC 10 9 8 7 6 5 4 3 2 1

One

Wyoming... Mid-May 1886...

Maggie paused to push back a strand of hair, hoping she'd dug the hole deep enough. Lord knew she was accustomed to hard work, but this was the first time the dirt and blisters on her hands came from digging a grave. Worse—it was her husband she was burying.

Shrugging off an urge to give up, she began shoveling again, not daring to stop for too long for fear her arms would give out. She flung more dirt high and to the left, then used her foot to push the point of the shovel into the wall of dirt at one end, starting another wedge in order to carve more soil to make the grave longer. The ground in these western plains didn't give like the soft earth of the old farm back home.

Dig-fling-dig-fling—over and over. With every shovel full of dirt she flung out of the grave she vowed to get revenge on the evil men who'd attacked her and James. Lord knew James Tucker had not been the easiest man to live with, and she'd never loved him the way she suspected a woman ought to love a man, but he'd treated her well. He didn't deserve to die the way he did, and she, by God, didn't deserve what happened afterward. There were moments when she wished that the filth who'd shot James had killed her too, but anger bolstered her determination not to cry or be ashamed.

Finally, groaning with exhaustion, she tossed the shovel up and out of the grave, then collapsed against a dirt wall and studied the length of the hole. *Lord, let it be long enough.* What a horror it would be to bury James all bent up because he didn't fit. And what if his body was already too stiff to bend at all?

Using what little strength she had left, she reached up and grasped the tall grass at the edge of the grave, hanging on as she dug her toes into the sidewall and gradually worked her way up and out of the gaping hole. She rolled onto her back and watched the rising sun turn from a huge red ball on the endless eastern horizon to its full yellow glory, bringing warmth to her aching body.

In spite of warmer weather, the nights were still bone-cold in this high country, and so far, the days still carried a spring chill. It felt good to lie here with the sun on her face. She struggled to banish the horror of last night, reminding herself that she was at least alive, able to breathe the morning air. An inner pride and stubbornness convinced her that what happened to her could not change who she was—Maggie McPhee Tucker, and proud of it. She was not about to let this bring her down.

A puffy cloud drifted by.

James, why didn't you listen to me and take up with a wagon train so we wouldn't be alone?

Grimacing, she rolled to her knees and managed to stand. She walked over to where James lay with a tiny hole in the center of his chest from a gunshot wound. One little hole, and life was ended. How could men be so callous and cruel as those who'd done this?

And after me cooking for those awful men—James offering our hospitality.

It didn't seem right that God allowed such deliberate killers to exist. She prayed she would find a way to make them die like James died. She'd done plenty of hunting with her father back in Missouri. She knew how to track game. It couldn't be much harder to track men, could it?

She headed for the canvas-covered wagon that had brought them this far and managed to find a flour sack among the remnants of what was left after the outlaws looted their supplies. She carried the sack over to where James lay and knelt down to kiss his forehead before pulling the sack over his head. She felt sick to her stomach as she tightened the drawstring around his neck. She couldn't bear to put him in that hole and throw dirt on his face. Once she got him into the hole, she'd throw a blanket over the rest of him before filling in the grave.

James was a stout man… short, big around, with wide shoulders and muscled arms. Moving his body would not be easy, but it had to be done. Mustering every ounce of her remaining strength, Maggie grasped him by the ankles and dragged his body to the side of the grave. She stood back then and judged the hole to be long enough. She could only pray it was deep enough to keep the coyotes and wolves away.

She knelt beside James and touched his shoulder. "I'm sorry, James. I could have loved you more. Lord knows you didn't know much about how to love somebody, but I never turned you away in the night or treated you bad or ever caused you any shame or tribulation. I came out here with no complaint. I don't know if I'll ever go back home, but I promise that before I do, I'll find the men who did this to you."

She rose and prayed the Lord's Prayer, then asked God to take James home to heaven. "He was a hard worker, Lord, and an honest man." She leaned down then and managed to push James into the grave. He landed face down. Refusing to bury him that way, Maggie took a deep breath and climbed into the hole. She managed to turn his body over, then scrambled back out, walked to the wagon, and pulled out a blanket to cover the body. She carried it over to the grave and tried to shake it open, but her fiercely aching arms would not even allow that much movement. She decided then that since James was at least in a proper grave, she could rest for a few minutes.

Lost in utter exhaustion and grief, she wrapped the blanket into her arms and lay down. Her muscles screamed with pain, and raw blisters burned her palms. She broke into deep sobs, hating to feel so lost and alone and afraid. She didn't like weakness. She'd never had room in her life for such things.

Amid the sobs and a battle against dearly needed sleep, she heard the soft thud of horse's hooves. Startled, Maggie's tears left her, and she bolted upright to see a broad-shouldered man sitting nearby on an equally broad-chested horse. He looked down at her, the afternoon sun behind him so that his face remained a shadow under his wide-brimmed hat.

"Ma'am? Can I help you?" he asked in a deep voice.

Maggie jumped up, realizing that she'd been so engrossed in the chore of burying James that she hadn't noticed anyone approaching, never even heard anything. How had he snuck up on her like this? She clung to the blanket and backed away, fear kicking in. Her recent ordeal with other strangers stabbed at her gut, and she turned and ran to her wagon, quickly pulling out an old Sharp's carbine that once belonged to her father. It was the only gun left behind by her abductors. It took all the strength she could muster in her overworked arms to raise the rifle and point it at the stranger.

"What do you want?" she demanded. "I'll have you know I've shot bears with this gun! I know how to use it real good!"

The stranger raised his arms outward. "I asked if I could help. I'm not here to hurt you. It's obvious something terrible happened, ma'am. There's a man dead, your dress is ripped up pretty bad, and your face is bruised."

Maggie realized then that her dress was torn half off in front, some of the skirt ripped away, revealing the one and only slip she'd worn, and showing some of her camisole. She struggled against deep embarrassment.

"I… you… throw your guns over here, and then we can talk," she ordered.

The man grinned a little.

He probably thinks I'm just a silly, helpless thing. "I mean it!" she spoke aloud. "I'll shoot your hat off! Do you want to take the risk of me firing so close to your head? I'm tired and hurting. My aim might be off!"

"Take it easy." The man lowered one hand, gripped the butt of his own rifle, and pulled it from its boot, then threw it aside. Keeping his left hand in the air, he pulled a six-gun from his holster and threw that aside also. "Now, put that thing down and rest. I'll finish filling in that grave for you."

"What's your name?"

"Name's Sage Lightfoot, and you're on my land. You could ride for miles more and still be on my land. This is my ranch—called Paradise Valley. I'm after some men who killed my best foreman and stole money from me. Figured maybe the same men made your acquaintance in an unpleasant way."

Maggie sidestepped her way to where his guns lay, keeping her own rifle in her right hand, while she picked up the man's six-gun and wrapped a couple of fingers into the trigger guard on his rifle, then managed to back away with all three weapons. She threw the rifles into the back of her wagon, but kept his six-gun and faced him with it. She'd never fired a six-gun in her life, and though she hated to admit it, the big man looking at her could probably jump off his horse and get the better of her easily, the shape she was in. He darn well knew it too, but he didn't make his move.

"I suppose they might be the same men," she answered him. She stepped a little closer, able to see him clearly now in the bright afternoon sun. His eyes were dark, set in a finely chiseled face. He was a big man, unusually handsome, and there was an honesty in his eyes that made her feel a little calmer in his presence. "All right. I… I guess I don't have much choice but to trust you… and I could use the help." She finally lowered the six-gun, her arms so tired she simply couldn't keep it aimed at the man any longer. "I'm Maggie… McPhee… Tucker…" The words trailed off as she felt blackness envelop her. The gun fell from her hand, and gravel stung her face as she hit the ground. Seconds later, she felt someone lifting her, then soft quilts beneath her, then more blankets covering her.

"Ma'am, you're in sore need of rest."

Maggie managed to open her eyes for just a moment, long enough to realize she was inside the wagon. All three weapons lay near her. The man left them, apparently, to reassure her she needn't worry about his motives. She heard a horse whinny, and that's all she remembered before drifting into sleep. She would later wonder if it was truly sleep, or if she'd simply passed out from shock and overexertion.

Two

Sage stretched his arms to relieve a slight ache from the repetition of shoveling dirt. He carried the shovel to Maggie Tucker's wagon and set it into hooks at the side of the wagon bed, then made a fire from wood tied to his pack horse. As he unloaded the wood and a sack of coffee beans, his thoughts were on the young woman whose lovely green eyes betrayed her show of bravery when she pointed his own six-gun at him. He could see she'd been as frightened as a rabbit in a foxhole, and from her appearance, he had no doubt what had gone on here.

Now he wasn't sure what the hell to do about Mrs. Maggie McPhee Tucker. Finding and helping her had already put quite a dent in his plans, and now, he was stuck with her. By the time he built a fire and made coffee, Sage detected movement near the wagon and glanced over to see Maggie climbing out. She still clung to a blanket. Her red hair was a tousled mess, her face and hands still filthy, her dress torn. As she approached him, he thought how her tiny frame made her appear more girl than woman, and he couldn't help feeling sorry for her, nor could he control a deep anger at the men who'd abused her in the worst way. No woman deserved that.

He kept his cheroot at the corner of his mouth as she hesitated once she drew near. She studied him as though he were a crouched bobcat, ready to pounce.

"Come have some coffee," he said. "You need it. And, ma'am, if you needed to be afraid of me, you'd know it by now."

She kept the blanket closed to her neck. "I suppose."

"I finished filling the grave. Was the man in it your pa or your husband?"

Maggie glanced at the grave. "My husband." She looked back at Sage. "Outlaws shot him and looted our camp and..." She walked around the other side of the fire, her voice hardly audible. "...and they weren't very kind to me."

"No need to explain." Sage removed the smoke from his lips and poured himself a cup of coffee, taking a sip. "I'm sorry for what happened, especially that it happened on my land. These are men I suspect once worked for me."

Maggie sat on a log across the fire from him. "So, you're pretty sure who they were?"

Sage nodded. "More than pretty sure. I'm damn sure."

Maggie swallowed. "Well, then, I'd be obliged if you'd tell me their names, Mr. Lightfoot, as I intend to find them and kill them."

Sage struggled to contain a snort of laughter at her matter-of-fact statement. Maggie Tucker looked to weigh maybe a hundred pounds at most. "Is that so?"

"Yes, sir. I'm good with my pa's old Sharps, and I

can't let those men get away with what they did to me and my husband. I just need a horse. Perhaps you'd sell me one. I have some money hidden in the wagon that those men didn't find. I can pay you."

Sage couldn't help admiring her. In spite of what she'd suffered, this woman was no shrinking violet. "Ma'am, I would never allow you to ride off with no idea where you're going, or how you'll find those men, or how in hell you expect to get the better of them if you do find them." He poured another cup of coffee and handed it to her.

Maggie took the cup, still eyeing him warily. "What I do and how I do it is none of your concern, Mr. Lightfoot."

Sage rolled his eyes in exasperation. "I just spent close to two hours filling in that grave for you. I cleaned up your camp a little and made you some coffee—and I let you sleep while I did it all because I figured you needed it. You owe me, so sit down, and tell me more about what happened here. Then we'll decide what to do about it."

Maggie looked at the grave again. "I guess I should thank you."

"I guess you should."

She took a sip of coffee. "You said this is your land. I don't see a house anywhere."

"That's because my house is a three-day ride from here."

Her eyes widened. "It takes three days to ride across your land?"

"Actually, about four, if you go beyond the house and to the other fence line. And that's if the weather is good. In winter, it takes longer. Sometimes out here, you don't go anywhere in winter. Snow's too deep." He swept his hand to point out the surrounding horizon. "All this is part of Paradise Valley Ranch."

Sage stuck the cheroot between his lips again, while Maggie drank more coffee. He wondered why she didn't appear to mourn her husband's death, but that wasn't his business. Besides, she was probably still in shock. She shifted restlessly, her demeanor reminding Sage of a nervous colt.

"Tell me more about yourself," he said, "how you and your husband ended up way out here alone. And I still need to know what happened here and what the men looked like."

Maggie wrapped one end of the blanket around the still-hot coffee cup and drank a little more of the stiff brew, then set the cup on the ground and folded herself into the blanket. "The man you helped me bury is James Tucker, my husband for the last four years."

Married for four years? Sage thought she looked barely fifteen or sixteen.

"We're from Missouri—lived there our whole lives. My grandparents came to America from the Scottish Highlands and settled there." She spoke quietly, staring at the crackling fire. "Last winter James decided we'd go to Oregon to farm in the Willamette Valley. He'd heard a lot about the place, what great land was there. The farm we had in Missouri was played out." She pulled the blanket closer. "There were other reasons we left, but mainly, it was to start over someplace new. My pa died, and there was nobody left—"

She stopped mid-sentence and blinked back tears.

Apparently, her loss was finally setting in. Sage waited for her to compose herself.

"James, he was a real independent sort," she finally continued. "He was one to make up his mind quick-like—didn't always think things out. We drove a wagon up to Omaha, then sold it for train fare to Cheyenne, where we bought that wagon over there and a team of mules." She looked at the wagon, then met Sage's gaze. "We left town and headed northeast, but we kind of lost our way. We got held up here because of a lame mule." She paused and closed her eyes. "Three men came along. They weren't very clean, but they seemed friendly enough. They wanted to know if they could use our fire for the night—said they'd been riding for quite a long time. My husband offered to let them eat with us, but after eating our food, those men started drinking. They got kind of wild—said things about me that alarmed my husband. He ordered them to leave our camp, but before he could get hold of his rifle to back up his words, one drew a gun and shot him." She met Sage's eyes again, her own showing utter devastation. "Just… shot him… just like that… point blank."

She turned her gaze to the fire again. A piece of pinewood popped, sending golden cinders upward. She jumped. "I was so stunned that I… well, before I could react… they were on me. When they were through with me, they stole what they needed from the wagon and rode off with the mules. I heard a gunshot after a little while. I expect they shot the lame mule because it would have slowed them down."

Sage wasn't quite sure what to say. He puffed on

what was left of his smoke then threw the stub into the fire. "I'm sorry for what happened."

She nodded, then suddenly jerked her head up and looked straight at him. "I'll have you know I'm a good woman. I was a good wife and true to my man. James had his faults, but he didn't deserve to be shot down like a rabid dog. And what those men did—that doesn't change who I am."

Sage shook his head. "I'm not a man to judge, Mrs. Tucker. I'd never think less of a woman because of something like that, and a bit of a thing like you couldn't have stopped it." He rubbed the back of his neck. "Can you describe the three men?"

"'Course I can. One was kind of fat, bald, maybe forty. Another was young, about my age, I guess. I'm twenty. The third man was older, like the first one. He had a beard and an ugly scar over one eye. All three wore buckskins, and they... smelled bad." Without warning, she suddenly turned sideways and vomited.

Sage got up and walked over to take the saddle from his horse, figuring he'd better unload some of the weight from his packhorse too. He wanted to give Maggie Tucker time to compose herself. He realized the woman couldn't possibly ride anywhere for now, and it was going to be dark in just another hour or so. They were stuck here for the night, and he had to decide what the heck to do with the woman come morning. His insides lurched with fury at what the three men had done, and by her description, he was sure they were the same men he was after. If only he'd caught up to them a little sooner...

"Is there any water nearby where I could wash

off the filth of those men and change my clothes?" she asked.

Sage turned to see she was standing near him. She'd wiped away her tears, smearing the dirt on her cheeks. God, she was small, and she sure didn't look twenty. "I can take you to a stream about a hundred yards from here."

She turned away. "I'd best go alone."

"Too dangerous. There are bears here about—and wolves—and sometimes, a renegade Indian." He reached for a nearly empty canteen. "Besides, I need to fill this." He faced her and read the doubt in her eyes. "Ma'am, like I said, if you couldn't trust me, you'd already know it. I even left my guns with you. So get some clean clothes, and I'll take you to the stream to wash. I'll turn my back and wait. I happen to be a man of my word."

Maggie slowly nodded. "All right. I see honesty in your eyes, Mr. Lightfoot, but something tells me you can be mean as an injured bear when you choose. Either way, I don't have much choice but to trust you."

"That's right, unless you don't want that bath."

Sighing with resignation, Maggie walked to the wagon and climbed inside. Sage followed, telling her to hand out his rifle and six-gun. "I'll be needing them. Can't very well guard you without my weapons."

After a moment of what Sage figured was another doubt-filled hesitation, Maggie handed out his weapons, then climbed out of the wagon with an armful of clothes and a towel. "Let's go."

Sage pushed back his hat, realizing she had a few freckles across her cheeks and nose. "You really twenty?"

"I am."

"You sure don't look it."

"Everybody says that." She looked around. "Which way do we go?"

Sage shoved his six-gun into its holster then shouldered his rifle. "This way." He turned and walked across rocky ground toward the stream.

"Thank you again for what you did—filling in the grave and all," Maggie told him as she followed.

"No problem." Sage scowled. Maggie Tucker's situation irked him. He hadn't been with a woman in a long, long time. Now this one was going to strip naked right behind his back. If circumstances were different…

Mind your business, Sage Lightfoot.

Maybe he should have left her sleeping and gone on without her.

Three

MAGGIE'S NEED TO WASH OVERCAME HER UNCERTAINTY about Sage Lightfoot. He sat with his back to her, and she supposed any man who would fill in the grave of a stranger then calmly sit and wait for her to wake up must be trustworthy. She lowered her naked body into the shatteringly cold creek water and scrubbed with a bar of homemade lye soap that stung her still-raw palms. She didn't care. Every bone in her body hurt, every muscle, every nerve ending. She imagined she was scrubbing away the ugly memories, ridding herself of real and imagined filth.

She bent over and washed the dirt from her hair, fighting an urge to scream at the memory of being shoved down hard to the ground and held there.

She stole frequent glances at Sage Lightfoot, making sure he stuck to his promise of not looking. He was certainly a handsome man, tall and well built, and he was clean. His stubble of a beard showed he was a man who got in a shave as often as he could. The hair that fell from under his wide-brimmed hat to the top of his shoulders was very dark, and she couldn't help wondering if he might have Indian blood. His build and facial features were mostly those of a white man, but when one considered his name and his hair and those high cheekbones…

Back home there were a few Cherokee still around, and many of them looked more white than Indian, but she wasn't going to ask this stranger strong enough to break her neck too many personal questions. She might say something to offend him. Something in those deep brown eyes sparked of danger, showed a man capable of pure violence if provoked. Yet there he sat, respectfully waiting for her to finish, understanding she needed to do this.

Still, respectful or not, she didn't want to be so vulnerable any longer than necessary. She quickly grabbed her towel and dried off the best she could. She wrapped her hair in the towel and scrambled to put on clean drawers, slips, and a camisole. She stepped into her blue gingham dress and shoved her arms into the sleeves, then realized that in her haste and confused state of mind she'd picked a dress that buttoned up the back.

How stupid! Now she had to ask Sage Lightfoot to button it for her. She breathed deeply for courage. "I'm done, Mr. Lightfoot—but I'm afraid I need your help with something."

Lightfoot rose and turned, walking closer. Maggie couldn't help feeling intimidated by his towering presence. She figured he stood over six feet tall, and she doubted there was a soft spot anywhere on his body.

"What is it?" he asked.

Swallowing her embarrassment, Maggie explained.

"I seem to have picked the wrong dress. This one buttons up the back. I'm sorry, but I have to ask you to button it for me. It's only from the middle up."

They stood there rather awkwardly, until Lightfoot cleared his throat and set his rifle against a rock. "Well, ma'am, I can be pretty clumsy at things like that, but turn around, and I'll oblige you."

Maggie turned, hugging the towel to her chest as he fumbled with the buttons. She shivered at the touch of his fingers, but his big hands were surprisingly gentle.

"There you go," he said when he finished.

"Thank you, Mr. Lightfoot." Maggie stiffened when he grasped her shoulders firmly and gave a gentle squeeze.

"Ma'am, you need to relax and stop shaking. You don't need to be afraid of me. I don't know how many ways to tell you."

He ran his thumbs over her shoulders in a way that caused Maggie to feel comforted by his strength. The frightened woman in her, perhaps even the little girl in her, wanted to turn and let him hold her for a moment, just to luxuriate in a feeling of safety and protection. But she couldn't risk this stranger taking such a bold act the wrong way. *Don't trust him*, she reminded herself.

"And call me Sage," he added, letting go of her. "Hardly anybody calls me Mr. Lightfoot."

"If you prefer." Maggie picked up her dirty clothes and her blanket. "And you may call me Maggie." She turned to face him. "I'd like to burn these clothes. I never want to wear them again."

Sage nodded. "I don't blame you." He shouldered

his rifle again and led her back to the campfire, where one by one Maggie held a piece of clothing over the fire until it burned. As each piece disintegrated, she started the next, fearful that if she threw the whole heap on the fire at once she'd snuff it out. Her dress took the longest to burn. She held it over the flames until they nearly consumed it. She jumped back and dropped the dress when the flames reached one of her fingers.

"You all right?" Sage walked over to look at her finger then noticed the deep red blisters on her palms. "From the shoveling?"

"Yes, sir."

"I'll put some bear grease on your hands."

"Bear grease?"

"An old Indian remedy. Smells bad, but it will feel good on those blisters and help them heal. Sit down."

An old Indian remedy? Maggie sat down on her blanket as he walked over to his gear and rummaged in one of his saddlebags, taking out a small, flat tin with a screw-top lid. "You hungry?" he asked.

"Just a little."

He fished a biscuit out of a gunnysack and brought it to her. "My cook back at the ranch house made these three days ago. I don't know how he does it, but his biscuits stay pretty decent for about five days. Might be a bit of a chew, but it's fresh enough that it won't have any worms in it."

"Thank you." Maggie bit into the biscuit, then laid it in her lap and held her hands out when Sage ordered it. He gently applied a light coating of smelly bear grease onto her palms. She noticed his own hands were those of a hardworking man—stained in the creases—the kind of stains that don't come clean with plain washing. He'd need a wire brush to get rid of them. He closed the tin and put it back in his saddlebag, then sat on a rock near the fire. He sighed as he pulled a cheroot from his shirt pocket. "We need to discuss what to do with you," he told her before lighting the smoke.

"Do with me? Mr. Lightfoot—I mean, Sage—you don't need to feel responsible to do anything with me."

He poured both of them another cup of coffee. "I found you, I helped you, and you're on my land. I can't just leave you here alone."

He studied her with those disturbing eyes, and it struck Maggie that part Indian or not, he was more handsome than she'd first realized. Given what she'd been through, she was surprised she'd noticed.

"Are you really twenty?" he asked again.

"That's the second time you've asked me."

"Well, now that you're all scrubbed up, you look even younger than I thought."

Maggie shrugged. "Think what you want. I've been through a lot in these twenty years—worked a farm back in Missouri, married James, lost a child to pneumonia... lost my heart when I put her in the ground... came halfway across the country, and then suffered something no woman should suffer—buried my husband..." Her eyes teared. "I guess that about sums up my life. I've worked like a man most of it. I reckon my pa wished I was a boy because I was the only child him and my ma ever had, so there you are." She wiped her eyes with the back of her hand and looked at Sage, who was studying her intently.

"You're going back to my ranch house with me," he told her. "I'll send a couple of men back here to put a marker on your husband's grave. They can bring extra horses and drive your wagon to the ranch."

"I'm grateful. But as far as going to your house, if you intend to leave me there while you—"

"That's exactly what I intend," he interrupted. "I have some men to find. Taking you to the ranch is going to cost me about a week, but I have a pretty good idea where the culprits who did this are. Once you're ready, one of my ranch hands can take you to the closest town, and—"

"I, too, have some men to find," Maggie interrupted. "I do not intend to go on with my life as though this never happened, not yet anyway. You said the filth who did this sounded like the same men you are after. I want to go with you to find them."

Sage shook his head. "Hell, no."

"I'd be no burden. You can count on that. I can ride. I can shoot. And I'm a good cook. I can keep up with any man."

Sage stared at her for a long, silent moment. "What happened to you last night is an example of why I can't take you along."

She held his gaze with determination. "I didn't have a gun on me. I won't make that mistake again." She stared boldly at him, warning him with her eyes he wouldn't get near her either, if he had such a notion.

"The fact remains you're no match if a man gets the better of you," Sage answered with a scowl.

Maggie looked at the biscuit in her lap. "If you ride off without me, then I'll just follow."

Sage rose and walked a few feet away, staring at the sun sinking behind the western mountains. He turned to face her then.

"The first thing we do is stay here for the night because it's too late. Come morning, we'll head back, and you'll rest for another day or two after we get to the ranch house. If you're still determined to go with me, I'll give you a horse and a packhorse to use, but you'd better keep up, or I'll leave you at the nearest town with enough money to get back on your feet, and maybe go home, or do whatever you think is best. Agreed?"

Maggie gave his offer some thought, then nodded. "That's fair enough, I suppose." Was she crazy to agree to ride off for days, maybe weeks, with a man she knew nothing about? "How sure are you that the men who killed my husband are the same men you're after?"

He closed his eyes, his jaw twitching in an obvious tussle with anger. "Your description fits them perfectly."

"Why are you hunting them?"

"We'll talk about that tomorrow. It's almost dark, and we have a lot of traveling to do, so for now, you'd better rest. I'll keep watch."

Maggie frowned. "Why are you doing all this? You don't even know me."

He removed his hat and smoothed back his thick hair. "Like I said, it's my land this happened on, and it was men who'd worked for me who killed your husband, so I feel responsible. Besides that, I can't very well just ride off and leave you stranded here like a newborn calf without its ma."

She picked up her towel and rubbed her wet hair, trying to dry it out faster. "I'd find my way if I had to." She shook out the tangled red tresses and met his gaze, trying to appear bold and determined, so he wouldn't change his mind.

Sage put his hands on his hips. "I expect you'd do your best to find those men on your own, but I'm not taking that chance and then feel guilty when I find you dead in the mountains. Speaking of which, what do you even know about survival in this land?"

Maggie looked around. Dark shadows stretched toward them as night came on. She remembered that yesterday she'd been contemplating how big this land was—beautiful and wild. "I guess I didn't need to give it a whole lot of thought when I was with James. We were pretty awestruck though—not sure how to get over those mountains."

Sage walked over and sat down again, drawing on his smoke before answering. "There are passes out here that will take you through the mountains, if you know the land, and you don't know it. I guarantee that if you set out after those men alone, you won't survive. It's real easy to get lost in the foothills, let alone in the mountains themselves. Then the elements would do you in… or maybe the wolves, or a grizzly, or a slide down a rocky slope, or a fall over the side of a cliff, or a boulder falling on you, or a renegade Indian finding you, or—"

Maggie held up her hand. "I get it. You're saying I need to be with somebody who knows his way—which would be you."

He took the cheroot from his lips and rolled the

thin cigar between his fingers. "I'm not guaranteeing I'll take you along, but I fear you mean it when you say you'd go anyway."

"We could go on from here."

He shook his head. "You need your rest worse than you think. Besides, we need to get you a horse, and I need to tell my men what happened and send a couple of them back here."

Maggie sipped her coffee. "I hope you're not angry with me for messing up your plans."

Sage took another draw on the cheroot. "You didn't mess up my plans. Those men did." He rose and stepped out his smoke, then took a sheepskin-lined leather jacket from his gear and pulled it on. He grabbed his rifle and a couple blankets, then propped the rifle next to his saddle and spread one of the blankets on the ground. He stretched out on it, resting his head on his saddle. "Finish that biscuit, and get inside the wagon where it's warmer. Get some sleep." Maggie picked up her blanket, shook it out, then walked to the wagon. She took a last glance at Sage Lightfoot to see he'd pulled his hat down over his face. She had a feeling that the man knew exactly what to listen for—that if a wolf came prowling too close... or an unwanted human... Lightfoot would know it, no matter how hard he slept. She suspected part of him belonged to this land as much as the animals that roamed beyond the foothills. It gave her mixed feelings of safety and danger.

She had no choice for now but to succumb to an aching weariness that far overwhelmed any distrust.

She climbed into the wagon and collapsed into a pile of quilts, pulling one of them over herself. She fell asleep wondering if Sage Lightfoot ever smiled.

Four

The wind blasted them with an arresting chill as Sage rearranged supplies on his packhorse so that Maggie could ride it. "You're so small. I don't think your weight will make a whole lot of difference," he yelled above the howling wind. "You do ride, don't you?"

"Of course. I've been riding since I was a little girl."

"I don't have reins for this horse." Sage looped the lead rope over the animal's neck then fashioned it into a makeshift harness. He handed her the extra length of rope. "Use this to hang on, and guide her the best you can. Her name is Nell. She's dependable."

Maggie shivered into a wool coat. She wrapped a shawl around her head and neck. "It was so calm and sunny yesterday," she shouted.

"Yeah, well, that's Wyoming for you. Spring in high country is damn unpredictable. Fact is, I smell snow in the air."

"Snow!"

"Yes, ma'am."

"But it's May!"

"And you're not down South." Sage placed his

hands around her waist and lifted her easily, setting her on the packhorse. "And don't expect the wind to stop blowing, even when it warms up," he added. "It's most always windy in this part of the country." He slid an old Sharps carbine between three ropes on the side of the horse. The gun was one thing the outlaws left behind after raiding Maggie's camp. Her father used it for hunting, and now, Maggie wanted to bring it along for her own protection.

"You said you know how to shoot this thing," Sage told her. "I hope that's true. In this country you never know when you might need it."

Their gazes held for a moment, and Sage realized she understood all too well.

"I've hunted black bears with this gun," she answered. "I expect I can use it on any animal out here... or any man."

Sage felt like an ass for saying anything. He looked away and stuffed his hat tighter around his head. "Hang on!" he yelled as he mounted the lead horse. "Come on, Henry. Let's make time before the snow hits."

He was worried. Sudden snowstorms this time of year could be dangerous. A blizzard could turn a three-day ride into ten if they had to hole up somewhere. He hoped the men he was after were also caught in this. That would hold them up too. If he were lucky, they'd get lost and freeze to death. His biggest worry was getting Maggie Tucker to safety... and hoping his men were able to stick to spring roundup. It was important that they find as many as possible of the scattered herd as quickly as they could. He was concerned mainly for the new calves. A heavy spring snow could bury the fresh grassland and the calves with it.

No amount of snow should last long this time of year, he told himself in an effort to soothe his own worries. He'd lived in this wild land long enough to know when a whopper was coming. He could only hope this one would be short-lived. He headed north, with the wind sweeping against them from the west, howling down the mountains like wolves. Henry balked a little, but the sturdy, dependable horse plodded on, which was why the roan gelding was one of his favorites. He glanced back at Maggie, feeling sorry for the way she hunkered down against the wind, looking so small. She'd been through more in the last two days than any woman should have to suffer in a lifetime. She knew absolutely no one else out here and had nowhere to go, but unlike another woman he'd once cared about, this one didn't complain.

Joanna. What a mistake that was, but it still hurt. Maggie Tucker was a far cry from that woman. He could tell she really meant what she said about finding her husband's killers, and foolish as the idea was, he couldn't blame her for wanting revenge.

Why in hell do you care? He had no answer for that one. After what happened with Joanna, it was stupid to care about *any* woman ever again. Right now, it didn't matter. The weather was worsening. They plodded on, and within two hours, blinding snow cut sideways in front of them, a solid white wall that blocked Sage's vision. He knew how easily a man could get lost in this, even one who knew every inch of the land. He'd known men to die two feet from their own front door, or to ride off a cliff because they didn't know it was there.

One thing he recognized now was Blackberry Wash. He knew it by the rusty red color of the wet sand the horses churned up with their hooves. If he turned west and followed the wash to the black rock formation a half mile ahead, that would lead them into a canyon that would get them out of the wind. In that canyon was a cave where they could take shelter. It was even big enough for the horses.

Damn it all to hell! This storm was making him lose precious time. Then again, he didn't expect to have a lot of trouble finding the men who'd done this, even if he ended up a week or more behind them. There was a time when he wasn't much different from their kind. He could think like them when he had to. They would most likely hide out for a while to the west or to the south along the Outlaw Trail… country he knew well. For now, he turned west himself, into the wind, and followed the red sand. He glanced back to check on Maggie, worried that she was so small the wind would blow her right off her horse, but there she was, bending into the wicked gusts and hanging on. The woman had grit—that was sure.

It seemed to take forever to reach the black rocks. When they finally came into view, Sage followed the wash right into Wolf Canyon, a place rightly named. He could only hope a pack of wolves weren't already holed up in the cave he planned to use tonight. He sat a little straighter as the wind eased within the shelter of sheer rock that now protected them. Still, the howling grew worse as the battering fury whistled hauntingly through precipitous cliffs and crevices above. He stopped Henry and motioned for Maggie to ride beside him so he wouldn't have to scream to be heard. "There's a cave not far ahead where we can take shelter till this blows over," he told her.

Maggie nodded. "Whatever you say. You're the one who knows this country."

They plodded onward until Sage spotted the cave. He urged Henry over layers of red rock and shale, careful to choose the most solid ledges until they reached the cave, which was curved inward to the west, so that when they rode into it, there was no wind at all. Still, it was damn cold.

Sage dismounted and walked over to lift Maggie down from her horse. "We'll have to stay here—probably for the night." He looked around. "I'm glad to see wolves didn't already decide to come here."

"Wolves?"

"This is Wolf Canyon. You'll know they're around come nightfall." He pulled up the collar of his sheepskin jacket, noticing how red her freckled cheeks were. "You gonna be warm enough?"

She danced around a little, huddling into her coat. "Oh, I'll survive. I just need a blanket or two. I'm glad we got a couple of quilts out of the wagon before we left."

Sage looked around, seeing a small pile of wood stacked in the corner. "Sometimes my men use this cave. Trouble is, outlaws like it too. Either way, whoever was here last left some wood. I think with what's here and the bundle we have tied on the packhorse, we can make a decent fire when it gets dark. If we can leave here in the morning, by tomorrow night we'll head into some timberland, so we'll have more fuel for another fire. We'll leave the saddle on Henry and the gear on Nell. They'll stay warmer that way."

Sage untied some blankets and pulled his rifle from its boot. He walked to a spot in the cave where there was soft earth rather than shelf rock. "This is the only spot that isn't hard on your hind side." He tossed Maggie the quilts. "Might as well sit. You can sleep if you want. Nothing else to do. Besides, we'll both need our rest. Likely the wolves will keep us up most of the night."

"Shouldn't we build a fire to keep warm?"

"No. There's only enough wood to make a fire after dark. We'll need it more to keep the wolves away than for our own warmth." He sat near her, wrapping a blanket around his legs and keeping his rifle close. "Nothing to do now but wait this out. I wish I could make something hot, but like I said, we can't build a fire yet. Out here survival comes before comfort."

Maggie shivered and pulled her wool scarf over her face and nose. "It's those outlaws who'd better think about survival… and not from this snowstorm."

Sage looked into her eyes… green as prairie grass, they were. He shook his head.

"Don't laugh at me, Sage Lightfoot," Maggie warned. "I mean it when I say I want those men dead, and I intend to help do it."

"Oh, I have no doubt about that." He didn't want to hurt her feelings, but he wondered how in hell he was he going to protect her on such a journey in wild country. *You're a damn fool, Sage Lightfoot.*

Maggie lay down and curled into the quilts, her back to Sage. He studied her a moment, thinking how much warmer they'd be if they got under those quilts together. He sure wouldn't mind it, but Lord knew she'd probably shoot him with her pa's old Sharps if he even suggested such a thing. He cursed the awkward situation he'd got himself into.

Five

Maggie jolted awake at a snorting whinny from Nell. Henry joined the mare in that kind of screeching cry a horse makes when frightened.

"Get up!" Sage told her, giving her a nudge. He laid a six-gun beside her. "They're here."

Maggie blinked, confused. She sat up, realizing only then how hurt she still was. Every bone and muscle ached, and laying on the cold cave floor the last few hours hadn't helped. The sound of low snarls brought her around to what was happening. She ignored her pain as she jumped to her feet.

Wolves!

"Try to keep the horses calm," Sage told her. "And keep that gun handy. You don't need to hit anything. Just firing it toward the entrance will help, but I should be able to hold them off that way myself. Stay with the horses."

Maggie noticed that while she slept Sage had built a fire near the cave entrance. By its glow she could see shining yellow eyes… several pairs! Fresh horseflesh was mighty tempting to wolves hungry from a long, lean winter. She picked up the six-gun and hurried to the restless, frightened horses. She laid the gun on a nearby rock shelf and grabbed Henry's harness just as Sage fired his rifle into the darkness beyond the light of the fire.

There came several yips and whines, and both horses reared slightly. Maggie took hold of the rope around Nell's neck, hanging on to both mounts as best she could in spite of her own pain. "Whoa, babies, whoa! It's gonna be okay."

"Keep them calm as you can," Sage said, adding another piece of wood to the fire, while he kept a constant eye on the cave entrance. "There's nothing in here to tie them to, and when they're this scared they could bolt and run. Those devils out there will get them for sure then, and we'll be stuck without horses or supplies. It doesn't take much for a man to die out here without his horse."

Restraining two good-sized equines was not an easy task for a five-foot-two, hundred-pound woman who couldn't name one body part that didn't hurt, but Maggie was not about to complain. She'd never had much experience with wolves, certainly not back home. Since coming west her only experience had been hearing them howl in the distant mountains and foothills.

This was different, and she understood now the real danger… and the stories she'd heard about how aggressive a hungry wolf could be.

Sage fired another shot, and Maggie controlled the horses with all her strength. She urged them farther back into the cave, keeping her voice calm.

Henry was the most difficult. His near-deafening whinnies hurt Maggie's ears, and he tugged so hard that she thought her arm would come right out of its socket. She wanted to scream to Sage that the horse might get away, but she was bound and determined to prove to Sage Lightfoot that she could hold her own and would be no bother when the time came to go after the outlaws who'd attacked her. She'd be damned if she'd do one thing to make Sage think she couldn't take care of herself. This was her first test, and she'd damn well pass it, pain or no pain.

Another gunshot.

"Whoa! Whoa! It's okay, big fella." Maggie talked constantly, making up anything she could think of, so that the horses constantly heard her voice.

More growls. More gunshots. A barrage of curses and name-calling from Sage. Somewhere deep inside, Maggie wanted to smile at the adjectives the man used to describe the vicious, snarling, preying beasts that would likely kill her and Sage in order to get to the horses… if not for Sage's constant shouting and gunfire.

"I'm from Missouri," she told the horses. "James and I had to go to Omaha before we came here. You should see it. That was the first time I'd ever been to a big city."

More gunfire. More cursing. More growling. More screaming whinnies. More yanking and rearing and snorting and head-tossing.

"Easy… easy… easy!"

Henry gave a sudden jerk that brought sharp pain to Maggie's left wrist. She nearly let go, but managed to keep her grip.

"At the train station in Omaha there were a lot of other people heading west. They had guides there too, with advice and maps and such," she continued, wondering how long this agony would continue.

More gunfire. More cursing. "...must be twelve or fifteen of them," Sage grumbled. "Now you know why this is called Wolf Canyon. Trouble is, they think they own this place. Actually, they do."

Another gunshot. "Tonight this cave is *mine*, you sons of bitches! And so are these horses!" Another gunshot. A loud whine from one of the wolves. More growls. "Go find yourselves a rabbit." Another gunshot. "And don't be going after my cattle!" Another gunshot.

Maggie hung on, telling Henry and Nell about her trip west, how different this country was from Missouri, how she wished her husband had traveled with a regular wagon train rather than striking off on his own. "I wouldn't be in this mess right now, and James wouldn't be lying in his grave if he'd listened to me. He was real stubborn, James was."

Henry seemed to calm down a bit. She pulled his head toward her and placed her cheek against his snout. "It's okay, boy." She managed to pull both horses farther from the entrance, praying there weren't bats hanging above her head. "James and I didn't really love each other the right way. I guess he wanted a woman to do the cooking and such, somebody to help on the farm." Maggie sometimes wondered how it would feel to be truly loved and adored.

More gunfire interrupted her thoughts. Henry shuffled and reared. When he came down, one hoof landed on Maggie's right shinbone. She cried out.

"You all right back there?" Sage yelled.

"I'm fine!" she insisted. "Whoa, boy, whoa!" Her leg hurt fiercely, but Sage needed to concentrate on the wolves. She'd tell him later about her leg. "I reckon I'm done with men, after what happened a couple nights ago," she continued more softly to the horses. "I've yet to find one who has anything soft about him. My ma died when I was only nine, and she never gave Pa a son, so he worked me like I *was* a son, and sometimes, he'd beat me. James—he was never mean to me, but he was never one to show much affection."

The horses calmed again. Maggie kept talking. Things quieted. After a few minutes, Maggie realized there had been no more gunshots. Soon, the only sound was the crackling of the fire.

"I think they finally gave up," Sage called to her. "I'd hang on to those horses awhile longer though. Are you able?"

"'Course I'm able," Maggie answered. *I think my wrist is sprained, my shinbone is cracked, and every part of me hurts so bad I need to cry, but I'm not about to tell you, Mr. Sage Lightfoot! You'll get no excuse to leave me behind when you go after those killers.* She prayed silently for the strength to hang on as long as necessary.

She began singing a lullaby she remembered her mother always used to sing to her. It had never left her, even after all these years since her mother passed. She remembered her mother was pretty, a small woman with red hair and pretty eyes—a soft voice—a gentle touch. She'd never known much about her—why she'd married somebody as mean as Maggie's pa was. She felt sorry for Louise Tucker. She, too, probably never knew the right kind of love from a man.

"*Sweet Maggie, my Maggie, you're soft to the touch. Let mama kiss you, she loves you so much,*" Maggie sang, realizing her mother made up the song. It was special, just for her Maggie. She wanted to cry at her only memory of gentle touches and loving arms. That was a long time ago, and she hadn't known anything like it since. The only thing that came close was the strange comfort she took when Sage Lightfoot grasped her shoulders so tenderly after he buttoned up her dress. No man had ever touched her that way, with reassurance, and that instinctive signal that she didn't need to fear him.

But then, he could be hard as nails. She reminded herself she knew absolutely nothing about the man, and she'd better be wary. There was one thing most men seemed to want and need an awful lot of, and she wasn't about to give that to any man ever again. James had made it a chore… and the outlaws had made it sickeningly ugly. If Sage Lightfoot decided he needed it too, he'd find a bullet in him!

She kept singing and talking, not sure for how much longer. She wondered if she might be asleep on her feet, or just in a daze from all the pain. A man's voice startled her.

"You can lie back down. I think the wolves are done with us." Sage took the rope and reins from her. "You all right?"

"I… Henry kicked me in the shin, and I hurt my wrist, but I'll be okay."

Sage grasped her arm and pulled her toward the

firelight. He kneeled down and pushed up the skirt of her dress to study a bruise and broken skin on her shin. "He kicked you, all right." He pressed around the bruise. "I don't think anything is broken, but you've got quite a welt here." He rose. "Let me see your wrist."

Maggie pulled away, afraid to appear weak. "I'm fine. Really. But it sure will feel good to sleep a little while. I think I'll bed down closer to the fire. It's so dang cold in here." She forced herself not to limp as she retrieved the six-gun from where she'd left it. "I'll keep this with me in case you need help again staving off more wolves."

She turned and busied herself with moving her bedroll closer to the fire, refusing to think about Sage's touch, his concern for her wounds. She absolutely could not let him see her as frail or unable to cope. Any time she had shown weakness around her father, he beat and belittled her. And James simply expected her to be strong and do her share of the work. He'd allowed no time for nursing aches and pains… not even after giving birth. The next day she'd gone right back to her chores. Men didn't like weakness in a woman, and she doubted that deep down Sage Lightfoot was any different.

She fixed her bedroll near the fire and sat down, laying the gun beside her. She leaned close to feel the warmth of the flames, while Sage tended the horses, talking soothingly to them for a few minutes before sitting down across from her. He kept his repeating rifle next to him and reached out to warm his hands over the fire.

Maggie winced with pain as she lay down and pulled a quilt over herself. How she longed for a real bed, or even the comfort of the extra quilts in the back of her wagon. "Are you sure they're gone?" she asked Sage. "I'll stay more alert if need be."

"They're gone, but I'll keep a watch and give you a nudge if necessary."

"You need to sleep too."

"I've gone all night without sleep before."

"It doesn't seem fair I should rest and not you."

"You've been through hell the last couple of days and nights. And Henry only added to your injuries. Get some rest. You'll get plenty more when we get to the ranch house."

"I'm just fine, thank you."

"No, you're *not* just fine. Quit trying to prove how strong you are. I can see that for myself. And by the way, you did a good job with the horses. That couldn't have been easy for someone your size. You're quite a woman, Maggie Tucker."

Maggie took pride in the remark. "I told you I could hold my own and wouldn't be a burden."

Sage put a last piece of wood on the fire. "That you did, ma'am. That you did."

It was the last thing Maggie remembered before weariness claimed her. Before she fell into a much-needed sleep, she wondered if Sage Lightfoot heard the things she said when she was trying to soothe the horses… about her life in Missouri… about her loveless marriage.

Six

Maggie was never happier to see the sun rise. The long, terrifying night was over, and the light brought no sign of wolves, other than the ones Sage had shot. He shoved the carcasses over a ledge. After drinking down cold coffee and eating one biscuit each, they packed up and left, watering their horses and filling their canteens from Blackberry Wash.

"If it gets any warmer, we'll have to be alert for flash floods," Sage warned.

Maggie couldn't help wondering at how quickly the weather could change in this country—calm one day, dangerous the next, then calm again. Apparently, a serene stream of water could suddenly turn into an angry river with one storm.

Thankfully, last night's howling wind had blown the snow into deep drifts in some places, but left the ground bare enough in others that they were able to travel without too much difficulty. As the sun rose, its light created an array of purple, green, and gray colors on the western mountains, all made more brilliant by a contrast of bright white snow.

If not for the pain that wracked every inch of her body, made worse by the bitterly cold morning, Maggie supposed she could better appreciate the beauty of this land. The mountains were higher and far more intimidating than she'd imagined when she and James first left Missouri. How foolish they'd been to think they could find their way over those imposing rocky peaks on their own. Now, as she and Sage rode along the foothills at their base, the Rockies appeared more formidable than from a distance.

They continued north, sometimes on obvious trails, sometimes up rocky slopes and through narrow crevasses. By noon, the sun warmed the air to the point that Maggie removed the wool shawl from her head, but kept it around her neck.

"How much farther?" she called to Sage.

"We should be home by late tomorrow."

"I'm sorry I've spoiled your plans for going after those men."

"Quit apologizing for something that's not your fault." Sage reined his horse to a halt and let the packhorse amble up beside him. He lit a smoke and studied the trail. "See those trees up there? We'll be riding through timber soon. There's a line shack in those pines where we can take shelter tonight. We might run into some of my men by then, for sure, by tomorrow. Beyond the trees is a big valley."

"Paradise Valley?"

Sage nodded. "That's it. The grass looks yellow now, but within a month or so it will be plenty green—prettiest sight you'll ever see. It took me some rough living to build this place—a few battles with renegade Indians and outlaws—but it's all been worth it. I'm up to about sixty thousand acres and counting. With the railroad going through Cheyenne, I can run my cattle down there and ship them off to the packing houses in Omaha and Chicago."

Maggie noticed a hardness in his demeanor—that hint of a man capable of violence. She wondered if all that land had been obtained lawfully. "No wife to share this with? No family?" she dared to ask. From the angry look that came into his eyes, she immediately regretted the question.

"Almost." He looked away, obviously upset. "She decided she couldn't take the loneliness of life out here." He hesitated and pulled his hat lower. "It's a long story, and this isn't the place or time. Besides, we don't know each other well enough for it to matter."

He straightened in his saddle and was quiet a moment before continuing.

"The men we're after worked for me," he told her, obviously changing the subject. "They were buffalo hunters I'd hired to hunt deer and other game to keep up my food supply. Sounds strange that a man who raises beef needs to hunt for meat, but why kill your own cattle when there's plenty of wild game? We were low on food, and we'd been through a rough winter. I needed every man to help find stranded cattle and to get a count on how many head we'd lost. One day when most of us were scattered on a cattle count, the bastards killed my best hand, an Indian named Standing Wolf. They raped his wife in front of their little boy, then ransacked my house and stole a good deal of money from me."

"How awful," was all Maggie could say.

"Yeah, well, I should have seen it coming, but I was too anxious about dying cattle to pay enough attention to my gut feeling about the sons-of-bitches. Sorry for the hard language."

Maggie noticed the flex in his jaw, and again, she felt the thick hint of violence in the man. "The way other people behave isn't your fault, Sage," she tried to soothe.

"Yes, it is, because there was a time when I wasn't much different from men like that, though I'd never hurt a woman. I've always considered myself a pretty good judge of men. I should have seen right through them. That's what riles me the most."

Maggie studied him, thinking how helpful he'd been so far. "I don't believe it when you say you were like them once."

"Believe it. That's why I know how to track them."

"Why didn't you at least bring some of your own men along?"

"It's roundup and branding time, and like I said, it was a hard winter. Barns and fences need mending. The cattle need to be culled into those that will be sold and those that won't. The ones too weak and sick for any use will have to be put down." He met her gaze again, and there was a chilling coldness now in his eyes. "Besides, this is personal. It's something I have to do myself."

The look he'd given her was unnerving. "Well, I hope you understand that I feel the same way, and that's why I'm going with you. Believe me when I say I can hold my own. I'll not be a burden."

He sighed. "I still need to think about that," he said. He kicked his horse into a gentle trot. "Let's go."

Sage moved his horse forward, saying nothing more as they moved across the wide grassland toward the trees. The horses plodded through deep snow in some areas, their hooves making swishing sounds in the soft grass and deeper drifts.

"When we reach the trees, we'll make camp," Sage called to her. "We'll have some fuel for a fire, and the trees will block any wind that might come up."

Within an hour they headed into a heavy stand of pines. Then it happened. No warning. A grizzly charged out of a thick stand of smaller trees before they, or even the horses, realized it was there. Henry reared in terror. Sage pulled his six-gun from the holster at his hip, but as he did so, the bear lunged, digging its claws into Henry's chest. The frightened, wounded steed twisted away. Horse and man crashed to the ground. Sage rolled away, and immediately, the bear was on him.

Seven

Henry took off running, and the pack mare skittered backward, then reared. Maggie hung on for dear life. "Whoa, girl! Easy!" Nell whinnied and shied even farther away as Sage wrestled with the grizzly. Maggie figured it was a she-bear and that a cub or cubs were close by. She managed to jump off Nell, then yanked her pa's old Sharps from the ropes at the horse's side before the mare bolted away.

"Please, God, help me!" Maggie yelled the words aloud. She brought up the Sharps and aimed, frightened to death that if she fired at the wrong time, she'd hit Sage instead of the bear.

Sage rolled himself into a ball to protect his face and chest. Maggie could see he was trying to unsheathe a knife from where it was strapped near his boot. Once the bear was on top of him again, Maggie squeezed the trigger. The old rifle boomed, kicking her hard in the shoulder. She stumbled slightly but didn't fall.

For a moment, everything went quiet. Then the bear rose and turned, looking straight at Maggie as though dumbfounded. Maggie fired again, aiming right between the eyes. The bear took two steps on its hind legs then fell. A stunned Maggie stared in amazement.

Everything happened so fast it was difficult to take it all in. She'd actually shot a grizzly! She'd shot a black bear once in Missouri, but the monster she'd just put down was many times bigger than anything she'd ever seen back home.

Sage lay still. Panic gripped Maggie as she hurried closer and nudged the bear with her rifle to make sure it was really dead. A bloody hole gaped in its forehead, and the animal did not stir. Maggie wasn't sure where she'd hit it the first time, if at all. Maybe the sound of the gunshot was what made the beast leave Sage and stand on its haunches.

She carefully walked around the bear then hurried to Sage, who'd rolled onto his back, groaning. Maggie gasped at a rip in his scalp and across his chest. Blood seemed to come from everywhere, and the right sleeve of his leather jacket was completely torn off, a large gash in his arm bleeding profusely. Quickly, Maggie ripped at the one slip she wore, tearing off a strip of fabric and pulling away what was left of the jacket sleeve. She wrapped the makeshift bandage tightly above the gaping wound in Sage's upper arm.

"Don't you die on me and leave me lost out here alone, Sage Lightfoot!"

His reply was another groan.

Maggie looked around, realizing the first thing she had to do was get the horses back. She and Sage would die out here without them. "I'll come right back! You hang on!"

Reluctantly, she left him and ran into the open

field beyond the trees. Both horses moved restlessly several hundred yards in the distance, calmer but still skittish. Maggie knew that once she got hold of them she'd have trouble getting them back anywhere close to Sage. They'd shy away again because of the dead bear. She'd have to find a place to tie them upwind from the carcass.

She hurried her stride, wanting to run, but afraid she'd scare the horses off again. She needed a canteen to wash Sage's wounds. Whiskey would be even better. She guessed Sage to be a man who didn't mind taking a swig once in a while, which meant she might find a flask of liquor in his gear.

She approached Henry, talking softly. "It's okay, boy. Nothing's gonna hurt you now." The horse whinnied, its nostrils flaring slightly. He balked sideways. "Poor thing. You were still spooked from those wolves last night, and now this. Remember me? I'm the one who held on to you last night and kept you safe."

She managed to get a little closer then grabbed his halter. "Good boy! You're okay now." She walked him closer to the packhorse, thinking what a good job Sage did tying on the supplies. Not one item had come loose during Nell's rearing and running. The mare hung its head and nibbled at the yellow grass. Maggie grasped the rope harness and led both horses to a spot in the trees. She checked the gashes on Henry's chest. They were already scabbing over, and she noted the horse didn't seem to be limping. She could only pray the wounds were superficial and that the faithful mount would be able to carry Sage to help.

She hurriedly rummaged through Sage's saddlebags

and found a pint of whiskey. "Just as I thought. You do imbibe." She figured she'd better find out if the man was a hard drinker before she left with him in pursuit of the outlaws. From what she'd witnessed of her father growing up, as well as the men who'd attacked her, it seemed liquor had a way of changing a good man into a beast.

No matter now. He could be bleeding to death. She loosened the canteen from around Henry's saddle horn, took a towel from the supplies on the packhorse, and ran back over to where she'd left Sage. He was on his hands and knees, trying to get up.

"Sage, stay down," she called to him. "Let me put some whiskey on those wounds."

He fell to a sitting position, looking at her with bewilderment in his eyes. "What happened?" He tried to wipe blood from his eyes.

"A grizzly was on you before either of us knew it was around," she answered. "Don't stand up. You've lost a lot of blood. I can't pick you up if you pass out."

Sage frowned, looking from her to the bear, then back at Maggie. "You all right?"

"I'm okay." Her hands shaking, Maggie poured some water from the canteen onto the towel, realizing that the urgency of their situation caused her own pain to leave her. "Sit still, and let me wash away the blood so I can see how bad things are. James was attacked by a wild pig once. Oh, man, it was something awful to see, I'll tell you. I swear a wild boar is just as dangerous as that big grizzly over there." She gently washed some of the blood from his face. "If I nursed James through that, I guess I can take care of you too. Soon as we get help, I'll make sure someone tends to Henry. He's got some cuts, but I don't think they're serious."

He grasped her wrist. "Did you put down that bear?"

"Yes, sir. I managed to yank my pa's old rifle from Nell's side as she ran off. That bear hovered right over the top of you, and that's when I fired. I'm not sure where I hit her, but she stood and looked straight at me. I'll tell you, I've never been so scared in all my life as when I realized that she-bear was going to come after me. I aimed for between the eyes and let go. When she fell you'd have thought we were having an earthquake." Maggie uncorked the whiskey. "Hold still now. I'm gonna dump some of this on the gash in your scalp and on your chest and arm."

Sage jerked and gritted his teeth at the sting.

"Sorry." Maggie pulled open his ripped jacket and shirt and poured more whiskey on deep gashes on his chest, then on the bloody bandage around his arm. "We've got to get you to help as quick as possible. You'll need stitches. I'm scared you'll pass out, and I'll get us both lost. Then you'll die, and I'll—well, I don't know what I'll do then. You sit here a spell, get your bearings, and then, maybe we can get you to the horses. They're tied not too far off, upwind of the bear."

With his good arm Sage grabbed the towel and used the damp part to wipe at his face again. "Hold up there." He squinted as a shaft of sunlight hit his face. "Do you mean to tell me you shot that bear? Then you got the horses, thought to tie them upwind, and find that whiskey—" He looked her over in a way that made Maggie a bit uncomfortable. "You're one hell of a woman—more than I even thought."

Their gazes held, and Maggie realized how close they were—that she'd just treated wounds on a near stranger's bare chest. She scooted back. "Well, I take that as a compliment." She handed out the flask of whiskey. "Here. Drink a little." Sage kept watching her as he downed some of the whiskey. She grabbed the flask from him then.

"That's enough. It's one thing for you to pass out from loss of blood—no sense having you pass out from too much drink. Besides, we'll need more of this to put on your wounds again later."

He closed his eyes and leaned sideways against a tree. "There's another flask… in my other saddlebag."

Maggie recorked the whiskey. "That so?"

He stole a sideways glance at her. "Yes, ma'am." He grimaced again. "Don't worry. I can handle my whiskey." His eyes looked glassy. "I think you're right about… these wounds… catching up with me."

"You're losing a lot of blood. We've got to get you away from here before the wolves get a whiff of that dead bear."

Maggie rose. She looked around for Sage's hat, then spotted it lying several feet away. She grabbed it and put it on his head, wanting to keep the wound there covered. "Can you stand? Lean on me, and I'll do my best to help you get to the horses. If you can get up in the saddle, I'll climb up behind you and put my arms around you, so you'll have some support. You just need to stay awake enough to tell me where to go."

Sage got to his knees, then leaned over and groaned. Maggie threw the bloody towel around her neck and shoved the flask of whiskey into a side pocket on her wool coat. She hung the canteen around her shoulder and then grasped Sage by his good arm. "Here. Stand up. We've got to get away from here."

"Hate to… waste good bear meat," he answered. "Too bad we can't… skin that thing and… keep the meat."

"Doesn't matter now." Maggie helped him get to his feet. He leaned on her shoulders, and Maggie almost went down under his weight. Together they stumbled haltingly to the horses. "Just a little more now," Maggie urged. "Try to get up into the saddle, Sage."

Using his left arm, he grasped hold of the saddle horn. Maggie helped him put his left foot in the stirrup. She was worried about his wounded right arm. God knew a man needed his shooting arm in a lawless land like this.

"Come on. We've got to get you to help and get you well, so we can go after those men, remember?"

Sage managed to climb into the saddle, then bent over and nearly slipped back off the horse. Maggie pushed him back up and quickly climbed up behind him. "Hang on to his mane, Sage. I'll take the reins. I just hope Henry is able to keep going too." She gently kicked the horse's sides and urged him over to the mare. She leaned over and untied Nell, holding on to the lead rope and keeping Henry's reins in her left hand. She said a quick prayer that she could keep Sage from falling out of the saddle. "Which way, Sage?"

He raised his head, looked around. "Wind around to… the path we were on when the bear came at us. Head north to get past the bear, then west to find the path again. It's one we… cleared a couple of years ago… cut down a lot of trees, so we could have an easier time… herding cattle through here. By the end of the day, you'll see the line shack. We can… hole up there. Ought to be some of my men around… by tomorrow morning."

"I hope you're right. First, we have to get through the rest of today without you falling off this horse." Maggie urged Henry forward. *God, help me,* she prayed. *And don't let this man die.*

Eight

Maggie could only hope Sage truly did know where they were. Most of the day he lapsed in and out of consciousness as she struggled to keep him on Henry's back and guide the horse at the same time.

"You're a damn good horse, Henry," she soothed, hoping the animal wouldn't balk or possibly even collapse because of the pain of his own injuries. "This is one fine horse, Sage. I can see why Henry's the one you chose for your trip. He's got courage, and he's faithful."

"From here on… you won't need to worry too much about leaving the trail," Sage answered, his voice so weak Maggie could barely hear him. "Henry… knows the way now."

"I hope you're right. I'm worried you don't even know where we are. I'm just following what must be the roadway you told me about."

"Line shack… not far…"

Maggie was afraid to stop and let Sage get down. She worried he might not be able to get back on the horse. At least it was warmer today, but she had no doubt they were in for another cold night. She didn't want Sage sleeping on the ground. It was imperative they reach the line shack by dark. She kept the horses going at a slow walk, so as not to wear them down, letting them stop once to drink a little water out of a puddle.

"Don't… overwater them," Sage warned.

"I know about horses. You just hang on till we get to that line shack."

They rode for another hour, until the sun settled behind the western mountains. With no cabin in sight, Maggie resigned herself to making camp, hating the idea of Sage being out in the cold tonight. She drew Henry to a halt. It was then she squinted at what appeared to be a light in the distant trees. Her heartbeat quickened with hope.

"Sage, look ahead! Is that the line shack?"

Sage clung to Henry's mane with his good arm. He managed to raise his head and looked in the direction of the light. "That's it. Somebody's there. Give me my six-gun, in case… they're not my men."

"You're too weak to hold a gun and Henry's mane at the same time," Maggie answered. "Besides, I doubt you can shoot straight anyway, the condition you're in. You leave that gun in its holster and just stay put. I'll see about this." She reached around Sage and quickly wrapped Nell's lead rope around the horn of Henry's saddle. "Can you stay on Henry if I get down?"

"Think… so."

Maggie wasn't sure Sage was completely aware of his surroundings. She dismounted, unsure how she'd managed to keep going against her own pain, which had gradually returned as she struggled through a long day of riding, while trying to guide two horses and hang on to a man. "You okay?" she asked softly.

Sage looked at her with eyes glazed from pain and loss of blood. "Not right… you taking chances for me. Should be the… other way around."

"You can't help it. Besides, you helped me when I needed it." She couldn't resist touching his arm lightly. She meant it as reassurance to him but found it oddly soothing to her as well.

Praying Sage wouldn't fall out of the saddle, Maggie pulled his Winchester from its boot at Henry's side and cocked the rifle. She limped from reawakened pain in her shin, making her way through brush and trees to a side window at the cabin. She cautiously peeked through a foggy glass pane to see two men inside sitting at a table, playing cards. One was slender, wearing a checkered shirt and leather vest. The other was bald and round. Both needed a shave and looked like they hadn't bathed in a while, normal for men who'd spent several days in the wilds looking for stray cattle, if indeed, that's what these men had been up to. She noticed a whiskey bottle on the table.

Just what I don't need… two drunk men I don't know anything about. She could only hope they were still relatively sober.

Good or bad, Sage needed help. She took a deep breath and walked around to the front door. She kicked at it with her foot. "You men in there work for Sage Lightfoot?" she yelled. She heard chairs scraping on the wood plank floor, heavy footsteps approaching. She backed away and held the rifle steady. The door opened. The hefty man stood in the doorway.

"Who the hell are you?" he asked, a bit wide-eyed at the sight of a woman standing there.

"My name is Maggie McPhee Tucker, and don't think I don't know how to use this rifle!"

The big man just laughed. "Hey, Bill, come over here and see what's standin' on the stoop. It's a little spit of a woman pointin' a rifle at me."

The slender man came to stand at his side. He grinned. "Well, now, ain't you the prettiest thing we've seen in months?" He chuckled. "She's just a kid, Joe."

"I'm woman enough to have shot a grizzly this morning. I don't have time now for small talk. I asked if you men work for Sage Lightfoot."

The big man leaned against the doorsill. "What if we do?"

"Hey!" The slender man frowned. "That's Sage's rifle! What are you doing with it?"

"Well, I guess if you recognize this rifle, you must be one of his men. Sage is out there a ways, about to pass out and fall off his horse. He was attacked by a grizzly this morning and needs help."

The smiles left both men's faces as they quickly shoved past her. "Where is he?" the big one asked.

"This way." Maggie led them to where she'd left the horses, and just as she feared, Sage was on the ground. The two men picked him up and lugged him to the cabin, while Maggie took care of the horses. She noticed a large shed nearby and led Henry and Nell inside, next to four other horses that were unsaddled and nibbling hay from a trough. She began unloading supplies off Nell's back when the heavy-set ranch hand came inside.

"I'll do that, ma'am." He tipped his hat slightly. "My name's Joe Cable. Sage said I should let you rest. Go on inside. There's stew on the stove, if you can stomach Bill's cooking. Sage gave us strict orders to be proper gentlemen."

Maggie wished she knew how much she could trust any of them. "Thank you," she answered. "If you have any bear grease or poultice you could put on Henry's chest, that would be advisable. A grizzly got to him when he reared up—put some pretty good scratches in his chest."

"Yes, ma'am, I'll look after him." Joe hung a lantern on a nail and studied her a moment. "Sage says you saved his life—shot a griz 'fore it could chew him up and spit him out. That's somethin', I'll say, especially for such a little thing like you."

"Well, I pointed my old Sharps and pulled the trigger. The rest was up to God." Maggie suddenly felt light-headed. "It has been a long day. I guess I'll take you up on your offer and go inside." She walked past Joe.

"How'd you end up travelin' with Sage anyway?" he called after her. "And what was he doin' headin' back home? He was supposed to be goin' after some sons of bitches that killed one of the ranch hands."

Maggie turned, realizing Sage had not explained the details of how they met. It was probably best for now. She didn't want the stress and embarrassment. "It's a long story, Mr. Cable, and I'm too tired to talk about it tonight." She wondered how these two and the rest of the ranch hands would look at her once they knew the truth. She held her chin up, reminding herself again that it didn't matter. It didn't change her morals or her pride.

"Bill's last name is Summers," Joe yelled before she reached the line shack.

Maggie could already hear Sage shouting a stream of expletives from inside. She shook her head, figuring Bill Summers must be doing some stitching. She headed inside, not terribly fond of the thought of sleeping in a one-room shack with three men tonight, two strangers, and the third likely to pass out from loss of blood, unable to help her if she needed it. Still, Sage had apparently given orders to treat her right, and she had a feeling his men were not apt to disobey the man.

Nine

Maggie felt removed from herself, a stranger in a strange land, surrounded by more strangers. She couldn't grasp the reality of all that had happened, or that James lay in that grave so far away. She longed to sleep soundly, in a soft bed, free of pain, free of ugly memories that tried to steal her sanity. Maybe once they reached Sage's ranch house she'd at least get the soft bed, and eventually, her injuries would heal. Healing her emotions and thoughts would take much longer.

She spent part of the night helping nurse Sage, who now lay on a travois Joe made from a couple of sturdy limbs from aspen trees and a buffalo hide secured between them. The buffalo hide was taken from the wall of the line shack… *brung this big fella down myself last year*, Joe had told her. *Ain't nothin' much more challengin' than a buffalo hunt, 'cept for facin' a grizzly.*

The man couldn't get over the fact that Maggie had actually shot the grizzly herself. Joe was big and rough, but amazingly kind and respectful, seemingly in awe of the abilities of "such a little thing." *The men are gonna have some fun teasin' Sage about this one*, he'd joked. *His hide saved by a woman.*

The trouble was, Sage's situation was no laughing matter, and Joe and Bill darn well knew it. It was difficult to watch Bill pull a big needle meant for leather through Sage's scalp and through the deep gash on his arm, sewing his flesh together with cat gut. They'd gone through half a bottle of whiskey dousing the wounds in hopes of staving off infection. Sage drank the other half and then some, and Maggie couldn't be sure his unconscious condition now was from loss of blood, or from being passed out from drink.

"Do you think Sage will be all right?" she asked Bill as he and Joe managed to tie Sage onto the travois.

The short, slender man faced her with true concern in his brown eyes. "I reckon if anybody can get over wounds like that, it's Sage Lightfoot. He's the toughest buzzard I ever knew. He was such a bloody mess you probably didn't notice the other scars from an old gunshot and a couple of knife wounds. His toughness comes from the Indian in him." He checked to be sure Sage was secured tightly to the travois. "I swear, human or not, an Indian is harder to kill than a white man, just like wild animals are harder to kill."

So he *was* part Indian, just as Maggie suspected. "What tribe runs in his veins?" she asked.

Bill shrugged. "Cheyenne, I think. He don't talk much about it, and he don't like bein' asked, so I wouldn't, if I were you." He looked her over curiously. "Ma'am, Sage told us not to ask any questions, but I figure if he run into you out there on the trail, then them outlaws he was after did the same. Me and

Joe know what they was like. You ain't complained none, and we're kind of surprised on account of you're limpin' some. You're pretty bruised up. Them men hurt you?"

Maggie turned away, embarrassed. She walked over to Nell. Joe had saddled the mare for her. He decided that Sage's gelding should simply be led by a rope with no weight on him because of his wounds. "They killed my husband, stole our mules, and took a good share of our supplies," she told Bill. "When Sage came upon me, I was burying James." She mounted Nell. She refused to add anything more, suspecting both men had a pretty good idea what else had taken place. "I'm limping because I got kicked by a horse back at Wolf Canyon."

She heard Bill heave a sigh. "Well, ma'am, I noticed you didn't sleep much last night, and I thank you for helpin' watch over Sage. You must surely be bone tired. Sage mumbled somethin' about you bein' up most of the night before last keepin' the horses calm, while he staved off some hungry wolves. Be assured you can rest up good when we get to the ranch house, other than helpin' nurse Sage, and maybe do some cookin' for him. The rest of us will have to get on with ranch work and roundup." He climbed onto his own horse. "I'm right sorry for all that has happened. Sage already told us the location where he found you—said we should go back and get your wagon once we get you to the ranch."

Maggie still could not meet his eyes. "I appreciate that. And if you could put some kind of marker on my husband's grave, I'd be grateful for that too."

"Yes, ma'am, we'll do that." Bill rode up beside her, leading a packhorse. The very hefty Joe rode behind them on a huge black gelding, leading the fourth horse Maggie had seen in the shed the night before. Sage's travois was fixed to straps tied around its belly.

"Main thing now is that Sage doesn't take a bad infection," Bill told Maggie as they left the line shack. "I've seen small wounds take down big men just because they festered into somethin' that ate up their whole body. You'll have to keep a good eye on those wounds and keep them constantly cleaned. Reason I said you'll have to do the cookin' is because the ranch cook is miles away with the cook wagon, way over to the northeast, I expect, where most of the hands are searchin' out the biggest share of the herd. We've lost a lot of them because of the hard winter, but it's not as bad as we thought it would be."

Maggie thought how she probably needed some nursing of her own, but it was natural for men to think that nursing and cooking were a woman's job whenever there was one handy. "I'll be glad to take care of Sage while you men get your work done. He'd want that, and I owe him for filling in my husband's grave and probably saving my life. I don't know what I would have done if he hadn't come along. I am swiftly learning that survival out here isn't easy."

"No, ma'am, it ain't. And wherever you want to go when you're healed, Sage will see that somebody goes along and gets you there safely."

Maggie sat a little straighter, her anger and hatred toward the men who'd turned her life upside down returning with a vengeance. "Where I'm going, Mr. Summers, is with Sage, soon as he's healed enough to go after those men. He's sworn to hunt them down, even if it takes weeks, and I'm joining him. I want to see them dead as badly as he does."

She heard Joe clear his throat and suspected he was forcing himself not to argue the matter, but the more talkative Bill shook his head and spit some tobacco juice before answering her. "Ma'am, that would be a foolish thing to do. You have no idea what men like that are like."

"Oh, I think I have a good idea, Mr. Summers." She stared straight ahead—sure he understood what she was saying.

"Well, I didn't mean it that way. What I meant was they'll head into country where there's more men just like them—country you don't want to venture into, and men you don't want to be around. Sage—he can handle them, but you'd be a real distraction—him worryin' about you and all... let alone the draw you'd be to men like that. Even all messed up and bruised up, like you are, a man can see how pretty you are. Believe me, that will make things real difficult for you and Sage if you go with him into outlaw country."

Maggie refused to let the thought intimidate her. "I've already proven I can handle a gun, Mr. Summers. And nothing can happen that could be any worse than what has already taken place. I'm sure you realize that. I'm not afraid of those men, and I have a right to go after them, and see them die, if I want. I hope to have a hand in killing at least one myself."

Joe cleared his throat again. Bill glanced back at him, and Maggie suspected they were sharing a smile.

"Don't underestimate me, Mr. Summers."

Bill adjusted his hat. "Oh, no, I'd never do that, ma'am. I expect the final decision is up to Sage."

"No, it isn't. It's up to me. If Sage won't take me, I'll follow him whether he likes it or not."

Bill chuckled. "I think maybe you would. Either way, while you're still with us, I wish you'd call me Bill. Mr. Summers just don't feel right. Me and Joe ain't exactly the gentleman types."

Maggie finally looked over at him. "You have both been perfect gentlemen since I met you last night."

"Well, respectful, maybe... but we ain't true gentlemen. You'd faint dead away if you knew all the things we've done in the past... Sage too. He'll be respectful too, but ain't none of us no angels, that's sure."

Joe let out a deep laugh at the remark. "That's puttin' it lightly."

Maggie felt a quick, tiny hint of how ruthless these men could be and probably had been at times. Still, she felt no fear around them, other than wondering how their demeanor might change if they drank too much. She was glad they'd used up most of the whiskey on Sage.

They finally cleared the trees and came into wide, open country covered with yellow grass, like Sage had told her it would be. Again the weather amazed her... a bitter snowstorm the day before yesterday... today, sunshine that actually warmed her through her wool jacket. For the first time since entering Wyoming, the morning brought no wind. She remembered Sage telling her that the wind never stopped blowing out here, and she wondered if the calm would last the whole day or just a little while.

She looked at an extravaganza of clouds that occasionally hid the sun as they moved on the higher elevation winds. Behind them the sky was a brilliant blue, and as always the Rockies loomed to the west, their towering peaks still heavy with snow.

She couldn't help appreciating the grandeur of the landscape, but for her it was a lonely grandeur. She felt small and alone and vulnerable, but she refused to show it. She'd grown up having to be strong, doing a man's work, and forced to hide the softer, womanly side that her father would not acknowledge. James never understood. The only thing that had brought it out in her was her baby girl… but her precious child was dead.

She was starkly alone in an unforgiving land, among rough-hewn men who couldn't possibly understand what she'd been through. She had no one on whom she could rely… no one but herself.

Ten

A fragrant breeze caressed Maggie's face as she and the others rode through a sea of grass heavy from melted snow. Already, she understood why Sage called this place Paradise Valley. Everywhere she looked she saw nature's beauty—colors and smells that soothed the soul.

She guessed that the crop of buildings below the vast slope they descended now was a good mile away. In this open land nothing was as close as it seemed. She and James had learned that lesson the hard way. About a hundred cattle grazed in scattered groups in every direction, and beyond them lay large, fenced corrals, some empty, others holding numerous horses. She could make out a couple of small cabins, a long building that was likely a bunkhouse, two large barns, a chicken coop, and several smaller sheds.

At the center was what she supposed was Sage's ranch house. As they came closer, she could see it was made of logs with a stone front, shaded by a wooden porch that ran along the entire front of the house. It wasn't fancy, but it was obviously sturdy, and much larger than any home Maggie had ever lived in. Everything about it, including a shake-shingle roof, fit the landscape. Out here a home of slat wood or even brick wouldn't look natural. She thought how the house fit the man—rough and sturdy and big… as well as good-looking.

She noticed several rosebushes along the front of the porch. Some looked dead, the rest barely struggling. Rosebushes were not something she'd expect a man like Sage to care about. Planting decorative shrubs was something a woman would do, and she remembered Sage's remark about "almost" having a wife and family. She couldn't help wondering what he meant.

"Nice place, ain't it?" Bill said as he dismounted.

"After living in a covered wagon the last month and spending a lot of nights sleeping on the ground, *any* kind of house would look nice," Maggie answered, wincing with aches and pains as she got down from her horse. "But yes, it's beautiful."

"Sage built it with plans to finally settle—maybe start raisin' a family."

"Thank God it weren't with that she-devil he brung here a couple of years ago," Joe spoke up.

Maggie frowned while tying Nell's reins to a hitching post. "She-devil?"

"Shut up, Joe," Bill warned. "You know Sage don't like anybody talkin' about it. This ain't the time nor the place, and Sage would figure it's nobody's business."

Joe dismounted, and Maggie suspected his horse was quite relieved to be rid of his weight. "Sorry, ma'am," he said as he tied the horse. "I spoke out of turn." He glanced at Bill, and the look they exchanged told Maggie that the woman Joe had mentioned was not someone for whom they had any good feelings. "We'd best get Sage settled inside."

Another man rode up to greet them—a Mexican man Bill called Julio.

"Blessed Mother what happened to the boss?" Julio asked in a thick accent as he dismounted.

"He run into a grizzly," Joe answered, untying Sage from the travois.

"I thought maybe those killers shot him."

"He never got the chance to catch up to them," Bill told Julio. "He came across this lady here buryin' her husband. Turns out them same men killed her man and took off with all their stock and some of their supplies. Left her out there to die. Sage was bringin' her back here to heal when he was attacked by a grizzly." He nodded toward Maggie. "This here is Maggie Tucker, and believe it or not, she shot the grizzly flat dead with an old Sharps rifle."

Julio's eyes widened. "*You* killed a *grizzly*?"

Maggie couldn't help a smile of pride. "I just got lucky," she answered. "Believe me, I was scared out of my mind, and I don't remember taking special aim. I just raised my pa's old rifle and pulled the trigger."

Julio shook his head and climbed down from his horse to help the other two men pick up the travois.

"Go open the door, ma'am, and we'll carry him inside," Bill asked.

Maggie hurried up the steps, across the wide porch to open the door. While the others carried Sage inside to a bedroom, she looked around the great room that took up the entire length of the front of the house—a good fifteen feet wide. Large stone fireplaces adorned each end. At one end sat two large leather chairs, a rocker, and a couple of small tables, a colorful braided rug at the center of the clutch of furniture. A hide from some kind of wildcat hung on the wall above the fireplace.

The other end was the kitchen, with a hutch, a rustic pine table, and hand-hewn chairs. An iron sink with a water pump was built into a long cabinet against one wall. A window placed just above the sink allowed a person… maybe the woman Sage "almost" married… to see outside while she scrubbed dishes. The hutch was filled with neat stacks of white china, finer dishes than any Maggie had ever owned. Some woman's presence prevailed. Maggie figured no home run by only men would have lovely china, furnishings, and conveniences men wouldn't care about.

The kitchen fireplace hearth was quite wide, with cranes on each side holding trammels where a woman could cook in two large pots at the same time, and a grate at the center where a coffeepot could be kept warm. Besides the fireplace, there was a wood-burning cookstove that looked barely used… perhaps a more convenient contraption Sage had brought here for the mysterious "almost" wife. Maggie decided that for however long she might be here, she'd not use that stove. The "almost" wife might come back and be offended to find some other woman using it.

For now, all that mattered was to finally lie in a real bed and sleep. Julio came inside with the two large satchels she'd brought along and carried them down a hallway. "Follow me, and I'll show you where you can stay," he told Maggie.

He headed down a wide hallway located at the center of the back wall of the great room. It led to four more rooms, one of which looked like a sewing room, one a bedroom where Bill and Joe were tucking Sage into a bed, the other two also bedrooms. Maggie could see this house had indeed been built with a wife and children in mind.

The Sage Lightfoot she knew didn't fit any of this… a nice home… a family. From what she knew about him so far, he'd had a pretty rough life, apparently even running with outlaws for a time. Surely somewhere, sometime in his youth, he'd seen some kind of family life, maybe even a loving family, and wanted it for himself… but something had gone awfully wrong.

"You can sleep here," Julio told her, setting down the satchels and nodding toward an iron bed covered neatly with a colorful quilt. Julio nodded toward a curtained doorway. "In there is a dressing room and a place to hang your clothing. There is also an iron bathtub. You can heat some water and take a bath if you like. No one will bother you. At the end of the hallway is a back door, and not far beyond it in the backyard is the privy." He backed out of the room as though embarrassed to be alone in a bedroom with a woman. "I am glad to meet you, Señora Tucker. I hope you enjoy your stay here. We will all help however we can."

"Thank you, Julio." After he left, Maggie walked to the bed and sat down, bouncing slightly to see what the mattress was like. Right now, any mattress would feel wonderful, but this one was better than most, thicker and softer than anything she'd ever slept on. Had it belonged to the mystery woman who'd apparently turned all this down? Had she and Sage slept on this mattress?

As soon as the thought hit her, she jumped up from the bed, amazed she'd even wondered about such a thing. It wasn't her business, and she didn't care. Still, what woman wouldn't be thrilled to live in a fine house like this? Compared to the plain little cabin Maggie lived in most of her life back in Missouri and the not much bigger one she'd shared with James, this house was like a castle. Sage Lightfoot had done a good job building a fine home to raise a family in.

She walked to the dressing room and pulled the curtain aside. There sat the iron bathtub. A couple of dresses hung on the wall. She could tell by their length that Sage's "almost" wife had been taller than Maggie, and the dresses were quite fancy, much finer than the plain gingham dresses Maggie always wore. She touched the lace on one.

From the look of things, the woman who'd worn these dresses had not just been an "almost" wife. She'd lived in this house, which likely meant Sage had been married to her. Maybe he still was… or maybe, they had divorced or split up, and the dresses belonged to nothing more than a fancy prostitute.

Eleven

When the men Joe sent for Maggie's wagon returned with her belongings, the fact that she'd never see James again hit her harder than she'd expected. Her life now was surreal, an adventure that seemed to be happening to someone else. In a sense it was, because she was not the same Maggie who left Missouri to come west.

Myriad emotions kept her awake most nights… her attack… fear of the unknown… and odd feelings of gratefulness mixed with attraction for Sage Lightfoot, who lay recovering in the next room. For nearly two weeks she'd nursed and fed him, wondering if he would even survive when a serious infection settled into his arm. The threat of losing the limb had sent Sage into a tirade of profanity and threats. He'd told Joe that he'd kill any man who tried to amputate. If they put him out first and did it anyway, he'd kill them when he woke up.

The men apparently took Sage's threat seriously. No one again mentioned taking off his arm. Maggie still knew next to nothing about Sage's past, but she could guess plenty, and her guess was that Sage and some of these men had once lived the outlaw life. She had no actual facts, but there wasn't one man on the ranch who wasn't pretty rough around the edges.

Still, probably thanks to orders from Sage, Maggie felt no threat. Bill told her that early on, just like his threat to kill any man who tried to take his arm off, Sage had threatened to take down any man who didn't treat Maggie with respect. She knew that by now, most of them had a pretty good idea of what had happened to her, but it didn't seem to make her any less worthy.

She was actually grateful for the constant care Sage required the first few days. It kept her busy and allowed time for her own healing. When Sage got a little better, he asked Julio's wife to stay at the house with Maggie, so there would be no suggestive talk of Maggie being alone there with Sage. Rosa Martinez Jimenez was a plump but pretty woman who didn't say much, mainly because she spoke little English, and Maggie spoke no Spanish. The two sons Rosa and Julio shared were grown and worked on the ranch, and Rosa often cooked outside for the entire bunch of cowboys who lived at the bunkhouse. The Indian woman who'd been raped had taken her son back to her tribe somewhere farther north, leaving Rosa the only other woman there.

The days turned into over two weeks of nursing, cooking, and doing laundry, and Maggie helped. The busier she stayed, the better she liked it… less time to dwell on the reality of her situation… a woman alone in a strange land amid a bunch of hardworking, but often rather unruly men, who liked to drink up a storm on Friday nights. She had no idea what she'd do with her life now, other than still being determined to go with Sage when he left to hunt down her husband's killers—the same men who'd made off with a considerable amount of Sage's hard-earned money. He'd never told her how much that was, but it was enough to create a real thirst for revenge and a dogged determination to go after them and get his money back.

Maggie stirred another large pot of chicken stew, what was left of a bigger batch she'd made for the ranch hands when Rosa took sick and stayed in bed at the little cabin she shared with Julio. Maggie felt pleased that the men loved the stew and praised her cooking. She wondered if perhaps, when her trip with Sage was over, she could come back here and work as a cook and laundress for a while, until she had some idea what to do, where to go. Part of her was falling in love with the ranch, this splendid home—the Wyoming landscape. She told herself she shouldn't start feeling too comfortable. When Sage Lightfoot was well, and he was now mending fast, he'd probably suggest she settle somewhere in town when all this was over.

Her biggest problem was Sage himself. She'd watched the hell he'd gone through healing from his awful wounds, watched as he grit his teeth against the pain of letting Bill reopen his arm to let the infection pour out of it, the groaning agony of allowing men to hold him down while Bill applied a red-hot piece of iron to the wound to cauterize it. Maggie could still remember the awful stench of burning flesh.

Sage Lightfoot was one tough man, and he had a way about him that made his men respect and obey his every word. If they once rode together against the law, Maggie had no doubt that Sage was the leader of the pack. It was difficult to put the man together—a wild outlaw who now owned a ranch and apparently tried once to settle here with a woman. When she thought about what a nice life this could be, she had to wonder why that woman left. Maybe Sage had a mean streak. Maybe he'd even beat her. As good as he'd been to Maggie when he found her, she couldn't quite picture that, but then a person didn't really know someone until they lived together. Maybe Sage was the type who was kind to a woman until he made her his wife, and then figured since she belonged to him, he could treat her any way he liked.

She filled a wooden bowl with the stew, then took a spoon and towel and carried the bowl to Sage's bedroom to coax him into eating lunch. She walked across the wide plank floor, down the hallway, and through the curtained doorway to Sage's room. To her surprise, he was standing at the window dressed in denim pants, but barefoot and bare-chested, except for the bandages wrapped around his arm and belly. To everyone's relief, he could use his arm quite well now, although it still caused a lot of pain. At the moment, he was raising it up and down, and Maggie couldn't help noticing the way his hard muscles rippled as he moved it, like a sleek, lean horse when it was in motion.

She drew a deep breath, feeling embarrassed at the thought. "You shouldn't be up," she told him. "You're still too weak."

Sage turned. "That's your opinion. Besides, a man doesn't get stronger lying in bed." He walked toward a small table next to the bed, where Maggie set down the bowl. "Is that more of that good chicken stew you make?"

"Actually, it's mostly broth. You and the others already ate most of the dumplings and chicken. I just didn't want to waste what was left."

Now that he was up and around and beginning to act like the Sage she'd first met, Maggie suddenly felt a bit self-conscious as he sat down on the bed to eat. It was one thing taking care of him when he could barely move, but seeing him at full stature and with no shirt on was something else. She was, after all, sleeping in his house. When the men realized he was better...

"Relax," he told her, apparently reading her thoughts. "Now that I'm better, I'll go stay at a bunkhouse the next couple of nights. Day after tomorrow we'll head out, if you think you're up to it, and you still insist on going with me after those men."

Maggie sat in a wooden chair near the table. "If I'm up to it? I can hardly believe *you'd* be up to it."

"Doesn't matter. We've already lost too much time. I'll have Joe pack us some gear, and we'll get this thing over with." He picked up the bowl and drank from it, rather than using the spoon. Maggie noticed that he spoke as though "this thing," which she knew was the killing of three men, was just another of his daily chores. As much as she hated the men who'd abused her, she couldn't look at killing them as just another job to do before going out to brand a steer.

"Well, I'm glad you still intend to take me along."

Sage shrugged. "Hell, I might come across another grizzly." He grinned, a strikingly handsome smile. His teeth were even and white, his smile genuine.

"So, you *do* have the ability to smile."

His grin quickly faded, as though he felt guilty for showing any kind of softer side. "Sometimes." He finished the broth. "Your good cooking must be why I'm mending so fast." He set the bowl aside. "You're a woman of many talents," he added, his dark gaze moving over her with a look she couldn't quite read. "You work hard, you braved a hellish attack without letting it bend you, you can handle a gun, you scrub clothes, and you're a good cook. Bill says you even killed and plucked the chickens yourself for that stew."

"I've killed and plucked chickens since I was about ten years old." Maggie picked up the bowl.

"Don't leave yet," he said when she rose. He nodded toward a dresser on the opposite wall. "There's a tin of tobacco over there—and some cigarette papers. Do you know how to roll a cigarette?"

Maggie set the bowl down and walked to the dresser. "Yes. James smoked too." She found the makings of cigarettes and rolled tobacco into the thin paper as tightly as possible.

"How are you feeling?" Sage asked.

Maggie licked and sealed the cigarette. "I'm fine—well enough to travel, if that's what you're asking." She struck a match and carried it to Sage with the cigarette, then held the match to it as Sage lit it.

Close… disturbingly close… all of a sudden too familiar.

Maggie fanned out the match and stepped back.

"Thanks."

"You're welcome," Maggie answered. Their gazes held for a moment, and Maggie felt a tiny bit of fear—something she couldn't explain—fear, yet not really frightened, if that made sense. She walked back to the dresser, making a pretense of straightening a few things sitting on it.

"You're some woman, Maggie Tucker," Sage commented. "How can I thank you for killing that grizzly? I'm a little embarrassed though. The men won't let me live that one down, but it sure shows me you can take care of yourself when we head out. Still, there's one thing I need to know. Have you ever killed a *man*?"

She stared at the cigarette papers. "Of course not."

"You can change your mind about coming with me if you want to."

I can't let you go riding off without me, she thought. She was already allowing herself to grow used to this wonderful house and the beautiful mountains beyond it... the rich life of living on a cattle ranch... and the thought of being in the company of Sage Lightfoot.

"I'm not changing my mind," she answered. "Even if I don't have a hand in killing those men, I want to see them dead." She faced him again. "But if the matter comes to hand that I need to use my own gun, especially if you're in a bad fix, I'll do it. You can depend on that."

Now came an even broader smile. It only added to all that was raw and masculine about him. Maggie wondered at how she could think such things after what she'd been through. How could a man's physical presence be so horrible on the one hand, yet seem like it could be wonderful… if it was the right man?

"Sometimes you talk like a man, but I swear, when you raise that old Sharps the whole picture is comical. It looks like too big of a gun for you to even lift, but by God, you can do it."

"'Course I can." Maggie pulled out a drawer then began straightening and refolding shirts. "Pa wanted a boy. I learned to adapt."

For a moment, the room felt too quiet.

"How are you at being a *woman*?" Sage asked.

What in God's name did he mean by that? Maggie stiffened, but kept her back turned. "I've never had much chance to be a woman." She wondered if he was testing her. What was he after? Did he think less of her after all… for the vile act those men committed against her? She wasn't about to let that happen! She faced him. "At least not the fancy kind, like the woman who apparently lived here for a time. I'm not like that. I suppose I can be enough of a woman to cook a good pot of chicken stew and make a good apple pie, yet I'm enough man to kill a grizzly and to help you find those outlaws. And if you try anything with me out there on the trail, you'll answer to my Sharps."

He shook his head as he drew on his cigarette. "Don't you know me better by now?"

"I don't know you at all! I'm grateful for you helping me out, but traveling together in good health for what could be weeks is another story. I know you like your whiskey. My pa did too, and he wasn't kind when he drank. I know enough about your background to suspect you have a wild streak that could change everything. You ever beat a woman?"

Sage's eyebrows shot up in surprise, and he actually chuckled. He laid his cigarette in an ashtray on the table. "Maggie, I've been around some pretty wild women, and the one who lived here for a time damn well *deserved* a beating, I'll tell you that. I never laid a hand on her or any other woman—ever. I'm not a man to do that." He ran a hand through his hair. "I only asked about you being a woman because I have a feeling you've never really had the chance to fix your hair fancy and wear a nice dress and really *be* a woman." He rose, looking her over in a way that caused her to avert her gaze.

Maggie walked past him to pick up the bowl.

"I heard some of the things you said when you were keeping the horses calm back at that cave," he told her, "about your pa and your husband. You can be pretty hard-nailed and matter-of-fact. Seems to me you don't know a whole lot about your softer side—and you have one—I've never known a woman who didn't. And it's that softer side I worry about if things get rough out there, and you think you need to look out for me. Shooting that bear is one thing, but bears don't shoot back. Going up against men like the ones we're after is a whole different story. I'm only looking out for your well-being."

Maggie scowled, backing away in an absently defensive move. "Well, you've seen enough to know I can handle myself. What happened to me would destroy most women, but not me! It just made me damn mad. What those men did is just… it's worse than a beating." She hurried past him to a window, studying the distant mountains. "Stop worrying about me having to face those men. You already know I can shoot straight. Think of me as another cowhand along to help you. Just make sure you don't see me as anything but a cowhand. Don't be thinking you can try going after that softer side you think I have."

She heard Sage sigh, felt him walk closer. "I'm no abuser of women," he told her firmly. "Stick that in your head, and remember it. For God's sake, how could you think anything different? If you're thinking I'd try to force myself on you when I get a need on the trail, forget it. I'll save those needs for when we hit the towns in outlaw country. Plenty of women in those places to satisfy a man. Quit worrying whether you can trust me."

Why did the thought of him being with another woman make her angry? Her fury deepened from the humiliation of the comment, designed, she was sure, to deliberately shock her. She refused to let him think it had worked.

"Fine," she answered. "Just so we're clear on the matter." She became suddenly aware of her appearance, wondering how she looked now that she wasn't buried under a heavy coat with her hair a disheveled mess. She wore it slicked back into a bun today, which she knew revealed every freckle on her exposed face. She probably looked like such a kid that he couldn't see her as a woman anyway.

My God, why does it matter? She put a hand to her cheek, a reaction she often had when trying to hide her freckles. "I'm glad you aren't making plans to leave here without me." She turned and finally met his gaze again. "When worse comes to worst, a person just does what he or she has to do to survive. That's why you can count on me."

Sage nodded. "I hope so." He turned and took a shirt from a hook on the wall to his right. "So, what do you think of this place?" he asked as he pulled on the shirt.

Maggie looked around the room. "I think it's lovely—a good, solid house—big enough for a family." She saw the hurt come into his eyes and knew he was thinking about the mysterious woman. Maggie was beginning to hate her. "You have quite a ranch here," she continued. "It's beautiful. I expect there's a lot to tell about how you got to this point in your life, but that's not my business."

"You're right. Meantime, you need to know there's a side of me you haven't seen yet, and you might not like it. You'd better be ready for it if you plan to go after those men with me. It's my temper you'd better fear, and the violence you might witness when I lose it, not against you, but against those men."

"I already figured as much." Maggie heard the front door open.

"Sage?" someone called.

Maggie recognized Hank Toller's voice. Sage's top hand was a short burly man who constantly chewed tobacco, but his friendly personality made it easy to ignore his stained teeth. Maggie hurried down the hallway into the great room. "Hello, Hank. Sage just finished eating." She turned to see Sage behind her. He was buttoning his shirt.

"What is it, Hank?"

"Well, it's good to see you up," Hank replied. He held out an envelope, and Maggie thought Hank seemed a bit upset. Usually, his jovial personality made up for his unkempt appearance, but at the moment, there was nothing jovial about him. "Joe just got back from the monthly mail run to town," he told Sage. "This here is for you."

Sage frowned. "Some kind of bad news?"

"Don't know. I don't read your mail. It's who it's from that's got me worried."

Sage took the envelope and glanced at the return address. "Jesus," he swore. He ripped open the envelope and pulled out the letter inside. "By the way, Maggie and I are leaving day after tomorrow," he told Hank as he read the letter. "Tell Julio to have Smoke and Storm ready, and a couple of pack mules."

"You sure you're strong enough?"

"I wish people would quit asking me that."

Receiving the letter had put Sage in a sour mood. His whole face changed as he read, a distant darkness enshrouding him. Maggie and Hank watched quietly as he finished the letter, then wadded it up and shoved it into his pants pocket.

"What does she want?" Hank asked.

"Something she can't have," Sage answered. "Go on, and tend to your chores. I'm coming to see how things are going."

Hank shrugged. "Whatever you say." He glanced at Maggie and nodded. "Ma'am, that chicken stew is awful good. The boys were wonderin' if you'd make more. Would you have time before you leave with Sage?"

Maggie smiled. "I'll make a big pot before we go."

Hank grinned. "Thanks." His smile faded when he glanced at Sage, who was grimacing with pain as he pulled on some socks he'd left with his boots at the door. "I take it you don't want me to give a letter to Joe to take back?"

"Hell no!" Sage shot back.

Hank turned and left. Maggie felt sorry for him. "You didn't need to be so sharp with him, Sage."

"Don't worry about it." He pulled on his boots, appearing to get angrier as he grunted in pain.

"Do you want some help?"

"No!"

Maggie decided that as dark as his mood was now, she'd better not say another word. She hung a kettle of water over the fire, needing to heat the water in order to wash dishes. She heard Sage's footsteps thump across the wood floor, heard him pull on his jacket, and then jumped when he slammed the door as he went out.

Maggie watched him through the window over the sink. He'd said nothing about the letter. Curiosity got the better of her, and she walked to the table to see who'd sent it.

Joanna Lightfoot, she read in the "from" corner. So, now the mystery woman had a name, and apparently, she was Sage's wife.

Twelve

June 2

Flour, sugar, beans, potatoes, ammunition, rifles, six-guns, a small shovel... *for burying the men we're after*, Maggie thought. Clean underwear, gloves, rope, tin plates and cups, a couple of forks and sharp knives, hardtack, jerky, a lantern, bedrolls, whiskey... *for medicinal purposes*, she mused. Four canteens of water, a porcelain coffeepot, one fry pan, a coffee grinder, sack of coffee beans, bacon, a hammer and nails for repairing a loose horseshoe if necessary, lye soap, a couple of washrags, and towels.

All items were packed neatly on two mules named Sadie and Rosa. Julio had named Rosa because she was *stubborn—like my wife*, he'd joked.

They were leaving today, and Maggie's heartbeat quickened at the secret she was carrying. She was overdue for her time of month. She told herself that maybe the trauma of what happened had messed up her insides and caused her to be late. She couldn't bear to consider the other possibility. Since her last time of month, James had not touched her. They were both too tired from their journey. The baby couldn't possibly belong to James, which left only one possibility. It made her shiver to think about it. Could she love a baby spawned through violence? Did she even want it?

Whatever her situation, if Sage had any idea she might be carrying, he'd put her in jail before he'd let her come with him. She was not about to spring the news on him now, especially since she wasn't sure yet. Still, she felt ill. Was it morning sickness, or just her nerves?

She continued tying supplies onto her own horse. She had decisions to make, and none of them would be easy. She adjusted the belt on the britches she wore. Sage insisted she wear pants, a pair of denims she'd borrowed from one of Rosa and Julio's younger sons who was small built. She brought along two extra pairs, as well as a couple of boy's shirts, everything far too big for her, but Sage wanted it that way. Riding for days on end wasn't something to do wearing a dress and slips, but that wasn't his true reasoning. He figured that from a distance she'd look like a boy, and the loose clothes hid her "feminine qualities," as Sage put it.

Maggie finished tying her share of supplies to the black gelding Sage picked out for her. He was a medium-sized, hardy mustang called Smoke. She climbed into the saddle, more pleased with the pants than she thought she'd be. She decided then and there that all women should be allowed to wear pants when the situation called for it. They were perfect for riding.

She touched the six-gun she wore on her hip, pulling it out and slipping it back into its holster to make sure she could get to it quickly. Sage's blacksmith had done a fine job cutting the gun belt down to a size that would fit her small hips. Feeling eager and confident, she decided not to worry about whether she was carrying. She couldn't think about that right now. A bigger worry was Sage's somewhat precarious physical condition and his ornery mood since he received that letter from his wife… or maybe ex-wife. Maggie was not about to ask at a time like this.

Julio handed her the lead rope to Rosa. Sage took up Sadie's rope and settled into his saddle.

"Thanks, Julio."

The Mexican grinned, showing several missing teeth. "Si, señor. You will ride easy the first few days until you are stronger, yes?"

Sage nodded. "I will."

Bill rode up to them then, greeting Sage. "I wish you'd take one of us with you, boss, and leave the woman here."

Sage glanced at Maggie. "She won't let me." He turned to Bill. "We'll be all right. I need every worker here. There's still a lot of branding to be done, and you need to cull those that should be taken to Rock Springs and on over to Cheyenne for market, plus there are fences to be mended. I'm depending on you to handle things." He put out his hand, and Bill shook it. "If I don't make it back," Sage continued, "you and Joe and Hank can divide this place up however you want."

Bill shook his head. "Won't be the same."

"You can do it. Just don't be giving any of it to Joanna, no matter how much she pressures you."

A look of disgust came into Bill's eyes. "Don't worry about that. She'll never get any of it."

Maggie sighed with the frustration of not knowing the whole truth about the woman called Joanna. "Come on, Sadie." She cooed the mule, kicking Smoke's sides and riding him out of the corral. She stopped to wait for Sage, gazing around the ranch grounds—the sturdy house, the barns and corrals, several hundred cattle grazing on the distant hills. It was all so beautiful. She'd been here long enough to hate leaving this place.

Sage cantered up beside her on a big Appaloosa named Storm. "You ready?"

"Yes, sir."

"Let's go."

As they rode past the outbuildings, Hank approached them from where he'd been culling a couple of steer. His big black horse lumbered close. "You sure you don't want one of us to ride along?" Hank asked Sage.

Sage pushed back his hat and glanced at Maggie before answering with a slight grin. "You men need to stop worrying. I've got a bear-shooter with me. That should suffice."

Hank chuckled, a laugh that—as always—led to a loose cough. He spit out some tobacco juice and turned his gaze to Maggie. "You keep shooting straight, ma'am, and watch your back. I wish you luck finding them men that killed your husband."

"Thank you, Hank." Maggie noticed Hank and Sage share a look that made her a little nervous. She knew Hank and the other men couldn't help but be a bit curious about her and Sage traveling alone together for what could be weeks.

"Take good care of that nice little lady," Hank told Sage with a wink.

Maggie thought how she didn't look like much of a lady now, wearing boy's pants and a sheepskin jacket covering whatever curves that showed under her shirt. She wore her hair in a bun under a wide-brimmed hat, another effort at looking like a boy from a distance.

"We'll be all right," Sage assured Hank. He kicked the sides of his horse and headed through the grassy valley, leading Sadie and scattering cattle as he rode past. Maggie followed, breathing deeply against the butterflies in her stomach. She couldn't help a little secret apprehension, but she wasn't about to back out now. And she was, after all, with Sage Lightfoot. She couldn't imagine any other man with whom she'd be safer when it came to facing the wrong kind of men. She just hoped it wasn't Sage himself she needed to watch out for.

Thirteen

AFTER SEVERAL MINUTES AT A GENTLE LOPE, SAGE slowed Storm to a walk. Maggie rode up beside him. "How can you be so sure where those men are headed?" she asked.

"Just a reasonable guess. They'll figure their best bet is to go someplace where the law won't go, and that's up by Lander or south toward Rock Springs, even into Utah and Green River. We'll go south first. I'm figuring they'll head for warmer parts. We'll check things around a place called Brown's Park. There are canyons and caves—a thousand places to hide. Some outlaws even run their own ranches there—with stolen horses and cattle, of course."

They rode for several minutes at a slower pace. "Did you ever steal horses or cattle?" Maggie dared to ask.

Sage leaned down and jerked up a piece of straw-like grass, then stuck it in his mouth to chew on. "How do you think I started this ranch?" He looked at her and grinned. "I don't care what anybody thinks. It's done, and I live by the law now… more or less."

More or less?

Sage cantered his horse slightly ahead of her again. This was their second day of travel. They made their way south through the same area they'd traveled before Sage's bear attack, and Maggie realized they must be just a day or so away from where James was buried. As though he read her mind, Sage circled his horse to ride beside her.

"We'll veer west soon—head toward Tipton, so we won't go by where I found you… unless you want to visit your man's grave."

Your man's grave… What happened to the woman she was before her attack? *Who am I? What am I doing here? What will I do when this is over?* "No," she answered. "If this is the shortest way, let's keep going. I don't want to go back to that place."

"I don't blame you." He threw down the straw. "Tell me more about yourself, Maggie. Is that farm in Missouri all you've ever known?"

Maggie shrugged. "Pretty much. It was a good distance from any decent-sized town. Every once in a while, my pa would get a newspaper when he did go to town, and I'd read about theaters and fancy stores—things like that."

"How did you learn to read?"

"I went to a little school a mile away three days a week… until my mother died. I was ten. After that my pa made me quit and stay home—do my mother's chores and help on the farm. There was a good neighbor lady about two miles from ours who taught reading and writing and math. She came over once in a while, mainly to bring books so I could keep up on my reading. She never stayed long because my pa didn't like her being there. It kept me from my work."

Maggie thought about that woman, one of the few kind people she could remember from her childhood.

"She was the closest thing to a refined lady I've ever known," she added. "Her name was Matilda, and she was from St. Louis, almost too fancy for the farm she lived on. I guess she loved her husband a whole lot because she left all that civilization to work in the fields."

"That's more than I can say for some women I've known."

Maggie figured he was thinking about Joanna. "Well, I guess Matilda did miss her old life some. I think it made her feel good to teach us kids and show us how educated she was. And her husband let her go back to St. Louis with her family for a week every year. She offered to take me once, but Pa said I was needed on the farm. Sometimes, I wish I'd have run off and gone with her anyway."

Sage reined Storm to a halt. "We'd better let the horses rest for a few minutes. I wouldn't mind one of those biscuits you brought along." He dismounted, and Maggie followed suit. She walked back to Sadie and pulled a couple of biscuits from a gunnysack, handing one to Sage. Because of his height, he cast a shadow over her, a relief from the bright sun.

She turned away and ate the biscuit, hoping that the small bit of food would stave off the nausea that kept visiting her in waves all morning. If she vomited, Sage might think she was weak. She shook off the worry over her condition and studied the high mountains in the distance. "Are we headed for those rocky mountains?"

"We are."

"They look intimidating."

Sage chewed on another bit of biscuit. "They can be," he answered then. "Those mountains remind me of a snorting bull, all brass and threat, daring a man to approach. But a bull can be put down, and so can those mountains, if a man respects them, understands the danger, and is prepared." He finished the biscuit. "We'll get through. There's a place we'll go around called Flaming Gorge. When you see that, you'll know you've seen heaven itself."

Maggie smiled and turned to face him. "Thank you for bringing me with you. I need to do this. Even if we don't kill those men, I need to face them again... show them they didn't beat me down to a sobbing, helpless woman who's ashamed of what happened. I'm not ashamed."

"You *shouldn't* be. I can't wait to see the looks on their faces when they see you're with me." Sage studied their surroundings. "Why don't you take that six-gun you're wearing, and see if you're getting better at hitting something?"

Maggie pulled out the gun, a single-action, forty-five caliber Colt revolver that belonged to Sage. "What should I shoot at?"

Sage grinned. "Sorry, but you do look funny handling that thing." He picked up the reins and ropes to the horses and mules and handed them to her. "Hang on to the stock while I go set up a target." He walked several yards and set some small rocks on a much larger rock. He returned to take hold of the ropes and led the horses farther away, tying them to a bush. "Try hitting those smaller stones."

Maggie supported her right wrist with her left hand because the revolver was so heavy. Wind blew a strand of hair over her eyes, and she paused to brush it away. "Were you telling the truth when you said the wind never stops blowing in Wyoming?" she asked.

"I was, but I should have said almost never. Once in a while, you get a calm day."

Maggie took careful aim then fired. She heard a ping, but none of the smaller rocks moved. "I think all I hit was the big one."

Sage leaned down behind her. He reached around her, supporting her hand with his own. "You jerked it when you fired. Hold it steady, and squeeze the trigger. Don't just suddenly pull it. That makes a handgun move too easy. Shooting this thing is a lot different from that old Sharps of yours."

Maggie tried to ignore the feel of his arms around her, the strength of his hand. She aimed carefully and did as she was told. One of the smaller rocks burst into several pieces and disappeared. "I hit one!" she exclaimed. She turned her head when she spoke.

So close. She felt a sudden urge to hug him, but checked her emotions.

Sage straightened. "Okay, try it on your own."

Maggie cocked the gun and took aim, again supporting her wrist. She squeezed the trigger as Sage instructed. Another rock went flying. She held the gun in the air. "I hit another one!" She danced in a circle.

Sage grinned and returned to the horses. "Reload

before you holster it," he yelled back. "You never know when you might need all six bullets. We'll practice every time we stop. Right now, we'd better get moving again. We have a lot of miles ahead of us."

Maggie did as she was told, wondering what he was thinking when their faces were so close. *Soiled goods, I'll bet… an unrefined farm girl who's had a husband and a kid and been taken by three other men… a freckle-faced, barely schooled spit of a woman no man could really want out of plain, old love.*

Sage walked up to her with the horses. "By the way, when we get to more civilized places, and people see that you're a woman, we'll have to say we're married. You'll be safer that way."

Maggie turned and mounted up. "If you say so. Just don't get any ideas about proving it."

Sage climbed onto Storm with the ease of a man accustomed to long hours in the saddle. "Now that you're learning how to use that side arm, I wouldn't think of it. You're dangerous enough with a rifle." He chuckled as he took off at a leisurely lope.

Lord knows, if you ever touched me gentle-like, Sage Lightfoot, I'd sure never shoot you for it, Maggie thought. Her stomach lurched then, and she quickly vomited, while Sage rode ahead. Thank God he didn't notice. She washed her mouth out with some water from her canteen and hurried to catch up.

Fourteen

The days were long, the nights cold. For Sage the cold nights were made worse by his constant battle with a growing attraction to Maggie Tucker. They'd been on the trail for sixteen days now, and she'd not complained about the heat, the cold, or the hard ground she had to sleep on every night. She knew how to tend the horses, pack the gear, handle a rifle, build a good fire, and cook decent food under rugged conditions. She could lift things no woman her size should be able to lift, and she never asked for help. There was a kind of spark and bravery about her he'd not seen in the pioneer women out here. She was as far a cry from Joanna as anyone he'd come across.

They rode over rocky ground and through high grass, over shale, through canyons, across streams and rivers, and up steep mountain slopes. Sage enjoyed the awe in Maggie's eyes when she viewed the immense red-rock canyon that was Flaming Gorge. He liked that she seemed impressed with this country that he loved—appreciated its beauty and respected its dangers. She learned fast and wasn't afraid of the unknown. At night they listened to wolves howling, and Sage noticed she never seemed afraid when that howling came a bit too close to camp. Even during that night they spent in Wolf Canyon, she seemed amazingly calm as she soothed the horses, while he kept watch for the predators.

"Are there wolves in Missouri?" he asked.

"None that I ever came across, but I suppose there can be wolves anywhere. All I know is you don't hear any howling at night where I come from."

Sage halted his horse to study the horizon—like a far-off rim of the world. "How is it then that you weren't afraid that night at Wolf Canyon?"

Maggie grinned, her freckles looking browner from days in the sun. "Oh, I was plenty scared. I just didn't dare let the horses know it. And you didn't need me whimpering and shivering when you were so busy watching for those yellow eyes in the firelight."

Sage nodded. "You're a straight-thinking woman, Maggie."

"Well, I guess out here, you need to think straight," Maggie answered. "Even back home I had to think about survival. Farm work isn't easy. And my pa would only beat me harder if I cried or complained."

Sage hated the thought of the hard life she'd led. He couldn't help wondering if she'd ever known true gentleness, ever wore a really pretty dress and went dancing. Long ago, he'd known a good life… when he was much younger and had a place to call home… until the reality of his heritage had slammed him in the face and taught him about surviving on his own. The only time he thought he had a chance at living a normal life again was when Joanna came along, but she'd destroyed that dream quick enough.

Now, here was Maggie Tucker, as different from Joanna as she could be, the kind it took to put up with life out here. The fact that she'd apparently been abused as a child and then lived in a loveless marriage worked on his thoughts every night. He didn't quite know what to do with these feelings because he'd vowed to never, ever let himself care about another woman again. Whores were the only kind he dared deal with. You could use a whore and then leave without worrying about feelings. Feelings could get in the way of a lot of things, and right now, he needed to avoid them if he was going up against men like those they were after. Feelings could get in the way of thinking fast and staying alive.

They neared a small ranch near Brown's Park, where Sage knew stolen stock was kept. Beyond this place lay some of the most lawless country that existed in the Rockies, other than up north at Hole-In-The-Wall. From here on, he needed to think like the men he was after, and that meant not caring about anything but staying alive and protecting his own back… and Maggie's. The thought of the bastards who'd abused her getting their hands on her again stirred a rage deeper than what he already felt for what they'd done to Standing Wolf and his wife.

He pointed to the scattering of buildings and corrals in the valley below. "The last I knew, that place was run by a man named Buck Kelley. In the sixties and seventies, he hunted buffalo. Of course, I didn't know him then—didn't meet him till after the money in buffalo hunting dried up, and most of the buffalo were gone. He turned to cattle rustling because back then it was good money, and for the most part, you could get away with it. Ranches had sprung up all over the place, so the pickings were easy. Buck and I rustled a lot of stock."

He saw the questions in Maggie's eyes. She was still trying to figure him out… was he good? Or bad? Sometimes Sage didn't know the answer himself. "I bought out my share of Buck's operation about five years ago," he continued, "including two good breeding bulls and eight cows. That was enough to get me going on my own. I've never had too much trouble with other rustlers, at least not those who knew who I was. They knew enough to leave me alone or suffer the consequences."

He pulled a cheroot from an inside pocket of his jacket as Maggie scanned the lush, fertile valley below. "It's pretty down there."

"Pretty, but full of men who'll give you a good look-over when we get down there, so don't forget you're my wife. You're wearing a wedding band, so that will help." He regarded her with amusement. "And Lord knows, you aren't terribly fetching in that getup," he teased.

She raised her chin. "I don't care to be fetching," she answered. "Not to any man for a long time."

Sage lit the smoke and drew on it to get it burning. "Well, Maggie, the men who live down there don't need much to get them excited. A new face is always something of interest. Don't take too much for granted because you aren't all gussied up. Some men want only one thing."

Sage regretted the words as soon as he spoke them.

"I am aware of that," Maggie answered coldly, staring straight ahead.

"I didn't mean to wake up the pain of it." Sage straightened in his saddle. "Buck up. We've got visitors..."

Maggie noticed that a few men were heading up the steep grade toward her and Sage. "By the way, I don't know the names of the men we're hunting," she told Sage. "That night... everything was too horrible for me to remember if they even called each other by name." She pulled up on Smoke's reins when he slipped a little on some loose rock. "Take it easy, boy."

Sage replied with the thin cigar sitting at the corner of his mouth. "The fat, bald one is Cleve Fletcher. The ugly one with the beard and a scar over his eye is Jasper. I don't know his last name. The young one called himself Jimmy Hart and thought he was good with a gun. I aim to test him on that when I find him."

"And the men headed up here? Will you know any of them?"

"Not likely. Those who ride with a leader, like Buck, come and go. He could have all new men riding with him by now, but it's likely Buck isn't around now. That's why we need to be careful. Just take it easy, and follow my lead no matter what. Don't go doing something stupid on your own, like pull that six-gun, or go for your Sharps. Understand?"

"I understand. The only men I care to pull a gun on are those who attacked me. I've got no quarrel with any others."

"Not yet you don't." Sage spoke the words as he watched the four riders come closer.

Fifteen

WET SOD SPEWED FROM BENEATH HORSES' HOOVES AS the rough-looking men made their way up the grassy slope, still soft from a recent snowmelt.

"Don't make a move," Sage told Maggie.

Maggie swallowed, anxiety tempting her to pull out her old Sharps. The men bearing down on them were no less menacing than the grizzly she'd shot. None bore a resemblance to those who'd attacked her, other than the fact that they weren't cleaner or less mean-looking. One was a big-bellied man who reminded her of Hank Toller. She wondered how his horse managed to keep up with the others, what with the weight it carried.

The second man looked pure Indian, his black waist-length hair flying in the afternoon breeze, a bandana tied around his forehead. He wore a heavy fur vest, and Maggie could see crisscrossed gun belts under it, packed with enough ammunition to fight a small war. In addition to that, a huge knife hung from one of his belts.

The third man was ordinary in looks—plain,

mousy brown hair that dangled in curls from under a stained hat. He wore a wool coat that looked too big for him.

The fourth man was built tall and strong, much like Sage, but he was fair, with steely blue eyes and blond hair that Maggie figured would look even lighter if it didn't need washing. He wore a long, black coat, under which Maggie had no doubt he carried more than one weapon.

Sage casually puffed on the cigar as the men rode within ten feet of him and Maggie. With a sideways glance Maggie noticed Sage nod. "Afternoon, gentlemen."

"Who the hell are you?" the blond man demanded.

"Name's Sage Lightfoot. I'm not here for trouble. Just looking for Buck Kelley. He still around?"

The fat man sniffed. "How do you know Buck?"

"Rode with him once, about five years ago."

"Buck ain't around no more," the fat man answered. "Broke his neck when a mustang he tried to bust threw him against a fence post. He's buried down below."

Sage straightened. "I'm sorry to hear that. He was a good friend."

"And that means you have no friends left here," the Indian spoke up, turning his dark gaze to Maggie. "What you doing comin' here with a woman you hide under men's clothes?"

"You the law?" the fat man asked before Sage could answer the first question.

"I already told you I was good friends with Buck Kelley, and he sure as hell didn't hang out with lawmen. Besides, what lawman would ride into a place like this with a woman along?"

"Then why is she here?" the Indian asked—then grinned. "You wanting to trade her for something?"

All four men laughed and whistled. The fat one looked Maggie over with unnerving hunger, and the Indian sneered. "I think maybe you will trade the woman whether you want to or not," he told Sage with a haughty grin. Sage's forty-five caliber was out of its holster so fast that Maggie never saw the movement. "This woman happens to be my *wife*," he growled, aiming the gun at the Indian. "Lay a hand on her, and you'll join Buck down there beside his grave!" He scanned the lot of them menacingly. "I'm looking for three men who killed a friend of mine and stole money from me." He glared at the big Indian again. "I lived with your kind long enough to know how to handle the likes of you, so don't piss me off. Fact is—I *am* your kind. Remember that!"

Maggie shivered. Everything about Sage spelled ruthless. He seemed no less dangerous than the Indian who glared back with pure hatred.

"Calm down, Lightfoot," the blond-haired man spoke up. "Around here we have to make sure what kind of man is riding in."

"Well, now you know, so tell these men to keep their eyes off my wife, or their guts will be slop for the pigs come morning."

The apparent leader of the bunch nodded. "It's done." He turned to the other three. "Ride back to the house. Tell Betsy to put on some food for these two, and get out a bathtub for the woman here."

The fat man and the curly-haired man left with scowls on their faces.

The Indian stared at Sage a little longer, obviously summing him up. "I think maybe I will go back and take a *cold* bath," he snarled. He yanked his horse around and rode off.

The blond man held his arms at his sides then. "I'm not going to use a gun, mister," he told Sage. "You can put yours away."

Sage slowly released the hammer of his revolver and slid it into its holster.

"Name's Whitey," the blond man told Sage. "The fat one is Stu. The one who rode beside me is Bo—a friend for years. I don't know their last names. The Indian, who I'll probably end up killing someday unless you beat me to it, is called Cutter." Maggie thought about the knife the man wore and felt a bit light-headed. The blond man nodded toward her. "What's her name?"

Sage took the cheroot from his lips. "Maggie," he answered for her.

Whitey took his smoke from his lips and flicked off ashes as he turned his horse. "Well," he called, "you're welcome to come down to the house. Betsy is a good cook." He looked at Maggie and grinned a bit sheepishly. "I, uh, hope you won't be offended by Betsy. She kind of belongs to all of us, if you know what I mean." Maggie couldn't imagine how any woman could share a bed with any of the men she'd just met. This was indeed a world she knew nothing about, but Sage seemed to know it well.

"We're obliged for a meal and maybe a bed for the night," Sage told Whitey.

"You've got it." Whitey turned back around.

"Don't worry, ma'am," he called out to Maggie. "Nobody will harm you."

He rode on down the hill, and Maggie pulled her coat collar closer around her neck. "I wish I could believe that," she commented.

She caught up with Sage. "You pulled that gun awful fast. It was kind of unsettling to see how quick you are with it."

Sage said nothing. Something about him was different… dark… still seething… an outlaw. "Is it really true that you're their kind?"

"I already told you that. You've been warned."

Maggie could see that "other" side of him wasn't going to go away soon. It was a side she wasn't familiar with… and it scared her.

"Just keep doing as I say, and don't make my job harder than it needs to be," he continued. "Don't forget that I didn't want to bring you along in the first place. What just happened is an example of why having you with me makes tracking those men more difficult."

"Don't take what happened out on me," she grumped. "I appreciate your skills, but it kind of scares me, now that I've seen the kind of men you used to ride with."

Maggie instantly regretted her words. Sage halted his horse and looked at her. It was as though she'd slapped him in the face. A surprising hurt passed quickly in his dark eyes, replaced just as quickly by a stiff pride.

"You saw it in Bill and Joe and the others back at the ranch too," he seethed. "Men can change, Maggie, and sometimes, they were good to begin with. Men like those down there were born bad and *won't* change. You have to know how to tell the difference out here. If those men see one weak spot in me, they'll jump on it, like a wolf on an injured rabbit. And believe me, you could be carrying an *arsenal* of guns, and they'd still get to you! Our best bet is to make sure they believe you're my wife. If they figure any different, then in their minds I have no real claim on you. Do you know what that means?"

Maggie stiffened. "I understand better than most." *You bastard!* Part of her wanted to scream, part of her wanted to cry. She didn't like this Sage Lightfoot.

Sage closed his eyes and rubbed the back of his neck. "I guess you do," he said quietly. He circled his horse. "Look, Maggie, you need to trust that I know men like those down there, and I know how to deal with them. You can't let anything I do cause you alarm over being with me."

Maggie looked away. "I guess it was the look of that Indian. I never saw anybody who looked more menacing, not even in the eyes of the men who..." She faced him again. "Could you... I mean... can you really take on somebody like that Indian if you have to?"

Sage's countenance completely changed. He actually laughed, shaking his head. "Jesus, you're something." His horse skittered, and he reined it to a halt. "I can take him on, as you put it. *Bet* on it!" He rode ahead again. "Think what you want of me, Maggie. I told you what it would be like if you came along," he called back. "And don't be surprised by anything that's said or done when we get to that cabin. Trust me."

You're a complex man, Sage Lightfoot. "I'd feel a lot better if I could figure out whether you're bad or good," she said. *I haven't seen you drunk yet.*

"You'll know by the time we get back to Paradise Valley."

That was sure. She'd seen his quick temper, and she'd been warned. She couldn't help wondering how furious he'd be if she told him she was carrying... all the more reason she needed to hide that fact until this was over. She was one hundred percent positive now. Too much time had passed, and every morning brought nausea that so far, she'd been able to control in front of Sage. Her belly wasn't any bigger, and even if it were, it wouldn't be noticed because of the way she was dressed. She remembered her first pregnancy didn't show for a good four months.

My little Suzie. Her precious girl lay buried back in Missouri... all alone... so tiny. Her baby had shown her the only real love she'd known in her life, other than what she remembered of her own mother. She longed for that kind of love again... pure, simple, forgiving, affectionate, sweet. More and more, she wanted the baby growing inside her now, but first she had to survive this trip and keep her secret from Sage through it all. He was enough like the men below that his attitude toward her might change if he knew the truth. She'd seen how quickly he could change, and even his good side could be intimidating at times.

Lord knew, nothing in her life had taught her she could trust any man completely.

Sixteen

Once Sage described the men he hunted, Bo and Whitey recognized them as three men who'd come by the ranch asking to sell three mules.

Maggie's mules, Sage figured. Maggie stayed in an adjoining room, an offer from Whitey that Sage welcomed. He wanted her away from the prying eyes and thoughts of these men.

"I traded one good riding horse for the three mules," Whitey told him.

"Which way did they go?"

"North."

That surprised Sage. "Not south?"

"Nope. That was about five or six days ago. They didn't seem to be in a hurry. I expect you have a good chance of catchin' up with them."

Sage took a drag on a fat cigar Whitey offered him. "Maybe they figured I'm not coming after them. They seem to be taking their time now."

"Could be," Bo commented.

"I'll leave in the morning."

Whitey nodded. "Out here, men don't rat on each

other, at least not without getting paid for it. In your case, the information is free because it was your wife they mistreated and not some no-account woman."

Sage tipped his chair back and rested the sole of one foot against the edge of the table. "I appreciate that. So does my wife."

The woman named Betsy reached down to take away his empty plate.

"Good steak, Betsy," Sage told her.

She leaned closer so that her very exposed breasts were near his face. "I'm good at a lot of things, mister."

The others snickered.

Sage met Betsy's blue eyes—eyes that showed a woman who'd lived a hard life. God only knew how she'd ended up this way. "No offense, Betsy. You're a fine-looking woman, but I do have a wife in the other room. I'd like to thank you for fixing that bath for her."

Betsy patted his face. "No problem, honey."

Sage put his chair down and leaned over the table to get Betsy's voluptuous cleavage out of his face. There was a time when he'd readily take advantage of her offer. What made matters worse was that before this night was over, he'd have to share a bedroom with Maggie. Sleeping on the open ground was one thing, but being together in a small room with a woman he was beginning to want while she lay right beside him in a soft bed was another.

"Break out the cards, Betsy," Whitey ordered. "And bring over another bottle. We're gonna take this newcomer for whatever he's got in his pockets."

"Might turn out I'm the one who's richer in the

morning," Sage shot back with a grin, trying to keep things jovial.

"We'll just see about that," Stu answered sullenly, still miffed about being threatened earlier with Sage's forty-five caliber. Sage judged Stu would need watching the rest of the night, but his bigger worry was Cutter. The Indian left before he and Maggie reached the cabin, and he hadn't come back.

"You boys deal while I check on my wife," he told the rest of them, momentarily putting out his cigar. He walked into the bedroom to find Maggie sitting at a dressing table in a flannel nightgown. She was brushing out her long, thick, red locks, and the sight was almost more than a man could take.

Maggie quickly put down the brush as Sage closed the door. She grabbed a robe Betsy had given her. "You could have knocked."

Sage put fingers to his lips to warn her to speak softly, so those outside the room wouldn't hear them. Then he stepped closer and kept his own voice down as he answered her. "What do you think those men out there would have thought if I had to knock before entering my wife's bedroom?"

Maggie shook her hair loose from the robe and tied the garment tightly. Sage noticed she could practically have wrapped the thing around herself twice—she was so small compared to Betsy. "I came to check and make sure things are okay in here," Sage added.

Maggie sat in front of the dressing table again. "It felt good to take a bath, I'll say that."

Sage could hardly stop staring. This was the prettiest he'd seen her. He wished she could always wear her hair down like that instead of the bun she kept it in. "I bet it did. Is there anything you want me to tell Betsy to get you? Coffee or something?"

She looked at him strangely. He could swear he saw something close to jealousy in her eyes.

"No, thanks, but from what I heard, there are other things she'd gladly help *you* out with," Maggie answered in a rough whisper. She turned and started brushing her hair again.

"That bothers you?"

Maggie laid down the brush. "Well, we certainly wouldn't look like the happily married couple if you cavorted in another room with a whore now, would we?"

Sage grinned. "No, ma'am."

"And if those men think you care so little about me, they might get ideas."

"Which is exactly why I turned Betsy down."

Maggie looked at him in the mirror, studying him with obvious distrust. "That's the only reason?"

Good God, does the woman have feelings for me? "What's wrong with you, Maggie?"

She closed her eyes. "I'm sorry. I don't know *what* to think when I see and hear how you interact with men like those in the other room, let alone with that Betsy."

He sighed with irritation. "I told you how things would be out here, and you swore it didn't matter. If what happened to you is going to get in the way, you'd better get out soon as we reach a place where I can put you on a stage back to Rawlins."

"No! Please don't!" Maggie picked up the brush and turned. "Please don't go drinking so much that you get ideas when you come back in here tonight," she added. "I don't want to worry… I mean… I know drinking can change a man. It used to make my pa real mean, and *you* can get real mean without even taking a drop of liquor."

The air hung silent for a moment. When Sage said nothing, Maggie added that he'd have to sleep on the floor when he came back. "I'll leave a pillow and blanket for you."

"Gee, thanks." Sage turned to leave.

"Sage," Maggie said.

"What?"

I'm carrying. That's why I need to sleep. "Please say you understand."

"Oh, I understand, all right. What I *don't* understand is why you think you need to tell me all this. Why don't you trust me? You've trusted me just fine up to a few hours ago."

She nodded. "I know, but you weren't… you weren't in this kind of situation… around men like those from your past."

"I *told* you, the men at the ranch *are* from my past, and you had no trouble trusting me *or* them."

"I know." She sighed and rose. "I guess… Sage, my whole life has been turned upside down. I hardly know what to make of it or how to abide by men like those out there. I don't know how you could have lived like this and then built such a beautiful ranch and settled." She took a deep breath. "I have to ask you, Sage. Are you married? I couldn't help seeing the return address on that letter you received before we left. Joanna Lightfoot."

Sage's brow deepened in a scowl. He hated how complicated women could be. He hated even more talking about Joanna. "She was my wife, but not anymore." He studied her eyes, realizing he often felt dangerously lost in their green depths. To his shock, it hit him that Maggie Tucker had enough feelings for him that she was jealous of Joanna, and of women like Betsy. For such a little thing who'd had no experience with men other than the obligations of a dutiful wife, she had a way of looking right through a man… maybe all the way into his heart, which of late, had begun beating through the wall he'd deliberately built around it. "Maggie, don't do this."

She blinked. "Don't do what?"

"Don't look at me like you are right now."

She turned away. "I was thinking how much I wish… I wish you could hold me, just for a minute. I'm scared, Sage. Please don't take it wrong, but… I'm grateful for your strength and protection, and I want to be sure you won't turn back into a man like those out there. Sometimes a woman needs some reassurance, if that makes any sense."

Against his better judgment, Sage walked up behind her and wrapped his arms around her shoulders. "I'd never go back to behaving like those men out there," he told her. Her hair smelled clean. She felt so small in his arms.

Maggie gripped his forearms. "Thank you… for bringing me along and all."

Jesus, Sage, let go before things go too far. He pulled away and gave her shoulders a reassuring squeeze. "Get some rest now. We have a lot more riding to do tomorrow."

He moved farther away and folded his arms. "Whitey and Stu saw the men we're looking for. They traded your mules for a horse, then headed north."

"North?" Maggie turned to face him. "Then we've gone right by them!"

Sage shrugged, glad for the diversion from the feel of her in his arms. "It's a big country, Maggie, and they obviously took a different trail. The point is they're trying to throw us off by backtracking. Then again, they're taking their time, so they might not suspect I'm on their tail at all. Taking so long to get started might benefit us." He grasped the doorknob.

"We'll leave early morning. Right now, I'm sitting in on a card game, just to keep things on a friendly note and to keep my eyes on those men till they go to bed. So don't be alarmed by how I behave or what I say."

He walked out, upset over the fact that he was starting to care way too much for Maggie Tucker.

He sat at the table and poured himself a shot. "Deal the cards, boys."

Seventeen

Sage tried hard to hide his foul mood. Too much whiskey, mixed with having to sleep on the floor while Maggie enjoyed the luxury of a mattress, led to an aching back and a headache. He could swear the hard ground was more forgiving than a wood plank floor. The only benefit was that being uncomfortable helped him keep one eye and both ears open for any attempt by someone from the other room to come inside. Whitey kept his promise that no one would bother them, but Cutter never did come back. That gave Sage a very uneasy feeling that led to a miserable, sleepless night.

He headed north on a straighter path that would keep them about a hundred miles east of Paradise Valley as they backtracked. They would literally ride right past the ranch. His intended destination was Hole-In-The-Wall, a place he knew well. If the men he hunted hoped he'd give up, they'd find out different. He had to make this right for Standing Wolf's sake… and now, for Maggie too. He arched his shoulders, again remembering that hard floor. "Sleep good last night?" he asked Maggie with a hint of sarcasm.

Maggie rode beside him rather than behind him. Again, she remained mostly hidden under pants, a wool jacket, and a man's hat pulled over her red locks, which were tied into a tail and tucked inside her jacket.

"Slept just fine," she replied, obviously aware he'd not enjoyed the floor.

"I know. I heard you snore." Sage kept an eye on the rocky outcroppings to their left, still worried about Cutter.

"What? I don't snore!"

"Oh, yes, you do."

Maggie laughed. "Why haven't I heard *you* snore yet?"

Her laughter warmed his heart. She seemed more relaxed today, probably because she was relieved to learn she had nothing to worry about last night. He'd not gone near her, a feat that turned out to be much more difficult than he'd expected.

"You haven't heard me snore because I always sleep with one eye open," he answered. "I never get to fall into a truly deep sleep… which reminds me… Cutter never came back last night. He's all Indian, which means he can be around without a person knowing it."

"Will *you* know it?"

"I'm not sure. It's been a long time."

"A long time since you lived like an Indian, or since you were around such men?"

"Both."

They rode quietly for several minutes before Maggie spoke again. "So you did live with Indians once. Dare I ask what tribe?"

Sage frowned. That was something else he didn't

care to talk about, and the mood he was in this morning, he found the question annoying. "I'd prefer we changed the subject."

"Okay. How old are you?"

"Old enough to have experienced just about everything a man can experience in life... and yet too young for all of it. I'm thirty."

"Have you ever seen a really big city? James and I got on the train in Omaha. That's the biggest city I've seen. We didn't live all that far from St. Louis, but neither my pa or James took me there."

More silence. The only sound was the creaking of their saddles and the occasional huff and snort of one of the horses.

"I lived in San Francisco for almost ten years," Sage finally answered.

"San Francisco!" His answer surprised her. "Is it true they have fancy opera houses there, and men walking around with gold in their pockets?"

Sage snickered. "Some do, I suppose—the ones who live on Nob Hill."

"How was it a man like you lived in a big city for so long?"

He shrugged. "Long story."

"Lord knows, we don't have anything else to do the next few days but talk. You told Cutter that you lived like him once. And you've already admitted to living with outlaws. You've been married. You run a big ranch. And now, you say you've lived in San Francisco. That's a lot of living in thirty years."

"Leave it alone, Maggie. I'll explain sometime when I'm in the mood, and I'm not in the mood."

"Don't get angry again. I don't like you when you're angry."

"And I don't like *being* angry, so quit asking so many questions."

Maggie trotted her horse farther ahead. "Are you still mad about sleeping on the floor?"

"That's another question."

She looked back at him. "Either way, the next time we get in a situation like that, I'll let you have the bed."

"Your thoughtfulness overwhelms me, but it will be a while before that happens. It's the hard, cold ground again for the next couple of weeks."

Maggie trotted Smoke back beside Sage. "Do you really think we'll find those men?"

"We'll find them. When someone betrays me like that, I don't let it go." The remark brought memories of Joanna—how she, too, had betrayed him. There was a time when he would have enjoyed wringing her pretty neck.

"I won't give up either," Maggie told him. "Whatever I've had to do in life, I never gave up. Mostly, I never gave up hope that things would somehow get better."

"I suppose that's a good way to—"

Sage's words were cut off by the whirring of an arrow that came so close the feathers at the end of the shaft brushed his nose. It all happened in a split second, and the next thing he knew, Maggie was screaming from an arrow in her thigh. She grasped her leg, trying to hang on to a startled Smoke. Storm also sensed the danger and reared slightly.

"Hang on!" Sage knew he had to act fast, before another arrow pierced him or Maggie. He grabbed Smoke's reins and charged toward a rocky incline to their left. He urged the horses higher, onto a ledge where a large, flat, overhanging rock hid them from whoever was above. He leaped down and pulled Maggie from her horse.

"Shit," he said. "It's Cutter! Lie low, and hang on to the horses the best you can. I've got to find him!"

"Don't leave me!" Maggie pleaded. "Oh, God, it hurts!"

"I can't help you till I kill that sonofabitch!" Sage propped her into the recesses of a pile of huge boulders and put the reins into her hands. "I'm sorry, Maggie. I'll come back. As long as you don't tug on that arrow, there won't be much bleeding."

She dug her nails into his arm. "What if he kills you?"

He took her six-gun from the holster she wore and laid it in her lap. "Try to stay alert, and keep this handy. I know you're in pain. I'll be back!"

Sage yanked his rifle from its boot and headed higher into the rocks.

"Sage!" Maggie screamed. "Don't go!"

The plea cut into him, but he knew he had no choice. That arrow was surely meant for him, and poor Maggie suffered for it. Apparently, Cutter was not as adept with bow and arrow as he was with his knife. Trouble was, both weapons were silent, so he had nothing to go by in locating the man. Cutter could be anywhere up here. He had to find him—and fast! Maggie desperately needed his help.

Eighteen

MAGGIE COULD NOT CONTROL HER SHAKING. THE PAIN in her thigh was excruciating, and the sight of the arrow sticking out of her leg only made the injury more terrifying. What if Sage didn't make it back? What horrible things would Cutter do to her with his knife? Even worse, what would he do to her before he killed her? Either way, if neither man returned, she'd have to lie here and slowly die alone in the wilds of Wyoming. No one but the buzzards would find her body.

"Sage!" she screamed again. Would Cutter kill him? It hit her hard then how deeply she would mourn his death, even more deeply than her husband's death. If that was a sin, then so be it, but bad or good, she realized she was in love with Sage Lightfoot, and there was no getting around it.

"Sage!" she yelled again, yet she knew she wasn't yelling at all. Her strength was fast leaving her. "I love you," she said softly, no longer able to raise her voice. She leaned her head against the boulder behind her and closed her eyes, listening.

Gunshots! They came from somewhere up in the rocks. She struggled to remain conscious, counted the gunshots… four… five… six… seven… eight. Everything grew quiet then. At some point in her weak condition, she'd let go of the ropes to the horses. Surprisingly, they remained nearby, although every time a gun was fired, their ears would perk up, and they whinnied and skittered slightly. Maggie tried talking to them and wished she could grab hold of the reins again, but the pain in her leg was too intense to get up.

Surely Sage would be all right. He told her he could handle someone like Cutter. He was strong and sure and able. He knew men like Cutter. Still, why was it so quiet? Had Cutter won? Was he slicing open Sage's throat and preparing to come for her? She clung to the six-gun Sage left with her, but she was so weak and dizzy she wasn't sure she could raise the weapon and fire it.

Maybe Sage was right in saying she shouldn't have come along on this journey. Maybe her presence was only making his job harder and putting him in more danger. If they hadn't been talking… if she hadn't asked Sage so many questions… he would have been more alert, maybe aware of Cutter's presence.

Her thoughts wandered, her vision blurred. Then, suddenly, pain ripped through her as someone jerked her up. Whoever it was tore the gun from her hand. She screamed in agony as a strong arm moved around her from behind.

Cutter!

The man grasped at her breast. "Now, you and me will have some fun, huh?"

Oh, God, Sage must be dead! She'd barely finished the thought when something broke the light in front of her. Maggie's vision cleared enough to see Sage standing there, his forty-five caliber in his right hand, rifle in his left. It looked like he was bleeding from his lower left side.

"Sage," she whimpered.

"Let her go, Cutter!" Sage growled.

"I think I *will* have my way with your woman before slitting her throat."

Maggie could see Cutter raising his right hand, aiming his gun at Sage. Everything happened as though in a strange dream. She had no idea how much time passed—a fraction of a second, she supposed. She saw the flash from Sage's gun, felt the bullet whiz past her right ear, and heard Cutter cry out. The man's grip on her weakened. Finally, they both fell to the ground. Maggie groaned from the awful pain in her thigh. She saw Sage come closer. He reached beyond her then dragged Cutter away by his long black hair.

"Let's see how you like the feel of your own knife slitting your throat!" Sage seethed.

Maggie watched Sage yank Cutter's knife from its sheath. Cutter's eyes were huge, his teeth gritted against pain. Sage kept hold of the man's hair and jerked his head back, slashing the big knife across Cutter's throat. Then he rammed the knife into the man's heart, yanked it out, and kicked Cutter's body over the ledge. He stood there a moment then—panting—watching Cutter's lifeless body tumble. At last Maggie knew what Sage meant when he told her she might be surprised by his dark side.

He threw the knife away and wiped sweat from his eyes with his shirtsleeve, then looked down and touched his bleeding side. He seemed to just realize he'd been shot.

"You're hurt," Maggie muttered. "I… can't… help you."

His dark eyes, still on fire with fury and ruthless revenge, met her gaze. He stood there briefly, as though to gather his thoughts and rid himself of the shroud of hard, angry darkness that enveloped him. "I think the bullet went right through," he said. "It's a flesh wound."

In a daze, Maggie watched him grab the horses to calm them. He took something out of his saddlebag. Gauze. He removed his shirt then wrapped the gauze around his middle. Maggie noticed the burn scar on his right arm where Bill had cauterized the bear wound. He was barely mended from those terrible injuries, and now he'd taken a bullet to protect her.

"I've got to take care of this to stop the bleeding," he told Maggie. "I'll be no good to you if I pass out on you."

"What if you… die?" Maggie asked. "Maybe we'll both die… out here."

"I'm not going to die, and neither are you," Sage answered briskly, tying off the gauze. He shoved what was left back into his saddlebag and came over to kneel beside her, studying the arrow.

"It hurts something awful, Sage. And when you pull it out, it's gonna bleed bad."

"I know."

Maggie cried out when he touched the area around the wound.

"I'm sorry, Maggie, but I have to figure out what to do about getting the arrow out. From what I can tell, it went through the muscle, but I don't think it hit the bone, which is good. I'm really sorry, but I've got to break off one end and push the shaft through your leg. You'd better drink some laudanum first."

"I'm so sorry, Sage. If I hadn't insisted on coming... this wouldn't have happened."

Maggie felt her strength and consciousness waning.

"Don't talk." He got up and walked to the horses again. Maggie watched his back muscles ripple as he took a brown bottle of laudanum from his gear and brought it to her, kneeling beside her again. "Drink some of this. Soon as you feel good and groggy, I'll get the worst over with. I might have to cauterize it before we're done, but if I can get the shaft out of there and wrap it good, I can get you someplace where you can rest better. There's a cabin not far north of here, if I remember correctly. It used to be deserted. If we're lucky, it still is." He leaned down and helped Maggie choke down some of the laudanum. She coughed and grimaced.

"I know it's awful," he said, stroking her hair. "But you'd better drink a little more. I want to spare you all the pain I can."

Maggie managed another swallow, and in minutes she felt her senses leaving her. She never realized until she thought he'd surely been killed that she'd want to die if something happened to Sage Lightfoot. "Did you hear me tell you that I love you?" she asked. Oh, God, did she really say that? Why couldn't she control her words?

Sage didn't answer. She felt him ripping at her trousers around the wound. Then came the horrible pain as he grasped the shaft of the arrow and broke off the feathered end. She hadn't drunk enough laudanum to kill the agony, and she passed out.

Nineteen

Maggie awoke with vague memories of being carried in a man's arms, while she sat sideways in front of him on a horse. She remembered how warm and safe she felt, remembered no pain… until now. She cried out as she came fully awake to realize she lay on blankets on the dusty wooden floor of a ramshackle cabin that had grass growing through the floor. Broken boards at one end of the roof left a hole big enough to shed a ray of sunlight inside. The minute she moved her leg even slightly, she groaned with pain. She lay still then, slowly taking in her surroundings as the wind outside rattled the cabin's shaky walls. She lay near a stone fireplace, where a fire burned for warmth.

One thing she'd learned in this land was that no day was the same. It was a little colder again, but if memory served her right, they'd moved into higher country as they headed for the South Pass. That would explain the weather. She pulled a blanket closer around her neck then reached down to feel for a second blanket caught under the top one.

She realized then that Sage had removed her outer clothing, leaving only her drawers.

"Oh, no." She groaned in embarrassment. She looked around the room, realizing she was alone. Tears filled her eyes from pain. She felt sorry for Sage for having to stop and take the time to care for her. On top of that, he'd been injured himself. She should be the one taking care of him, after insisting on coming along.

She heard footsteps then, and the front door creaked open. Sage stepped inside carrying a bundle of wood. He stopped short when he noticed her watching him.

"So, you're awake."

"Yes, and I've never hurt so bad. Where are we?"

Sage carried the wood over near the fireplace and dropped it in a pile. "About three miles north of where we left Cutter's body to the buzzards, and somewhere a bit southwest of Flaming Gorge. God knows who originally built this old cabin. The roof is already splitting from sun rot, but it will do for a place to hole up."

He rose, removed his hat and jacket, and ran a hand through his hair. "It's chilly. If I make a fire now, we'll get this place heated up enough to keep us warm tonight when the sun goes down." He walked to a table with one lone chair and sat down gingerly, obviously in pain himself. "While you were passed out from laudanum, I broke off that shaft and pushed it through. That's the only way to get an arrow out without tearing up the wound even worse. I dumped a lot of good drinking whiskey into that wound. I hope I can keep what's left for something more enjoyable."

He gave her a smile, but Maggie could see the pain in his own face. He was trying to cheer her up, probably to keep her from thinking about how serious her wound really was.

"What about your side? Did the bullet go through like you thought?" Maggie asked him.

He shrugged. "It'll heal. I'm far more worried about your leg." Sage reached into his shirt pocket for a cigar, then rose and walked to the fireplace to pull out a thin piece of wood and light the smoke. Maggie felt deep embarrassment at the thought of him undressing her. "Where are my denim pants? Are they ruined?"

"I'd say so. I had to cut off the pant leg around the wound. I don't think you'll have much use for a one-legged pair of britches. Good thing you brought along a couple extras." He walked back to the table and sat down.

Maggie looked away. "Thanks for making sure I was mostly unconscious when you took out the arrow." A tear slipped down the side of her face. "I'm so sorry."

"For what?"

She wiped at the tear. "I don't know. Everything, I guess. If not for me, you'd have caught up with those men by now."

"Don't worry about it. Life has a way of handing us things we never asked for." He sat quietly smoking for a moment.

"There's coffee on the fire, and I'll make us something to eat soon. Do you have to... you know... relieve yourself?"

"Oh, my God," she whispered, covering her face with both hands. "I'm so embarrassed at all of this."

Sage rose. "A wound is a wound." He set his cigar in an old dish on the table, then leaned down and lifted her, blankets and all.

Maggie thought how easy it seemed for him, even though his side must surely hurt. "You'll make your wound start bleeding again."

"I've suffered worse—that bear attack—for one thing. And I know what an arrow wound feels like, as well as a gunshot wound. I'm the one who's sorry for not realizing that bastard was around."

What kind of a wild, unsettled life had this man led? Just hours earlier she'd watched him slit Cutter's throat with no sign of feelings or regret. Yet now, he showed that he could be incredibly gentle and caring. He held her in sure, strong arms, careful not to jostle her too much. When they got outside, he took her to an old outhouse, where he managed to get the toe of his foot in the door and force it open. Inside he lifted her blankets and placed them around her shoulders for warmth.

"I swept this thing out and checked for spiders, so don't worry about any of that. This is as far as I go. You'll have to get those drawers down and sit on your own. I guess I could do that for you too, but I don't think you want me to."

"I think I have to hang on to your arm to steady myself."

"No matter. I'll look away."

He stood there while Maggie held one of his forearms and managed to get her drawers down enough to sit. The whole situation was so unbelievably embarrassing, but she had no choice, and Sage handled it matter-of-factly. "You can go now. I can't do this with you in here," she admitted. She let go of his arm and steadied herself with both hands on the wooden seat, hoping there weren't any remaining spiders lurking in the old dark latrine.

Sage went out, but held the door open a crack so she'd have some light. She quickly took care of things, worried she'd pass out from pain. She held on to the wall with one hand while she managed to pull her drawers back into place, and then pulled the blankets around herself again. "Okay," she called out. He opened the door and picked her up again, carrying her back to the cabin.

"Thank you," Maggie told him, her head on his shoulder.

"Well, you can't say I'm not a gentleman at times." He carried her inside the cabin and carefully laid her down on the bedroll near the fireplace. "I'll have to check that wound pretty soon. Do you want coffee for now? I'll heat up some beans and bacon for us."

"I'd love some coffee, but at the moment, I could use a drink of water. My mouth feels like sand, and my head is beginning to ache something fierce."

"Laudanum will do that to you, same as whiskey. I wasn't feeling too great myself this morning when we left Whitey's place. I intend to get some decent sleep tonight. We should be pretty safe here for a couple of days." He took a tin cup from a shelf nearby and wiped it out with his shirttail. "This ought to do." He poured coffee in it and knelt near her. He set the cup aside and carefully scooted her—blankets, bedroll, and all—closer to a wall, so she could lean against it. Then he handed her the coffee.

"I'll be right back," he told her. "I have to bring in the rest of our gear and check the horses. I'll bring you some water and a shirt to put on, then I'll make us some grub." He stopped at the table and picked up a small brown bottle, bringing it over to set beside her. "Laudanum. I know you've had your fill, but go ahead and drink a little as you need it for pain."

"Thank you. I wish I could do more to help."

"I don't want to hear any more apologies. I'm glad you're all right, but you aren't out of the woods yet." He walked to the door then hesitated. Back when he killed Cutter and quickly tended to her wound, she'd blurted out that she loved him. Was it just the pain talking, or did she mean it? He wanted to ask, but decided not to. Weeks on the trail together were causing their relationship to become too damn personal. He didn't know what the hell to do about this feeling that he was losing control of this whole situation.

He glanced at Maggie. Maybe she didn't remember what she'd said so sincerely in her pain and terror. She looked pitiful and small and helpless sitting there under those blankets.

"Get some rest," he told her before walking out.

Twenty

Maggie nervously drank her coffee, feeling groggy and disoriented. She had a vague memory of blurting out that she loved Sage. Had she really said that? Did he hear and remember?

The terror of an arrow in her leg and the fear Sage would die had got the better of her, but she knew deep inside that she meant what she'd said, even though it was too soon to be thinking such things, let alone saying them out loud. What in God's name was Sage thinking right now?

She ached with indecision, then grabbed the laudanum and took a swallow, hoping it would numb the renewed pain in her leg. Maybe it would even give her more courage. By the time Sage finally returned, her coffee was gone, and she was uncomfortable sitting against the wall.

Sage said nothing as he plopped an armload of supplies on the floor and tossed her one of the extra shirts from her gear. He proceeded to put together an old rusted tripod perched near the fireplace, while Maggie quickly pulled on the shirt before he might glance her way again. She wondered if his gaze had lingered on her nakedness while she was passed out.

Sage set the tripod over the fire and hung a small pot from it, then took a wicked-looking knife from his back pocket and used it to slice open a can of beans.

Maggie watched silently, wary of the fact that Sage, in turn, was awfully quiet. He dumped the beans into the pot, then went back to the supplies and pried the lid off the small barrel that held bacon packed in lard. He used a large spoon to dig out some bacon and added it to the beans, lard and all.

"All this fat will help you keep warm and give you energy to heal," he said casually, stirring the concoction until the lard melted into the beans. He knocked the residue off the spoon and set it on a flat stone beside the fireplace. "Want any more coffee?" he asked.

"No, thanks."

Sage grabbed a towel from one of his saddlebags and used it to grasp the handle of the porcelain coffeepot he'd left near the base of the fire. He poured himself a cup of brew, then set the pot aside, pulled the one and only chair in the cabin closer, and sat down. He leaned back and let his long legs sprawl in front of the chair, almost to the point of touching Maggie's feet. His dark eyes met her gaze.

Maggie would have given her right arm to be able to read his thoughts.

"You're still a pretty fresh widow," he spoke up.

Why on earth did he say that? Maggie felt confused, not sure how to reply. Men like Sage Lightfoot were damn hard to figure. She swallowed before answering.

"Well, I guess I'm not the typical widow, seeing as how my marriage was arranged and didn't have anything to do with love." She dared to meet his gaze. "I think maybe you're remembering something I said when I was hurt." She took a deep breath. "I'll say it out for you, Sage. I said I love you." She looked away. "I expect that's something a man like you doesn't want to hear, what with you still upset over a bad marriage, and us not knowing each other all that long. I know you don't have such feelings in return, but… well… I guess I pretty much meant it. If not for the pain, I wouldn't have said it this soon… maybe not at all, but when I thought you might die, and me in all that pain… the words just came out. I didn't mean to burden you with such feelings."

Sage struck a match and lit his cigarette. "Burden me?"

Maggie shrugged. "Lord knows I've piled enough troubles on your shoulders without you wondering what to do about… you know… personal feelings."

Sage studied her intently. "You're a beautiful young woman, Maggie, and traveling together like we have, it's hard not to care, but it's also hard to know your real feelings when you become so dependant on each other." He drank more coffee. "Sometimes that closeness can be mistaken for something else."

Maggie nodded. "Yes, sir, I expect so, but maybe I could sort out my own feelings better if I knew more about you and your past. You keep refusing to talk about it."

"Yeah, well, the truth can really hurt sometimes—and I'm talking about the teller, not the listener."

Maggie saw sorrow in his eyes. "I just want to understand you."

"For now, just understand this. I'm not real eager to get mixed up with any woman. When you're stronger, I'll explain more."

Maggie frowned. "I'm sorry somebody hurt you so bad that you don't ever want to care again. Seeing that beautiful house you must have built for the woman called Joanna makes it hard to understand why she would give all that up."

He smoked quietly. "It wasn't enough for her." He got up and stirred the beans and bacon, then scooped some onto a tin plate and handed it to her with a spoon. "Eat. It will make you stronger."

"Thank you." Maggie took the plate and ate as much as she could handle, while an awkward silence hung in the air. God knew she dared not complicate things even more by telling Sage she was carrying.

It was growing dark outside, and Maggie heard the distant howl of a wolf somewhere in the hills. She thought she also detected a rumble of thunder. She finished most of her beans and set the plate aside, feeling uncomfortably exposed now that he knew she felt something more for him than a partnership formed out of a need for revenge. Anything more would bring a whole new perspective to their situation, yet she'd grown accustomed to his protection and strength, and from all she'd seen back at his ranch, this man truly could care if he'd let himself. He'd been so gentle with her after she was hurt, so respectful when he took her to the privy, so caring and patient. On top of that, his very physique was hard to ignore. He was boldly handsome, arms whipcord strong, a rugged jawline and dark, moody eyes. She swallowed for courage and decided to get a conversation going again. "In a way, you're lucky, Sage, having loved a woman so much that it hurts to talk about her. I wouldn't know what it's like to be loved like that. I guess we've both had a hard life."

He shook his head. "You aren't part Indian. That doubles the hardship."

Maggie shrugged. "I have to admit that when I first met you I was pretty sure you were part Indian, but it only bothered me because coming from Missouri—what did I know about Indians? I only knew the things I read a time or two in the papers… always bad stuff. I wondered if you might get mad at me and scalp me, or something. But when you took care of camp, and you kept your promise not to look when I washed in that stream… I knew you were good at heart."

To Maggie's surprise, he chuckled. "You thought I might scalp you?"

Lord, you're handsome when you smile. "Well, I do have red hair."

He laughed harder. "Jesus, Maggie, you say the damnedest things sometimes." He walked over and leaned down. "You'd better get some rest. We'll be here two or three days, until we're sure you don't get an infection, and you're able to ride. There's plenty of time to talk about things and sort out feelings."

Maggie reached up to hold on to his arms as he helped scoot her all the way to the floor again. He met her gaze, and for a moment, it was all there. Maggie could see he wanted her… but he'd been hurt like no good man ought to be hurt. She couldn't resist wanting to comfort him… or resist her own sudden desire to know what it was like to *want* to be with a man. Acting on impulse, she caught his mouth with hers. His lips were full and soft and gentle, and for a brief moment, his own kiss became more demanding.

Suddenly, Sage pulled away. He reached over and positioned the only two pillows they'd brought under her head. "Go to sleep. The faster you heal, the sooner we can get going again." He stood. "You're walking dangerous territory, Maggie Tucker. If you weren't injured and my side didn't still ache, that kiss might have led to more than you bargained for."

He picked up her plate and cup and set them on the table. "You aren't playing fair, Maggie. Don't take too much for granted when it comes to feeling safe around me."

"You don't scare me, Sage Lightfoot."

"Oh?" He faced her, folding his arms. "You mentioned that day at the creek—that you began trusting me when I kept my promise not to look."

"What about it?"

"For your information, I did take a peek."

Her eyes widened. "You did not!"

"I'm a man, for God's sake, Maggie. And I can tell you right now, my ability to be trusted has never been so sorely tested as it has been ever since that day. Right now, I'm a man who hasn't been with a woman in a long time, so I need to know any desire I might have for you isn't just because of that. You're scared, and I'm all you have. So you need to know that it isn't just those things making you think you love me. I am never going to let a woman use me again, like Joanna did."

He dumped what was left of their beans back into the pot, then put a lid on it and took the pot from the fire. He set it and the coffeepot aside as he stirred the coals and added wood to the fire.

But I would never hurt you, Maggie wanted to answer. It struck her that if he knew about the baby she carried, he might think the only reason she was after him was so she could claim him as the father and save herself the shame. He'd feel used, and he already told her Joanna had used him too. "Will you tell me one thing, Sage?"

He faced her. "What's that?"

"The letter from Joanna. It upset you real bad. What did she want?"

A flat, angry look came into his dark eyes. "To come back." He snickered. "She claims she realized she still loves me, but that's bullshit." He took his jacket from a peg on the wall.

"Will you take her back?"

Sage opened the door. "Never!" He walked out and slammed the door.

So, there it is, Maggie thought. *He still loves her, all right.* Her heart had never pained her like this. For years she'd had a man she never wanted, and now, she wanted a man she couldn't have.

Twenty-one

Another day passed and Maggie spent most of it asleep from laudanum. Sage wanted her to sleep, not just because she needed to heal, but because he was angry with himself for doing so much talking earlier. He'd allowed their relationship to go from just a man and woman traveling together tracking outlaws to something too personal.

He swallowed more whiskey, thinking how blatantly open and honest Maggie was.

She loved him? Hell!

More whiskey, that's what he needed. He'd drunk a little to kill the pain in his side, wanting to save the laudanum for Maggie. But the more he drank, the more he wanted Maggie Tucker. The last time a woman professed to love him it had ended in disaster. And everyone else he'd ever loved, or who he thought loved him, either abandoned him or was taken from him. Maggie still didn't know the whole story—why it was so hard for him to trust anyone in this world.

Still, Maggie Tucker was different, wasn't she? She

wasn't one to use a man. She wouldn't know how if she tried. There was much about her to be admired.

He shifted in his bedroll, trying to get comfortable, but he couldn't get his thoughts to fade. By the soft firelight, he watched Maggie sleep. He was glad the laudanum was working so well. It had torn at his guts to rip that arrow shaft out of her leg two days ago. Sometimes she reminded him of a little girl who just needed holding, but he knew damn well what holding her would lead to, because she *wasn't* a little girl. The worst thing he could have done was to put his arms around her two nights ago at the cabin, let alone allow that kiss earlier. She was a lot of woman for such a small frame… and damned if she wasn't pretty. He didn't need to see her all gussied up to know that.

He'd seen her slender legs… bare. God, they were pretty. He wanted to feel them wrapped around his hips, wanted to show her what it was like to take on a man she really loved and wanted. He hated her father for working her like a horse and forcing her into a loveless marriage, and he hated her husband for treating her like his personal whore… and now, more than ever, he hated the men who'd abused her.

He had to admit it—at least to himself. He was falling in love with Maggie Tucker. He wanted to taste her lips again. Maggie was different. She and Joanna were like night and day—Joanna being the night. A man could be sure of someone like Maggie. He'd never need to wonder about ulterior motives or worry about how to keep her happy.

Yesterday a storm had passed them far to the north. Late this evening, another storm moved in, this one coming right over them now. There came a sudden popping flash of lightning, and a terrific boom of thunder immediately followed, so close that it literally shook the cabin. Maggie let out a short scream, startled from her sleep.

"Let me in!" she yelled. She sat up then, and Sage could see by the dim light of what was left of the fire that her eyes were wide. She looked confused and terrified. "Don't leave me out here!"

Sage threw off his blanket and went to her, kneeling down near her. "Maggie? It's me—Sage. What's wrong?"

She looked at him, blinked. "Sage?" She glanced around the darkened room. "I guess I was dreaming. I heard the thunder—"

Another loud boom made her jump. Sage touched her arm. "It's just a storm. They always seem closer in the mountains. What were you dreaming? You screamed something about letting you back inside."

She put a hand to her hair, pushing a piece of it behind one ear. "I was remembering." She grasped his hand. "Once when Pa beat me for burning his supper, he shoved me outside in a thunderstorm and tied me to the back of a wagon. He knew I hated storms. He told me I should think about how it felt to be hungry and cold. Maybe then I'd be more careful about burning his supper." She met his gaze, and Sage saw an agonizing sorrow in her eyes. "Liquor did that to my pa—made him mean." She looked away again. "I had to sit out alone in the rain all night."

"Jesus." Sage squeezed her hand.

Maggie shivered. "I was sure the lightning would strike me dead. It was a terrible storm, high wind and pounding rain. I was so scared."

Reason told him not to, but Sage stretched out beside her, then pulled her into his arms. "You're safe here, Maggie, and you need your rest. Go back to sleep. No one is going to turn you out in the storm."

The rain came down in torrents then, pounding the old shingles of the cabin roof. Sage could hear it dripping inside where the roof had split, but things remained dry on their end. Maggie rested her head against his chest.

"The laudanum worked good, Sage. My leg doesn't hurt much right now."

"I'll check it again in the morning. If it's not red and swollen, we might have avoided an infection."

They lay there quietly while the rain kept coming down. Another clap of thunder and flash of lightning caused Maggie to wrap her arms around Sage. "I want to tell you something, Sage. I hope you won't think the worse of me for it."

He leaned down to smell her hair. "What?"

"It doesn't matter if you love me or not. I want to know what it feels like to take a man I really want." She looked at him, her lips close. "Make love to me, Sage."

"You don't know what you're asking. It's the laudanum talking."

"No. It's me. I need to know what it's supposed to be like. I need to forget the pain of what happened… before. Please, help."

"Damn it, Maggie, I've been drinking. A drinking man doesn't have any common sense."

"I don't care." Maggie reached up to meet his mouth.

He returned the gesture with a hungry, yet tender kiss. "God, Maggie," he groaned, moving his lips to her neck. "Don't ask me to stop."

"I won't. I've never felt like this," she said in a near whisper.

"I don't want to wake up ugly memories for you."

Maggie could barely comprehend this wonderful yearning for a man. She wanted every part of him, to feel his strong hands move over her body… under the shirt he'd given her to wear… over her breasts. "Touch me, Sage." She took his hand and put it against her breast. She wanted to feel his hard, heated body move on top of her like he was doing now. She relished his deep kisses… arched up to him when he pushed the shirt open and leaned down to taste her breasts.

"Sage…" she whispered. This was nothing like it had been with James, who'd always been quick and demanding… no gentleness to his touch, no concern for what she might want or enjoy.

She breathed deeply as Sage moved down to kiss her belly, groaned when he pulled off her drawers and did something magical with his fingers that sent her into a relaxed ecstasy far beyond anything the laudanum could do. Rain continued to pound the roof, and thunder rolled in the distant mountains. By the dim firelight she could see intense desire in Sage's dark eyes when he came back to meet her mouth in an invading kiss. The way he touched her made her forget any remaining inhibitions… forget everything that had come before.

Now she was the one taking pleasure. She moved

her hands over Sage's hard muscles, pulled his shirt open so she could feel his chest. A wonderful sensation of wild need engulfed her then, a pulsating, desperate want for this man. She lay in a near daze of desire as she waited for Sage to remove his clothes, felt no pain in her thigh as he moved between her legs.

"Maggie, are you sure about this?" he asked.

Never before had she actually wanted to touch a man's nakedness, but she wanted to touch Sage Lightfoot. She moved her hands over his chest, down to his hips. She gently grasped his hardened shaft. "I'm sure," she whispered.

She guided him into her, and he responded with a slow, deep invasion that sent her reeling. It was like he actually wanted her to enjoy it. He filled her to near painful glory, making her cry out with sheer ecstasy. She raised her hips rhythmically to meet his every thrust, drinking in his glorious masculinity when he grasped her hips and got to his knees, lifting her to him.

Maggie thought how he could have forced this on her whenever he wanted during all the time they'd been alone together. He could have used the excuse that she'd been used by other men already, that it shouldn't matter if a man took her again for his own pleasure, but in Sage's dark eyes she saw only respect. He understood.

She'd never known a man like this… never actually wanted to lie completely naked and let a man look at her as he mated with her. But she wanted Sage to look at her, to enjoy her just like she was enjoying his own nakedness… enjoying the feel of him inside her.

She felt his life spill into her then. How she wished now that it was Sage Lightfoot's life in her belly.

She pushed back the thought. She couldn't worry right now about how she was going to tell him about the baby. She only wanted to enjoy this moment of surrender, this moment of sheer pleasure.

Sage relaxed and pulled away then. He kissed her again before rising and walking over to stoke the fire and add wood to it. Neither spoke. Still naked, Sage grabbed his own blankets and pillow and brought them over beside Maggie. He arranged them and laid down next to her, pulling the blankets over both of them and letting Maggie nestle against his chest.

"You smell good," she told him. "You have a natural good, manly scent. James never smelled good like you do. You smell like leather and the outdoors and strength."

Sage grinned. "Strength has a smell?"

"Yes, it does. It's the kind of scent that makes a woman feel safe."

Sage caressed her hair. "If you say so. Are you okay?"

She kissed his chest. "I'm wonderful. I've never felt like that. Thank you, Sage."

He sighed. "You're thanking me? I think it should be the other way around. I've wanted you since before we left."

But do you love me? He hadn't said that yet, but she'd promised he shouldn't feel obligated. She could only hope he'd learn to love her as much as she knew for certain she loved him, but Sage was Sage... not a man to let on... and the fact remained there was still another woman in his heart, whether he wanted to admit it or not. Right now, she hated that woman.

"I want to do it again, Sage."

"You need your rest—and I'm afraid I'll hurt your leg."

"I told you I'm fine."

"Neither of us is thinking straight right now."

"I am perfectly aware of the needy, confused condition we're in."

Sage moved on top of her again. "You're some woman, Maggie Tucker."

"And you're some man."

Sage met her mouth, his kisses full and tender and delicious. She opened herself to him… and took him twice more before they finally slept.

Twenty-two

Maggie awoke to see Sage stoking the fire. He'd thrown on more logs and poked at them with a bit too much punch.

He was angry. She could tell.

He was fully dressed. She'd not heard him rise and go out for more wood. She felt groggy, yet warm and wonderful and satisfied. She pulled the blankets closer, then realized she had to use the privy. She managed to get up, keeping the blankets around her. Surprisingly, her leg didn't hurt so much when she started walking, but she stumbled a little from sleepiness and catching a blanket in her toes.

A frowning Sage came over and picked her up. "You shouldn't be getting up on your own yet."

"I'm much better—just a little dizzy."

"Too much laudanum last night. Too much of a lot of things."

Maggie put her head on his shoulder as he carried her out. "Why are you angry with me?"

"I'm not. I'm angry with myself. I did a stupid thing last night, thanks to too much whiskey. Whiskey and reason don't mix. I'm sorry as hell, Maggie."

"Why? I *asked* you to make love to me. You tried to discourage me."

"That doesn't matter. Laudanum acts on you the same as whiskey when it comes to thinking straight."

"It wasn't the laudanum, and I'm a big girl, Sage. I knew what I wanted, and I'm fine with it."

Sage set her on her feet in front of the privy. "You okay on your own now?"

Maggie was a bit worried. Did he see last night as nothing more than taking his pleasure? Were there no feelings involved? She'd told him it didn't matter, but deep inside she dearly hoped it did.

She kept her blankets wrapped tightly. "I'm fine. You can go back inside and make us something to eat. I'm famished."

From all the lovemaking, she thought. *It was wonderful, Sage. Please tell me you thought so too.* She went inside the privy and closed the door. When she came out, he was gone—back in the cabin. She saw their horses and mules grazing nearby. It was a pleasant morning—cold but still. She'd almost forgotten how quiet things were in high country when the wind didn't blow.

She felt alive and beautiful. Everything around her was beautiful too. The sun shone brightly against gorgeous mountains of green and purple. Last night seemed like a dream... but it was ever so real. She was in love with Sage Lightfoot, and that was that. She'd learned that giving herself to a man could be beautiful and enjoyable, when she truly wanted and needed him.

Her biggest problem now wasn't finding the outlaws, or even Sage's mood this morning. It was the fact that Sage still didn't know about the baby. She feared telling him more than ever. She'd likely lose him for good. He'd think everything she'd done last night was to trap him into marriage to save her honor. She decided that, for now, she would enjoy the chance to lie in Sage Lightfoot's arms, whether he loved her or not. It felt wonderful to know he was attracted to her, that he'd wanted her. He had a way of making love that made her feel treasured. He'd taken away the ugliness of her attack with a touch amazingly gentle for his size and strength. He was beautiful to look at, beautiful to touch, and beautiful in the way he could please a woman.

She remembered his words from the night before… *I've wanted you since before we left.* He could growl and scowl and do all the pretending that he wanted. It didn't matter. Sage Lightfoot loved her. Maybe he didn't realize it himself yet, but he did.

She walked gingerly back to the cabin, determined to ignore the pain in her leg and not let it slow them down. She went inside to see a pan of bacon cooking over the fire. Sage sat watching it, his back to her. "Coffee's hot," he told her. "You need help getting dressed?"

"Do you *want* me to get dressed?"

He remained quiet.

"What I meant was—are we leaving today?" she added.

Sage shook his head. "You need to stay off that leg as much as possible for a couple more days. I let you walk back in here on your own just to see how you'd do. Do you want some stockings?"

"No, I'll wrap myself in these blankets for now.

I'll clean up after I eat." Maggie limped back to her makeshift bed.

"I should look at that wound again—change the dressing," Sage suggested. He walked to their supplies to take out more gauze.

Maggie noticed he'd gathered his blankets and pillow and put them on the other side of the room, as far from her bedroll as possible. So... this was his message. Last night was last night, and it wasn't going to happen again.

We'll see about that.

Maggie sat down and pulled her blankets away enough to expose her thigh. There was blood on the gauze, but it was dried blood—nothing fresh. "I think I'm going to be fine," she told Sage as he came over with whiskey for the wound and clean gauze to wrap it. He remained quiet as he gently untied the old gauze and carefully unwrapped the wound.

Maggie winced, more at the sight of the wound than how it felt. "It looks awful! Will it leave an ugly scar?" She noticed Sage refused to meet her gaze.

"Maybe not an ugly one, but it will leave a scar, all right." He tossed the gauze aside and dribbled whiskey on the wound. Maggie grimaced at the sting.

"Sorry. Can't be helped."

Maggie studied his strong hands as he rewrapped the wound. "Does it look okay? I mean, no infection?"

"Not so far. Believe me, you wouldn't have walked on your own if it was infected. I'm amazed at how good it looks and the fact that you can walk on that leg. Either that wound wasn't as bad as I thought, or you're a good healer." He finally met her gaze. "Maggie..."

"It's okay." Maggie touched his lips, sensing he felt guilty about last night. "I told you what I wanted, and you shouldn't feel obligated. I'm not the kind of woman to make demands, Sage. I'm scared—and all alone in this big country. You make me feel safe." She looked away. "And it's okay if you just needed a woman. I wanted you no matter what your own reason was. It was another kind of healing."

Sage rose and took the pan of bacon off the fire while they talked. "It's not okay," he told her. He sat beside Maggie, facing her. He reached out to push some hair off her face. "Look at me, Maggie."

She met his eyes—eyes that could show wildness and anger—but now, they were gentle, searching.

"You deserve to be appreciated for the strong, beautiful woman you are—the respect of being loved the proper way."

Maggie's heart had never felt so full of love and joy. "Are you saying… you love me? I meant it when I said that I'm not asking anything like that from you."

"You *should* ask it, because you deserve that much."

She thought about the baby. "Maybe I don't," she answered. *I'm carrying a bastard child.* Why couldn't she bring herself to tell him? The man appreciated honesty.

"Maggie… I'm telling you not to expect too much from me right off. The way I feel about you… it's a whole different thing from Joanna. You're a far better woman than she'll ever be."

Maggie smiled through tears. "It makes me feel good to hear you say that. No matter what happens, I can honestly say that I've never been this happy. If it lasts only a little while, I'll still be glad." She leaned close and wrapped her arms around his neck, kissing him deeply before he could move away, loving the taste of his mouth, the delicious way he had of kissing her back.

"Damn you." Sage whispered the words through deeper, searching kisses. "I didn't intend to do this again."

"I did."

Sage moved his lips over her neck, down to her breasts, lingering there to taste and enjoy. Maggie relished allowing him his pleasure. She was still naked under the blankets. Nothing more was said. For the moment, neither wanted to worry about the right or wrong of it. Sage removed his pants and long johns, and Maggie drank in the sight of his firm thighs, his heated erection—the almost intimidating size of him. Leaving his shirt on, he knelt over her.

Maggie moved her fingers into his thick, dark hair and opened herself to him. He surged inside her, groaning with the want of her, reaching down to grasp her bottom while kissing her wildly. He moved his lips to kiss her hair, and Maggie breathed in his scent, snuggled her lips into his neck, and relished the glory of his manhood until his life pulsed into her again.

He relaxed, and they lay there together quietly for a while. Maggie moved her hands over his muscled arms and chest, adoring every part of him. Finally, Sage kissed her once more before pulling away with a deep sigh.

"Now, we definitely need to wash up somehow," he told Maggie, "and I need a shave." He rose and stretched. "There's an old washtub hanging at the back of the cabin. If it's not full of holes, I'll heat some water and fill it for you. I have a lot of repacking to do, and the horses to tend." He pulled on his long johns. "We'll eat breakfast, and then I'll leave you alone to clean up. I'll wash outside as soon as we eat." He looked down at her. "Maggie, we can't do this anymore—till this is over. The last thing we need is for you to end up carrying my baby in your belly when we don't even know—" He turned away.

"Don't know what?" Maggie asked. "Whether we love each other? I already know I love you, Sage, with everything that's in me, but I know there's something in your heart for Joanna. You're bothered by that letter."

He walked to the fireplace and set the pan of bacon on the fire. "I don't want to talk about Joanna." He glanced back at her. "And so you know, I think I love you, Maggie Tucker. I just don't want it to get in the way of what we have to do. I've got to think straight and be alert, and so do you."

"What are you trying to tell me?"

He turned the bacon, his back to her again. "Well, for one thing, I don't want to worry about getting you pregnant."

Her heart pounded with dread. "It's a little late for that, don't you think?"

He shrugged. "Maybe not. We can at least try to avoid it from here on." He pulled the cabin's lone chair over by the fire and sat to watch the bacon fry. "That means two things." He glanced at her. "Either we stop doing this, or we get married. Somebody like you would make a good rancher's wife, but God knows, getting married now would be ridiculous."

"Because you still love Joanna?"

That look of dark anger came into his eyes again, the look she saw the day he got the letter. "No. Dealing with Joanna is a necessary evil that will need taking care of." He turned away. *It's okay, Sage. Once you know the truth, you won't want to marry me anyway.*

"Sage, for now, I don't mind pretending to be married till this is over," Maggie said aloud. "With Joanna wanting to see you again, you'll need to get your feelings worked out before you make a decision as big as getting married again."

I'd marry you right here and now if we had a preacher… if you knew the truth, accepted my baby, and were over Joanna.

Sage rubbed the back of his neck. "Maybe in the next town we can find a doctor—get some protection for—"

"No!" *A doctor might figure out I'm carrying. He might tell you.* "I'm afraid of strange doctors," she told him. "I'd be too embarrassed."

Sage grinned almost sheepishly then. "Well, then the only alternative is to visit one of the local whorehouses. Prostitutes know all kinds of ways to keep from getting pregnant."

"I expect you'd know more about that than I do." Maggie bristled. "Is that the only plan you can think of?"

Sage smiled. "I can't think of any other."

Maggie sat up and wrapped herself in blankets again, not fond of the idea of a wild, handsome man like Sage Lightfoot visiting a whorehouse. Sage rose, still smiling. He helped her stand then pulled her into his arms. "I have no plans to see any prostitutes for reasons other than getting something for protection," he soothed. "Until then, I'll try my best to keep my hands off you, but it won't be easy." He pulled her chin up so she had to face him. "Right now, there's no other woman I want, not even Joanna. Understand?"

She saw only honesty in those dark eyes. What was she getting herself into by not telling him the truth? She threw her arms around his neck. "I love you so."

I just hope I don't have to tell you good-bye when this is over. His strong arms came around her, and for the moment, she enjoyed the luxurious safety and comfort of his embrace.

Twenty-three

THEY LEFT, HEADING NORTH. MAGGIE FELT MELANcholy leaving the crumbling cabin where she'd found real love for the first time in her life. But there were still too many unanswered questions, too many obstacles in the way of their love—outlaws to be hunted, miles to be covered, another woman Sage needed to deal with... and a baby Sage didn't know about.

"Are you ever going to tell me more about yourself?" Maggie asked. "You keep saying you'll tell me the whole story, and here we are, riding through grassland with nothing to do but talk."

Sage didn't answer for a tense few minutes, and Maggie let him mull over his reply.

"I expect you deserve to know more about me, so you can make up your mind once we get back to Paradise Valley," he finally spoke up.

Relieved, Maggie waited patiently for even more silent seconds, afraid one wrong word would change his mind.

"I was raised by a Cheyenne mother and a white trapper father," he told her then. "He was French, and I remember him being tall. I get my build from him, I guess. My mother's name was Bending Flower Woman, and I have only good memories of her. I have no idea if my father is still alive. His name was Franco Cherborne. He left for parts unknown when I was about eight, right before Colorado volunteers attacked the perfectly peaceful camp where I lived with my mother at Sand Creek in southern Colorado. Their intent was to murder every last person there, mostly women, children, and elders. I watched them cut my mother's belly open." His voice dropped lower as he revealed the ugly memory.

Dear God, Maggie thought.

"I ran—an eight-year-old boy lost and scared. One of those volunteers chased me down and shot me."

Maggie drew her horse to a halt. "You were just a little boy!"

"To them I was filth that needed to be eliminated." Sage turned his horse and faced her. "The bullet grazed my neck in such a way that I fell unconscious and couldn't move. White missionaries found me. When I came to, I was in their wagon." He started riding again, and Maggie trotted her horse up beside him. "They kept me so sedated I couldn't fight them or run," Sage continued. "Even later, I couldn't leave because I was partially paralyzed for several weeks. They took me to their headquarters in San Francisco, and I came to realize I was better off where I was for the time being. They tended my wound, fed me. By the time I was able to move around, I figured I wouldn't know which direction to go if I did leave, and I was still just a kid, so I stayed because I had food and a roof over my head. They took good care of me. They schooled me, taught me about religion and all that, let me live with them—showed me off in church as their 'saved' Indian boy."

He hesitated, lighting a cheroot.

"They sound like good people."

Sage grunted a rather evil laugh then took a draw on his smoke. "Yeah, well, I thought so at the time," he continued. "I thought I meant something to them, believed they loved me. I came to think of them as my parents, loved and trusted them like parents. Trouble was, there was a wealthy family who lived up the street and often donated money to the church. They had a daughter about my age."

Maggie felt his instant tension. "Joanna?"

He met her gaze, and there it was... the deepest hurt Maggie had ever seen in anyone's eyes.

"Joanna." He turned away. "Her parents invited me and my so-called Christian adoptive parents to their house a few times—I believe more as a curiosity than anything else—and to show friends and neighbors the good their money was doing." He snickered. "Saving the savages, so to speak."

He shifted in his saddle, and Maggie could tell he was struggling with anger.

"What they didn't realize was Joanna and I felt a real attraction to each other. We began making secret plans to meet. She was—I don't know—about sixteen, I guess. I was eighteen. One thing led to another, and we got caught in some pretty heavy kissing and in a rather compromising position behind a barn. We were dressed and all, but what they saw was enough for the good Christian people who raised me to instantly condemn me."

He rubbed a hand across his forehead and adjusted his hat again. Maggie sensed his restlessness was a way to keep from exploding.

"I was dragged away and severely beaten by several men. I think they would have hung me if they could have gotten away with it. Joanna was promptly sent to some fancy finishing school in the East. My so-called parents who 'loved' their fellow man banned me from church and said they were disappointed that all their years of teaching hadn't rid my savage soul of Satan's lusts. They gave me ten dollars, told me I was old enough to make my own way in the world, and out the door I went. I think they had orders to get rid of me or lose whatever donations Joanna's parents made to their church."

Maggie closed her eyes, aching for him.

"Life sure can punch you in the gut sometimes," Sage continued with a sigh, "and I've been punched more than once. I headed back toward where I'd come from, not sure what the hell I'd do. Most of the Cheyenne were on reservations, which I wanted no part of. I did find one renegade band—lived with them awhile, even raided with them. But I'd lived the civilized way too long, and I knew the time would soon come when they, too, would end up on a reservation, and me with them, if I didn't light out. So I left. I ended up in northern Utah working for a rancher who turned out to be a horse thief. His ranch was a way station for stolen stock—horses and cattle both. They treated me well, befriended me, so I fell in with that life—helped steal horses and cattle—even robbed a stage once. I learned to like liquor and bawdy women. Hell, I'd gone so far to the other side of life that no respectable woman would have anything to do with me anyway."

He stared ahead at distant mountains.

"Through it all, I never forgot Joanna—always wondered if she thought about me anymore." He turned to Maggie. "After one last robbery, I gave up my share of the profit in return for some real fine horses and a few head of cattle, and I headed away from outlaw country. I wanted to find a place to settle. I brought three men I knew I could trust. You've already met them—Joe Cable, Bill Summers, and Hank Toller."

"And you settled in Paradise Valley."

Sage nodded. "I came upon that valley, and I knew that was where I wanted to be. That's why I named it Paradise. It was far enough from civilization to let me mind my own business, and far enough from outlaw country to not worry too much about getting robbed. I promised the men that if they helped me build a ranch, they'd get their fair share of whatever I earned. When I filed a claim on the land, I used the white name my missionary parents gave me, Sage—for finding me amid sagebrush, I guess—but the last name they gave me was theirs—Graham. I figured I'd have an easier time with claims using that name, which I did. I got the land—one hundred sixty-two acres under the Homestead Act. The men with me each filed for another hundred sixty-two acres adjoining it, turned them over to me, and we kept claiming more and more land through fake names, then putting it in my name until—well, I just kept spreading out and finding ways to keep it going. Now it's a good sixty thousand acres. I've never used the name Graham for anything besides claims. I hated the missionaries for trying to make me deny my Indian blood. My Cheyenne name was Lightfoot. From what I remember, they called me that because when I was born, one foot was whiter than the other, I guess."

He smoked quietly then, and Maggie couldn't imagine the hurt he'd suffered—the terror a little boy would feel at watching his mother being mutilated, the abandonment of his father, and then being banished by the only other people he'd learned to trust.

"I guess I grew out of the white foot thing because there's no difference in my feet now." He looked at Maggie and smiled sadly. "Anyway, I kept the name and built the ranch, and I eventually built the bigger log house I live in now, hoping to settle with a wife and have kids."

Maggie winced with pain in her leg as she shifted in her own saddle to get more comfortable. "Obviously, you found Joanna again?"

He smashed out the cheroot against a concha on his saddle and put the stub back in a vest pocket to smoke later.

"Oh, I found her all right. I should have left well enough alone, but I wrote a letter to the Grahams back in San Francisco to let them know how I was doing. I wanted to make sure they knew I'd made something of myself in spite of what they did to me—that I was worth a lot more than the ten bucks they gave me when they turned me out. In the letter I asked them to please let Joanna know where she could find me, if she cared to. A few months later, I got a message that a Joanna Hawkins was in Cheyenne—wanted to know if I'd come for her."

He leaned forward and rested his arms on his saddle horn.

"I figured the Grahams must have told her about me after all, but later, I learned Joanna found the letter after they died. Either way, I couldn't believe I'd found her. I charged down to Cheyenne as fast as I could—and there she was, at the rooming house where she said she'd be—and God, she was the picture of heaven—ten times prettier than I'd remembered."

He looked away. Storm bent his head to graze.

"She fell into my arms like all the years in-between never happened—said how glad she was that I wrote that letter—said she never forgot me."

Maggie could feel his mood darkening.

"She claimed she still loved me and wanted to marry me—share Paradise Valley with me, raise a family there. We married two days later. I took her back to the ranch, and the men were all struck by how pretty she was—things were fine… for a few weeks."

He shook his head. "It wasn't long before she began asking why we didn't go to town more often… why we had to live so far out in the wilds… why couldn't we live in Cheyenne or Rock Springs, since I was the boss and could just tell the men what to do and let them take care of it. She wanted a fancier house… wanted to throw lavish parties… wanted to order dresses from back East… wanted to spend weekends in Cheyenne—maybe help establish a library in our name—an opera house."

He took off his wide-brimmed hat and ran a hand through his hair. "As I'm sure you know by now, it's obvious I'm not cut out for the fancy life," he continued, repositioning his hat. "And an ex-outlaw who's half Indian isn't exactly welcome in the circles Joanna liked to run in. She gradually got more demanding, showing her true colors and the real reason she'd looked me up. Once she threw it back at me that maybe her parents were right—that the Indian in me would never go away, and I'd never behave like a white man, no matter how much money I had."

He pulled on Storm's reins to stop the horse's grazing.

"Finally, after another big argument, she admitted her parents were both dead, and they were so far in debt that the estate left her nothing. She almost married another man in San Francisco, but someone told him she'd once been caught behind a barn with an Indian, so he left her. She was desperate, so she came to Cheyenne to find me—figured if I had such a big ranch, I must have decent money, and that's all she really wanted. She hated ranch life and the smell of cattle, and the fact that I, along with half my men, were former outlaws. I hated her so much that to keep myself from wrapping my hands around her pretty throat and squeezing until her face was purple, I threw her and her things into a wagon—drove her to Cheyenne—never saying one word. I drew money out of the bank, took her to a lawyer for a quick divorce, handed her the money, and told her to have a good life in San Francisco. That was a year ago and the end of our relationship… until I got that damn letter."

He kicked Storm into a faster gait. "And that's that, Maggie. That's the whole story, and I'm done talking about it. It's not easy for a man like me to admit he's been roped and tied and castrated by a woman."

Maggie watched his back as he rode away. How could any woman do to a man what Joanna had done to Sage? No wonder he didn't like talking about it. No wonder he wasn't sure about marriage.

Why on earth had Joanna written him about coming back? What did she want this time? The thought crushed Maggie's heart. Joanna still had a hold on the man—of that Maggie had no doubt. And from Sage's description, Joanna was beautiful, sophisticated, and educated… all the things Maggie wasn't. She figured she was pretty enough… but not beautiful in the way someone like Joanna must be.

Maggie decided that all she had was the here and now, and she vowed to love Sage Lightfoot as best she could—the way he deserved to be loved—until the day came that she would likely lose him to another woman… or because of the secret life she carried.

Twenty-four

MAGGIE STUDIED THE SCATTERING OF BUILDINGS below. Atlantic City. On this journey through the most rugged country she'd ever seen, she still found it astounding that anyone stayed in such remote places after the mines played out, but according to Sage, that's what happened here. It didn't look like much of a "city," but maybe they could find a place to stay where they could sleep in a bed instead of on the ground.

She rode behind Sage, wondering whether they would share a bed if they did find one for the night. He'd not come near her since they made love clear back near Flaming Gorge. That sagging old cabin would forever hold a special place in her heart, but Sage had followed through with his determination not to get her pregnant, which filled her with guilt. She could probably tell him now that she was carrying, and he'd believe it was his, but she could not bring herself to deceive him that way.

For now, she'd watch him—love him—drink in the man's masculinity and enjoy the safety of his arms. There he was, set against the vast, barren hillsides that surrounded the weathered, mostly tin-roofed buildings below. Sage was a man who fit this land like the wild mustangs. She'd grown to love this rugged, unforgiving, yet splendidly beautiful country, almost as much as she loved Sage Lightfoot. Every day brought new scenery and astounding beauty. Jagged mountains lined their surroundings all the way here. They'd ridden along ridges hundreds of feet high, below which ran the Green River like a satin ribbon, winding its way into an endless horizon.

The nights were cold, with black skies that exploded with stars—the sound of wolves and coyotes howling and yipping throughout the distant hills and canyons. The almost constant wind groaned through thick stands of pine and aspen, or whipped at a person wildly when riding through open, endless grassland.

Wyoming did something to a person. It had a way of making its way into a man's... or a woman's... blood and heart... or was it men like Sage who got into the blood and heart? Men out here tended to blend right in—big, sometimes mean, with jagged edges—yet they held a strange code of honor. They were a confusion of personalities. Even Whitey, who'd probably shoot a man for looking at him wrong, had proved he could be trusted.

And then there were women like Betsy, who seemed relaxed and unafraid, even though she lived in that cabin with a bunch of outlaws. Maggie suspected not one of them had ever laid a hand on the woman wrongly... except for Cutter. Betsy was probably glad the man never returned. When Maggie remembered what Sage had done to Cutter, it didn't seem possible that he could be so gentle with her just hours later.

How did a woman handle a man like that? She'd never known anyone quite like him, a man capable of extremes when it came to violence and goodness. She remembered his remark about how some men were basically good, and some were bad through and through, and she'd need to learn to tell the difference.

Sage held up, waiting for Maggie to ride up beside him.

"We should be able to find a room at Ma Pilger's place," he told her. "If Ma is still there. She was in her late forties when I stayed at her rooming house a couple of times. Even then, she looked more like seventy."

He cast Maggie a sideways glance. "That's what the dry air out here can do to you." Maggie figured he was thinking of everything he could to make sure she knew what she was getting into if she stayed in this country. "Do you think any of the men we're looking for could be down there?" she asked Sage.

"Hard to say, but from here on, we need to keep our eyes open and stay alert. They could be anywhere now, unless they've turned on us again and headed for other parts. My gut tells me they're here in outlaw country though."

"How long should we keep looking?"

"Till they're found," he answered matter-of-factly. "If we have to head south again, I'll leave you at the ranch and go on from there."

"But you promised—"

"I've kept my promise," he interrupted. "But the time will come when you've been living like this long enough. I'll take you back, and that's that. No more arguments."

His tone told Maggie this wasn't the time to protest. They reached the outskirts of Atlantic City, and Sage halted Storm and shifted in the saddle, meeting her gaze again. "We'll get a room together tonight to make things look right." Sage adjusted his wide-brimmed hat. "And whether you like it or not, there are women down there who can fix me up with something we can use for protection, so I intend to pay them a visit."

Maggie felt the heat of the flush that came to her cheeks. She hated the thought of him with that kind of woman. "Just don't stay too long. I'm sure they'd like to fix you up in more ways than one. You're an awfully handsome man, you know."

Sage grinned and shook his head, then turned his horse and headed into town.

Maggie followed, studying their surroundings as Sage halted the horses in front of a dry goods store. "Might as well stock up on a few things. Then you can rest, clean up, and change while I have a look around town."

And visit the prostitutes, Maggie thought. Two women dressed in neat frocks and wearing bonnets stood conversing near the doorway of the supply store. Both studied her curiously as Maggie climbed down from her horse. She felt self-conscious of the way she was dressed. She needed another bath after several more days on the trail. She nodded to them as she followed Sage inside the store. They nodded in return, and as Maggie stepped through the doorway, she heard one whisper, "It's a girl!"

Much as Maggie preferred wearing pants for days of riding horseback, she was eager to look like a woman again, partly to remind Sage she could be pretty when cleaned up. He'd promised they would eat in a real restaurant tonight, a relief from the work of campfire cooking.

The store clerk approached Maggie. "Help you, sir?"

Maggie pushed her hat back slightly and met his gaze.

"Oh, sorry! I mean… ma'am?"

Sage chuckled. "She's my wife, and we've been on the trail a long time. Pants make an easier ride for a woman."

The clerk reddened. "I see! Well, I didn't mean any insult, ma'am."

"None taken," Maggie answered. She repositioned her gun belt.

"You figuring on getting into a shoot-out?" Sage teased.

Maggie waved him off. "I'll shoot *you* if you keep making fun of me," she answered.

Sage turned to look at a variety of tobacco under glass. "Look around, and see what you need." He glanced at the clerk. "You got any good face creams?"

"Oh, yes, sir." He pointed to a shelf to Maggie's left. "Right over there, ma'am."

Maggie glanced at two old men who sat near a heating stove in the center of the small store. A pipe from the stove ran through the ceiling, and a kettle of water sat on top of the wood burner. The two old men looked her over, grinning. Maggie wasn't sure if it was out of kindliness, or humor at her appearance.

The plank floors creaked as she walked to the shelf of face creams. She studied them, while Sage ordered tobacco and cigarette papers, as well as four flasks of whiskey.

"We'll also need about ten pounds of potatoes, three or four cans of beans, five pounds of flour and sugar, lard and bacon, a couple of large towels, laudanum, and ammunition."

"Yes, sir." The clerk called to a young boy in back. "Sammy, come out here and start filling this man's order." He turned back to Sage. "What kind of ammunition do you need?"

Sage rattled off the caliber of bullets and shotgun shells he needed—bullets for Maggie's Sharps and his repeating rifle. Maggie picked out a jar of cream then noticed several spools of brightly colored ribbon, thinking how she'd like to tie them into her hair. She had some money of her own left, and she asked Sammy to cut some of the ribbon for her. Maybe tonight she'd wear a real dress and put one of the ribbons in her hair… for Sage.

"Ma Pilger still have a rooming house a couple blocks north?" Sage asked the clerk.

"Yes, sir, she's still there. Do you know her?"

"I do. It's been a few years though. I wasn't sure she'd still be around."

"Are you here to stay awhile, or are you passing through?" the clerk asked.

"Passing through."

"Well, sir, if you're here at least for tonight, you might want to take your wife to the spring barn dance. It's just about the equivalent of four blocks east. Ma can tell you where it will be. There'll be food there, lots of desserts. Perhaps if you've been on the trail a long time, your wife would enjoy putting on a dress and going to a dance. You're certainly welcome."

Sage began rolling a cigarette. "Well, now, that's not a bad idea. We were going to go out to eat, but if we can get the same thing along with some socializing, I think my wife would like that just fine." He glanced at Maggie.

"A dance and homemade eats sounds wonderful," she told him. She walked back to the counter with the cream and the ribbons. "I don't know if I have a fancy enough dress though."

"I'll take care of that," Sage told her.

Maggie wasn't sure what he meant by that, but he seemed pretty sure of it, so she decided not to question him in front of others. She looked at the clerk. "How much are these ribbons?" she asked, reaching into her pants pocket.

Sage grabbed her arm. "I'll get it all. You don't need to be spending that money I gave you, honey."

Honey? Sage gave her a warning look that reminded her that a wife wouldn't be paying for supplies when her husband was with her.

"Go pick out some peppermint," he told her, "and some rouge, or something like that if you need it."

Maggie did just that, stifling an urge to burst out laughing. They finished with their supplies and paid. When they walked out to pack them onto Sadie and Rosa, Maggie noticed the two women were gone.

"We'll unload this stuff at Ma's, and I'll take the horses and mules to a livery—have their hooves and shoes checked, feed them some oats, and give them a good rest," Sage told Maggie.

She faced him. "We can really go to that dance tonight?"

Sage kept his cigarette at the corner of his mouth. "If that's what you want."

"I'd love it."

"And I'll be there with the prettiest girl."

Maggie put a hand to her freckled cheek. "I sure don't look it right now." She frowned. "And what did you mean about taking care of a dress for tonight?"

"Don't worry about that. Let's get you to Ma's and get you a bath and some rest." He grabbed her around the waist and hoisted her onto Smoke's back. "And try to remember, we're married. Don't be paying for things yourself when I'm along."

"Yes, sir."

A big, bearded man in a black coat and hat rode up just then. Maggie watched Sage stiffen as he stepped away from Smoke and watched the man dismount and tie his big roan gelding to the hitching post. The man turned, and for a tense moment, he and Sage glared at each other. Finally, the bearded man grinned.

"Well, I'll be goddamned if it ain't Sage Lightfoot," he said, pushing his coat behind his gun as though he might need to draw it. Maggie cautiously moved her hand to her own six-gun.

"Leave it be, Maggie," Sage told her, as though he could see her from the back of his head.

The bearded man glanced at her. "You got a woman protectin' you now, do ya?" he asked Sage.

Sage moved away from Maggie and the horses,

keeping his eyes on the bearded man. "More like me protecting her from the likes of you."

The man chuckled. "Well, I heard you married some fancy woman from San Francisco a while back and was all settled on that ranch stocked with stolen cattle, Sage." He glanced at Maggie again then back to Sage. "She don't look like no fancy San Francisco woman. Fact is, she don't look like a woman at all. You takin' a fancy to the young ones now?"

Sage took the cigarette from his mouth and stepped it out. "What have you been up to over these years, John?" he asked. "You still robbing and killing? Still beating up on innocent women?"

The bearded man lost his smile. "Ain't a whore alive who's innocent, nor one who don't expect a man to be a little rough once in a while. Some of 'em actually like it."

"I asked what you've been up to." Sage looked around as though making sure the man didn't have some friends about.

"The usual… same as when you run with us. Not a bad life, Sage, if you remember. Money when you need it, plenty of liquor and cards, all the women a man could ask for." John put his hands on his hips. "Which makes me wonder how in hell you go from bein' married to a fancy lady and settled on a ranch to showin' up here in outlaw country with a little whip of a woman who looks like she's tryin' to hide her curves under boy's pants and a big hat."

"None of your business. We're only here for tonight so stay out of my way."

The man snickered. "Oh, I'll do that, all right.

Last time we mixed, I ended up with a broken jaw, a broken nose, cracked ribs, a broken wrist, and according to the doctor, I had a punctured lung and a lacerated liver—but I didn't have my gun on me then. A gun makes a big difference."

"If I hear you've done anything like what you did last time we mixed, fists or guns, it won't matter. You'll be in worse shape… most likely, dead. I was hoping that's how I left you back then."

Maggie could tell the bearded man was only pretending not to be afraid. He glanced at Sage's gun then backed up slightly. "Hey, Lightfoot, it's only by chance that we happened into each other after all these years. You're goin' your way for your own reasons, and I'm goin' mine, so no sense in us tanglin' at this late date."

Sage nodded. "Glad you understand that. And the woman on that horse is my wife, so get your filthy eyes and thoughts off her. You already know I've got little patience for a woman beater. Wouldn't take much for me to be offended at one who looks wrongly at my own wife."

The bearded man tipped his hat to Maggie. "Ma'am…" With one last glance at Sage, he turned and walked into the store. Maggie breathed a sigh of relief. Sage mounted Storm and took the reins to both packhorses.

"Let's go," he told Maggie.

Maggie followed him up the street. She could already see a sign that read *Ma Pilger's*. She cantered Smoke up beside Sage's horse. "Who was that?" she asked Sage.

"Just somebody from my past," he answered.

"Name's John Polk, and he doesn't have much respect for women... decided to beat the hell out of a prostitute we all used to do business with down at Brown's Park. I decided to show him how it felt to get beat on. I liked that girl. The other men had to drag me off him. By the time I'd got done, I thought maybe I killed him, but he obviously survived. We all rode off without him after that, and I never saw him since... till now."

Again Sage's violent side came into perspective. From the injuries John Polk mentioned, it must have been quite a beating... and over a woman. If Sage could beat such a big man so violently over a prostitute, what would he do in defense of a woman he loved enough to marry?

"Do we need to worry about him?" she asked Sage.

Sage stared straight ahead. "From here on, we have to worry about pretty much every man we come across." He glanced her way then. "But let *me* do the worrying. You're going to Ma Pilger's to rest and clean up—and tonight I'm taking my beautiful wife to a dance." He gave her a wink and galloped Storm and the pack mules up to Ma Pilger's place.

Twenty-five

"There ya go, honey." Ma Pilger tucked a rhinestone comb into the last curl atop Maggie's head. "Now, take a look. I've got to say, you're the prettiest thing that's passed through Atlantic City in a hell of a long time. You looked like a kid when Sage walked in here with you, and you're goin' out a full woman."

Maggie turned to look at herself in the full-length mirror in Ma's bedroom, where the crusty old woman had let her bathe, then take a good, long nap before helping her dress. Rather than wear the ribbons she'd bought, Ma coiffed her red hair into a mass of curls bedecked with combs and tiny flowers.

Maggie sucked in her breath. "Ma!" She literally stared at herself. Never had she felt like a pretty woman, but she did now. "I've never looked like this!" She touched her lightly rouged cheeks, ran her fingers along the tiny daisies that decorated the bodice of her baby-blue checkered dress, cut slightly off the shoulders—just low enough to show she was a woman without revealing too much. She put a hand to her small waist. As with her first baby, she showed no signs so far of being with child. "I've never seen myself like this," she told Ma. "And my hair—" She touched the curls. "I don't even look like myself."

"Ain't you ever been dressed up fancy?" Ma asked her.

Maggie smiled. "No, never this fancy."

Ma Pilger was a sweet woman with almost comical features—skinny arms and legs, wide around the middle. Sage was right that Ma looked far older than her years. He'd figured she should be about sixty now, but she looked ninety with so many lines in her face it would be impossible to count them.

"Back on the farm in Missouri I knew nothing but farm work," Maggie told Ma. "A trip to the closest town once in a while, but only to get what things we needed—never for something fun, and never a reason to dress fancy."

Ma's deep brown eyes remained bright in spite of her aging features. Her kindness and friendly personality made up for her lost looks, so much so that after a mere couple of hours of knowing her, a person didn't notice the incredible wrinkles, and the fact that when she smiled she showed only two teeth. "Well, you'll have fun at the dance," she told Maggie. "You and Sage hit town at just the right time. And I sure am glad to see Sage has took a wife. I ain't seen him since he was still a hell-raiser and ridin' with outlaws. I'm glad to see him happy and settled."

Maggie decided not to explain that Sage had already been married once. Maybe Ma knew, but decided not to ask questions. "Sage said he'd take care of me having the proper dress for tonight," she told Ma.

"He sure kept his promise. Where on earth did he get this? I don't remember seeing a dress shop, but then I haven't seen the whole town."

She wondered what Ma's first name really was, or if she'd ever been married herself. Sage told her no one in town knew much about Ma—only that she'd come to Atlantic City one day, paid to build a rooming house, and then settled there. By then, she was already getting old.

"Well, now, there ain't much to the town, darlin'," Ma answered. "Far as that dress, you'll have to ask Sage. He said I shouldn't tell you."

Maggie felt a tiny sting of jealousy, suspecting the dress came from his visit to a local prostitute—maybe more than one—to find something they could use to keep Maggie from getting pregnant. He'd dropped off the dress without an explanation and left to visit a bathhouse. Maggie worried about the man called John Polk, but as far as she knew, Sage had no more trouble with him.

"I have to say, you're lucky he found a dress small enough to fit ya'," Ma added. "You're about the tiniest woman I've ever met, 'sides Louella over at—" She covered her mouth, and her eyes widened as though she'd been caught red-handed at something. "Don't tell Sage I said anything. And he didn't have no choice. There *is* a dress shop in town, but they didn't have anything that comes near to fittin' you. I'm the one who told him about Louella over at... well... over at Delight Cabin. It's a saloon. There's only two girls that work upstairs, and I knew one of 'em was about your size. She's right nice. Really. And Sage... I can see in his eyes how he feels about you. You shouldn't ought to worry where he got that dress."

Maggie almost felt sorry for her. She looked ready to cry at accidentally revealing the source of the dress. "It's okay, Ma. I already suspected." Maggie looked in the mirror again. "Thank you so much for doing my hair. I've never worn it like this before. I hate to take it back down after the dance, but I sure can't ride the trail looking like this."

Ma smiled, but kept her lips closed, obviously a bit embarrassed about her lonely teeth. She walked closer and tugged on one curl to make it dangle a bit longer. "You sure can't—not in this country."

Someone knocked on the door. Ma opened it, and there stood Sage, in clean denim pants and a white shirt with a black string tie. He looked wonderful, and the stunned look on his face made Maggie feel even more beautiful. He shook his head in wonder. "By God, Maggie, you're—"

"Beautiful, that's what she is," Ma finished for him, chuckling. "Now, you two get on to the dance." She glanced at the six-gun that hung in its holster at Sage's side. "You gonna wear that thing? It's a friendly dance."

Sage glanced at the old woman, scowling slightly. "Do you really expect me to leave my weapon behind in this country, with a woman on my arm who looks like Maggie, and with the chance of running into the men we're after? That doesn't include the fact that John Polk is probably still around."

Ma shrugged. "You know the code out here. Ain't no men gonna give you trouble at that dance, 'specially knowin' Maggie's your wife. And from your description, I ain't seen any of the men you told me about. You know me. I don't miss much in this town. Ain't like we're a big city where nobody knows his neighbor. Far as that Polk fella—none of the other men will let him bother anybody at that dance."

"We can't be too careful, Ma." He looked at Maggie again. "Ma is right. You *are* beautiful. I already knew that, but I didn't expect anything like this, even after all the time we've been together."

Maggie felt like crying. "Thank you… for the dance… for this dress."

He walked closer, leaning down to kiss her cheek. "Let's go, Mrs. Lightfoot."

How she wished that really were her name… Maggie took his arm.

"Wait." Ma walked to a wardrobe and opened the doors, reaching into the bottom of the closet and taking out a lovely knitted shawl. She brought it to Maggie. "You might need this later. There's always a chill in the air in the mountains at night. This belonged to me when I was young… and pretty… a long time ago. I haven't worn it for years, but it's too special to give away, so I've always kept it. My own ma knitted this for me."

Maggie took the shawl, marveling at the softness of the yarn used to make it. "It's beautiful. Thank you so much." She threw it around her shoulders, wondering at the old woman's past and the secrets it held. "Are you going to the dance, Ma?"

The old lady waved her off. "Ain't nobody gonna dance with me. I'll be takin' over a couple of pies and cakes later, but I ain't stayin'. I'll keep the coffee hot here for you two."

"You're wrong about nobody wanting a dance," Sage told her, giving her a wink. "Most of the men in town would love at least one whirl with you, and I'm one of them."

Ma chuckled. "Go on with you now." She gave both a light shove. "Have a good time."

Maggie left with Sage, wishing every day from here on could be this wonderful.

Twenty-six

Maggie couldn't remember enjoying herself this much in her whole life. The local citizens had transformed the livery into a real dance hall, having cleaned the stalls and pushed the hay aside. A table along the back wall boasted a variety of cakes and pies, as well as a huge bowl of strawberry punch. A three-man band made up of two fiddles and a banjo played a mixture of slow tunes and fast-paced dances with moves called by a bearded man wearing bib overalls. Maggie's only experience at dancing came from when she would whirl around her house or in the fields alone back home. This was all new to her, and being raised by missionaries and then running with outlaws, Sage's own experience with legitimate social frolics was limited. He'd confessed that what little he did know came from dancing in saloons with not so legitimate women. Together they managed to move to the slow dances with reasonable ease, their personal emotions taking over in a natural rhythm that helped them move about the hard-packed dirt floor with few stumbles. Neither wanted to try the square dances, but others helped them learn the whirling movements and partner changes that had everyone laughing and stomping their feet.

There were only five other women present, three of them wives of local business owners, and two of those being the women Maggie had seen standing near the supply store earlier. They introduced themselves as Mary Calus and Elizabeth McKenzie. One of them asked Maggie if she was the same girl they'd seen at the store. When Maggie proudly declared she was, they all had a good laugh.

The fourth woman was the daughter of an older couple. Maggie guessed her to be perhaps sixteen, but she was big as a man—nothing feminine about her. Still, the oversupply of men there seemed happy to dance with any female, manly or not, and the girl was flirting unmercifully with all of them. At times, for lack of feminine partners, men danced with each other, which led to hilarious and colorful remarks.

The fifth woman was a middle-aged widow named Alice Beemer. She'd come here with her husband and opened a laundry. According to Elizabeth, Alice's husband was killed trying to stop a man from robbing him. The rest of the townsmen promptly caught and hanged the murderer… one of the strange forms of justice in a lawless country. Alice stayed on and continued with the laundry service.

Maggie realized that any number of these men had likely committed crimes and acts of violence outside this haven for outlaws, but inside their own community, they adhered to their own unwritten—and unspoken—laws. Outlaw country seemed removed from the rest of the world, its own little kingdom with its own citizens and its own set of rules.

No one was dressed in frills and suits. Maggie had a feeling few people in this remote little town even owned fashionable clothing, but it didn't matter. They were simply having fun the best way they could, celebrating the coming of warmer weather after what Ma told her earlier had been a miserably cold, snowy winter that kept most inside for days on end.

It felt good to be off the trail, happy and relaxed. What made it even better was knowing that tonight, she and Sage would sleep together in a real bed. She looked at him now as he turned her to another slow dance, telling herself she couldn't think about James or her pregnancy or the real reason she and Sage were here in Atlantic City. Tonight was too wonderful. She felt adored and protected.

Another dance ended. Sage struck up a conversation with a local rancher, asking if he'd lost many cattle because of the harsh winter. Maggie saw Ma Pilger setting a pie on the table. She walked over to greet the old woman.

"Ma, you have to stay. Sage will be upset if you leave without at least one dance."

"Oh, no. I'm not even dressed up."

"It doesn't matter. I'll bet every single man here will want at least one dance." Maggie took hold of the woman's hand and urged her to where Sage stood talking. The fiddlers struck up another waltz as Sage turned to greet Ma. He put out his arms and told Maggie to slice him some pie while he danced "with the prettiest woman here." He began turning Ma

Pilger about the room, while the other men whistled and got in line to cut in.

Maggie walked back to the pies and moved between the table and the wall so she'd be at a better angle to cut into a pie.

"Well, now, ain't you the best lookin' woman this side of the Rockies?"

The voice sounded familiar. Maggie looked across the table then felt as though her heart dropped to her feet, along with all her blood. There stood the fat, bald man Sage told her was called Cleve Fletcher, one of the three men who'd raped her. He grinned.

"What's yer name, honey?"

He didn't even recognize her! She'd been nothing to him, a woman without a name, someone to poke, then leave lost and alone in a cruel land with her dead husband lying beside her!

"What the hell is wrong with you?" Cleve said with a frown. "You look like you've seen a ghost. I ain't that ugly, am I?" He laughed a familiar, ugly laugh and reached across the table, grabbing her arm. "Come dance with me, darlin'. I just rode into town and heard the music—figured I'd come see what's up."

Maggie's thoughts converged in a mixture of panic, revulsion, and hatred. Sage! Cleve would recognize him the minute Sage turned around! She had to protect Sage!

There was no time to think—no time to run to Sage and warn him. And tonight, she was completely taken by surprise—she wasn't carrying a gun.

She never expected it all to happen this way. She looked past Cleve, wondering if his two friends were with him, but she saw no one familiar. His eyes darkened more, anger moving into them.

"You gonna dance with me, or do I have to wait outside to catch you for somethin' more than a dance?"

Maggie jerked her arm away. "Let me get around the other side of the table." She hurried so she'd be near the main dance floor. The anger left Cleve's eyes, replaced with the same hideous hunger she'd seen only weeks ago. His cheeks were so fat that his eyes were more like slits in his face.

Quickly, Maggie bolted, hurrying after Sage and grasping his gun.

"What the—" Sage let go of Ma as Maggie turned, raising the six-gun and aiming it at Cleve, whose eyes widened as he went for his own gun.

In an instant, Sage grabbed Maggie's arm and tackled her to the floor, ripping the pistol out of her hand.

"You!" he heard Cleve yell.

Sage rolled face up to see Cleve's gun out of its holster. Women screamed and ran. Sage fired, and Cleve stood there a moment, his own six-gun half raised.

"Lightfoot!" he mumbled.

Her elbow hurt from being tackled by someone more than twice her weight. Maggie half sat up, staring at Cleve as he continued to stand there while blood spread outward from a hole in his chest. Maggie ripped the combs from her hair.

"And me!" she screamed. "Remember me?" She let her hair fall. "Remember the woman and her husband alone on the plains south of here?"

Recognition finally sparked in Cleve's eyes. The

life oozed out of him, and his legs folded as he plunked to the floor butt first. Sage got up and walked over to him, grabbing Cleve's gun from his hand. "Where are the other two?" he demanded. "Are they here in town?"

Cleve looked at him. He shook his head. "...Lander," he choked out, before the last spark of life left his eyes. He died sitting up... staring.

Sage shoved the man's six-gun into the waist of his pants and placed his own revolver back in its holster. He put a foot on Cleve's chest and forced his body out flat before it could completely stiffen. He knelt down then and rummaged through the dead man's pockets, pulling a leather money pouch from inside his jacket. He grabbed some bills and counted them while everyone stared. Then Sage ripped a chain watch from the man's belt.

He rose, shoving the money and watch into the front pocket of his pants. He glanced around the room. "This man and two of his friends once worked for me. They killed my best ranch hand, abused his wife, and stole money from me. I intend to get all of it back. Anybody here object to me taking what money this one had?" He rested a hand on his six-gun.

People shook their heads.

"You got a right, mister," one man spoke up.

Others nodded.

Suddenly, a man bolted out of the barn, as though frightened.

"Polk!" Sage shouted. He ran after the man. Maggie wondered when on earth John Polk had snuck inside... and what he might have to do with what just happened. Ma Pilger and Elizabeth helped her to her feet. Outside, a shot was fired.

"Sage," Maggie muttered. Was he all right?

Everything became so quiet inside the barn that they all heard a horse gallop away.

To Maggie's relief, Sage stormed back inside and up to Maggie. "The sonofabitch got away!" he growled. "I couldn't keep shooting into the dark for fear of hitting someone else." He took hold of Maggie's arm supportively and then scanned the staring crowd. "The man I just killed is called Cleve Fletcher," he explained. "The others I'm looking for are a younger one called Jimmy Hart, and an old bearded man called Jasper. The one who just rode off is a big man called John Polk. He's an abuser of women. Has anybody here ever heard of them?"

Nearly all shook their heads, most still watching in shock and surprise. Finally, Ma Pilger walked up to Sage. "You'd best take Maggie back to the rooming house," she told him. "She's lookin' pale, Sage. The men here will take care of that one." She glanced at Cleve's body.

Maggie looked at Sage and knew by his demeanor that he was angry with her for grabbing his gun the way she did.

"Maggie and I will be heading out in the morning," he told Ma. "Dying men usually don't lie, so I'm figuring Fletcher told the truth about the other two being in Lander. I have a damn good idea that's where Polk is headed too."

He looked around the room again.

"Sorry for ruining the dance, folks. Go on with the

music. There won't be any more trouble." He turned to Maggie, who suddenly felt ill. Being surprised by Cleve reopened ugly memories that got the better of her. She started to sway, felt someone lift her. "Sage," she murmured.

He picked her up and carried her out.

Twenty-seven

Maggie felt Sage's anger. He was stiff with it. She closed her eyes and rested her head on his shoulder. "I was afraid that if I called out your name, or if that man noticed you first, he'd shoot you before you realized he was there. All I could think to do was grab your gun and shoot him first."

Sage didn't reply. He kept walking until they reached Ma's place. He set her on her feet, then took her arm and led her to their room. He turned up a lantern Ma had left lit.

"I forgot Ma's shawl," Maggie said.

"She'll find it." Sage began undressing. "Get your clothes off. We'll both need our rest. We'll leave early for Lander." It was an order. He'd become the angry outlaw again.

Maggie began undressing. She stepped out of her dress and let it fall, then removed her many slips and unlaced her camisole. The magic of the night was ruined, and she wanted to cry. She took off the camisole and laid it aside, then pulled on her robe.

She walked to the other side of the bed, her back to

Sage as he finished undressing. She unlaced her shoes, something else Sage bought from the harlot named Louellen. The air in the room seemed too heavy. Everything was different. *Sage* was different. In spite of the warm night, Maggie felt cold.

"I only got six hundred dollars off that bastard," Sage grumbled. "They took four thousand. I hope I find the rest on the other two. If they divided it up, maybe I'll at least get another fifteen hundred of it back. God knows how much they spent on horses, whores, and gambling. And now, I'm wondering what John Polk might have had to do with all this."

Maggie didn't reply, not sure what words might soothe his anger or make him madder. She sat on the side of the bed… waiting… not sure what for. A beating? No—not from Sage Lightfoot. A good tongue-lashing? Surely, she'd get that much. She felt the bed moving and noticed the room dim as Sage apparently turned down the lantern. His arm came around her then, and he pulled her under the covers… and into his arms.

"Damn it, Maggie, did I hurt you when I pushed you down?"

"I don't think so. I'm still in shock." Maggie shivered. "I never expected to see that man's face, Sage. I couldn't believe it."

Sage pressed her closer. "I should have been more alert. This is an example of why you can never let your guard down in this country. Promise me you'll never try to take things into your own hands again."

Maggie snuggled her face into his neck. "I promise."

Sage wrapped a hand into her hair. "Seeing that son of a bitch must bring back ugly memories."

She moved an arm around his middle, loving the feeling of safety in his arms. Sage stroked her hair, and in the next moment, he covered her mouth in a fiery kiss as he pushed open her robe.

"Let me take it away, Maggie," he offered, his voice husky with desire. "Let me help erase the bad memories."

She closed her eyes and enjoyed the taste of his mouth, the gentle strokes of his hands. "Sage," she whispered. "His face… that awful face…"

"Look at me, Maggie."

She gazed into his eyes.

"It's me. Sage. And I promise you, men like that will never touch you again."

Maggie melted into him, needing to remind herself how good and beautiful this could be. She felt him move inside of her, gently burying himself deep, claiming her, owning her, taking away the ugly memories Cleve Fletcher had revived. This was Sage… and he knew how to make this a matter of ecstasy and joy. Maggie responded from the sheer pleasure he quickly awakened, meeting his gentle rhythm, until she gasped with the splendor of his manhood.

Soon his life spilled into her. He relaxed then, and Maggie could tell most of his initial anger had finally left him. He rolled away from her and scooted up against the headboard.

Maggie put an arm across his solid stomach and rested her head against his chest.

"I shouldn't have made love to you without protection." He sighed. "I swore I wouldn't do that. I just… I wanted to take it all away, Maggie."

"It's okay. I *needed* you to take it all away." Maggie

couldn't help wondering if the dead man back at the barn dance might be her baby's father. How could she tell Sage such a thing?

"Still, I'm sorry." Sage caressed her hair. "After seeing that bastard, you probably weren't ready for taking a man."

"I'm the one who's sorry, Sage. I reacted in all the wrong ways."

He squeezed her closer. "Just don't grab for my gun again. If I didn't quickly realize it was you, I might have swung around and clobbered you full force. I could have hurt you really bad before I realized what was happening."

"I know."

"Do you see what I mean about the possibility of you being caught without your gun? What if he'd waited till you walked outside? You'd have been as helpless as that night on the prairie."

"But what if he saw you first? I did what I did so he couldn't take you off guard."

"Maggie!" He leaned on one elbow and made her look at him. In the dim light, she could see the determination and sureness in his dark eyes. "How often do I need to remind you that I rode with men like that for years? I've handled men far more dangerous than Cleve Fletcher—believe me. Get that through your head, or you'll get us killed. You might have got Ma killed tonight, or some other innocent person."

Maggie wilted against him. "He came out of nowhere. And when I realized he didn't recognize me at first… realized I'd been nothing but a faceless woman that night he and the others—"

Sage put a hand to her lips. "They actually never touched you, Maggie. That's how I see it. They didn't touch what's inside… here." He ran his fingers between her breasts. "From what you've told me, not even your husband touched you that way. I'm the only one who has, so put the others out of your head. I'm the only man you've ever given yourself to willingly."

The words stabbed at her heart. She reached around his neck and pulled him to her, tasting his mouth willingly. "Make love to me again, Sage… the right way."

He gladly obliged, and the way he moved over her… the way he took her yet again… made her feel beautiful, cherished, protected.

They settled under the covers for some badly needed rest. Tomorrow they would leave for Lander. Soon, this part of their journey would be over. They'd go back to Paradise Valley. Maggie hoped that by then Sage would love her so much that when she told him the truth, he'd actually accept it, and it wouldn't change his feelings for her. She clung to him, wishing she'd never have to let go.

Twenty-eight

Sage worked the horses and mules hard, in a hurry to reach Lander. Every day was the same, not much talk, a lot of riding, few stops. More than once, Maggie was grateful for the sure-footed steeds Sage had chosen for the trip. One trail took them several days over mountainside cutouts barely wide enough for the animals. They finally reached a point where they had to dismount and lead the horses by the reins—"Just in case one goes over the edge," Sage told her.

Maggie dared to glance over the side into what seemed a bottomless canyon. "Just so one of *us* doesn't go over the edge," she muttered, more to herself than to Sage. She felt sick to her stomach, unsure if it was her pregnancy or the reeling height. "How much farther before we start going down instead of up?" she spoke louder to Sage.

"A half mile maybe." He stopped and looked back. "You okay?"

Maggie took a deep breath. "Well, on this whole journey, whenever we were high, it was always someplace where there was still plenty of ground under us. We've never been on such a narrow path."

Sage turned and kept walking. "It gets a little wider not much farther ahead. Just keep your eyes on the path, and don't look down."

Sure. Maggie did as he said. "What happens if we meet someone coming down?"

"Then they have to figure out a way to turn around and go back up till we reach a place wide enough to pass each other."

Fine. Simple. Maggie thought how, if she wasn't so damned scared, she'd enjoy stopping to drink in the stunning view. Across the awesome canyon she spotted a cascading waterfall. A green-gray haze drifted lazily around rocky spires that jutted upward from the canyon. Ahead lay endless peaks that stretched into the horizon.

"How far do you think we can see from here?"

"Forty-fifty miles... probably more. Hard to tell. Damn big, isn't it?"

"Big isn't a fitting enough word. I've never felt so small in my life," she called aloud. *Fifty miles—maybe more.* Again, as had happened so often since her attack and James's death, Maggie couldn't fathom she was really here. Never in her wildest dreams did she imagine she'd end up carrying an outlaw's baby, while traveling through the most desolate, frightening landscape one could travel... with a man she'd met only eight weeks ago, yet she had already slept with him... already fallen in love with him.

Who was Maggie Tucker? She'd lost her identity... her perspective... her husband and the life she thought she'd be leading, perhaps in Oregon by now. What if her attack had never occurred? She'd have spent the rest of her days in a loveless marriage, working a new farm, never knowing this kind of adventure… never meeting Sage Lightfoot. She remembered once, when she was little, her mother told her that God had a plan for everyone. If His plan was for her to fall in love with Sage, then she could only pray it would last.

Still, how could Sage possibly care about some other man's child? If he turned her out, she'd find a way to raise her baby and never tell him or her about its beginnings. She'd make something up about the father—make him sound like the most wonderful man who ever lived.

She couldn't think of a better man than Sage. What a strong, protective father he would be… *could* be… if he chose. He'd built his fine home big enough for children, but he'd planned to have those children with Joanna. Why would he want to raise the bastard child of an outlaw? Her heart fell at the thought of how easily his love for her would likely blow away with the Wyoming wind once he saw Joanna again.

A few rocks let loose and went tumbling, disappearing into the chasm below and bringing Maggie's thoughts to the current situation. Sage stopped and looked back.

"I'm all right," she assured him.

"They say that on this trail even the horses and mules pray."

"I have no doubt they do," Maggie answered.

Minutes later, as Sage promised, the roadway finally widened. How the road even came to be was a mystery.

How many men had died when they first searched for a way over this mountain? How many more died chipping at the mountainside, probably using dynamite to create this excuse of a road?

After another hour of walking as close to heaven as Maggie figured she'd ever be without dying, they headed downward. Maggie soon realized that going down was no less harrowing than going up… maybe worse.

"Do we have to come over this trail when we head back to Paradise Valley?" she asked Sage, nervously wanting to keep a conversation going.

"No," Sage answered. "To get back to the ranch, we'll head farther east first, then south. That country is more open. We'll mostly be looking at the mountains instead of traveling through them."

Thank God.

They finally reached an area where the path widened considerably for a good half mile.

"We'll camp here. The horses need a rest after that climb."

The *horses* need a rest?

"Going down is about as difficult as coming up," Sage continued. "I don't want the horses trying to fight gravity and loosen stone when they're tired out."

Heaven forbid. Maggie breathed a sigh of relief. "I'm all for stopping," she agreed. "Will we be able to make a fire?"

Sage looked at the scrubby growth on the side of the mountain. "Not from anything up here, but we should have enough left from the wood bundle we brought to make one later. We'll wait till it's darker. It'll get pretty cold up here, even though it's plenty warm now in the valleys." He unloaded some of his gear.

Maggie watched him thoughtfully. Again, while they traveled, he'd said nothing about loving her, and nothing more about their encounter with Cleve Fletcher. Once they were on the trail, he was all business, and now, more than ever, he was zeroed in on finding Fletcher's friends, as well as John Polk. He reminded Maggie of a hound on the scent. They'd traveled so hard and fast that neither had the energy at night to consider making love, let alone how uncomfortable it would be.

They made camp and ate some cold biscuits Ma had given them. The old woman hugged them before they left, wished them luck. Maggie liked Ma. She had a feeling the old woman would have understood what she was going through right now. Maybe Ma could have given her some advice.

Darkness came rapidly, as it always did out here. Sage built a fire, and they spread their bedrolls close to it.

"We'd better take turns keeping watch of the horses and mules," Sage told her. "There could be wolves or grizzlies up here—usually not this high, but you never know."

"Well, after being so tense all the way up here, I could use some sleep first, if you don't care," Maggie told him.

"Fine with me." Sage rolled and lit a cigarette. "By the way, you aren't carrying, are you?"

The question took Maggie by complete surprise. Her heart pounded. Did he somehow know? "What?" she asked, hardly able to find her voice.

"Back there in Atlantic City… I still feel guilty that I didn't use protection. I was so damn mad and worked up over what happened that I just didn't care."

Maggie breathed a little easier, but his question made lying feel like she was stabbing him in the back. "I wouldn't know this soon. It would take me another month to know for sure."

Sage smoked quietly. "Good. By then, we should be back at the ranch where we can talk things out."

Talk things out? Was he having doubts? Was he thinking about that letter from Joanna and how he'd feel if he saw her again?

"Sage."

"Yeah?"

"No matter what happens, I love you and always will." Maggie watched the red embers of the end of his cigarette as he drew on it. He exhaled as he walked to where she stood and wrapped his arms around her. Maggie breathed in his now-familiar scent.

"Same here," he answered. "Now go to sleep. You'll need your rest for tomorrow."

Maggie knew that's all she would get out of him. *Same here*. That was better than nothing at all. For now, he was Sage Lightfoot the hunter. Tender moments would be scarce while on the trail of men he intended to kill.

Twenty-nine

Mud splattered everywhere as Sage and Maggie headed toward the main street of Lander, Wyoming, another town Sage frequented in his outlaw days. He often wondered how and why he'd managed to survive the wild, lawless life he once led, constantly on the hoof, and never sure when the man behind him might shoot him in the back. How many of the men he once rode with were gone now… dead from violence or disease or too much drink? Being back in this country and around men like Cutter and Cleve Fletcher reminded Sage of the life he'd gladly left behind when he settled in Paradise Valley.

He finally had a place to call home… and he missed it. He even missed Joanna, but not the Joanna who'd left him. He missed the Joanna he'd loved in his youth.

Now there was Maggie Tucker to consider, an up-front, no tricks, no-strings-attached woman who fit ranch life like one of his cowboys. She was brave, rugged… yet beautiful in a tiny, fragile way. Her outward appearance belied her tough innards, and in someone like Maggie, a man had a true partner.

Woman or not, and despite her size, in many ways she was his equal. And damned if she couldn't, by God, bring him right down to her size when she wanted.

Two days of steady rain, highly unusual for this time of year, left them drenched and eager for a dry bed. They passed a lumberyard, where a team of sixteen mules pulling a wagon piled with logs headed into the street. The wagon's wheels were a good foot wide and made of iron—the wagon itself obviously reinforced to carry extra weight. Sage figured so much lumber must be for a pretty big building, maybe a school.

He shook his head at the thought of a school in a place like this. On a distant hill he noticed a steeple… a *church*. This once-wild town might become a settled, law-abiding place after all. It was a lot bigger than the last time he was here. They rode past a bank, a dry goods store, a livery, lawyer's offices, a doctor's office, a billiards hall, a feed store, a leather goods store, hat shops, and of course, several saloons.

Sage recognized three of the saloons, but the others were new since he was here last. At least the place was big enough now that there should be a decent hotel or rooming house where he and Maggie could again sleep in a real bed.

He glanced at Maggie, huddled under her floppy leather hat as rain dripped off its brim. The trip over the dangerous mountain trail had taken its toll, let alone riding in the rain the last two days. Sage continued to be impressed by her dogged determination to complete this journey. Most women would have given up a long time ago. Joanna would never have come along in the first place.

He kept a watchful eye on the people who eyed them from the boardwalks and from the stoops of buildings. Lander was not so big that its inhabitants didn't notice newcomers, which meant he should be able to find Jimmy Hart and the man named Jasper, as well as John Polk, if indeed, they were here. He decided he'd first get Maggie settled in a decent room where she could bathe and rest, then he'd pay a visit to the saloons and whorehouses, the most likely places to find the men he was after.

He'd much rather Maggie wasn't along when he found them. He hated the risk of her getting hurt, and he worried she'd make another rash decision if she saw them. The crazy woman kept thinking she could do this herself, as well as thinking she needed to protect him. He shook his head at the memory of how she'd shot that grizzly, staved off wolves, and then decided she'd shoot Cleve Fletcher. He could smile about it now, but it sure wasn't funny at the time.

They reached a side street where he saw a sign on the corner that read *Kate's Rooms*, with an arrow pointing to the right. Sage reined Storm in that direction. He had no idea if the rooms were decent, but the rain came down so hard now that he was ready to take shelter no matter what kind of place it was.

Thunder rolled in the distance, and Storm balked. Sage thought about Maggie being afraid of storms. He needed to get her inside. Lightning flashed, and another clap of thunder quickly followed. He looked back to see Maggie calming an unsettled Smoke. He rode back to grab hold of the horse's bridle. "I'll get you out of this quick," he told Maggie. "Come on."

He kicked Storm into a faster gait and headed for the two-story frame house called *Kate's*. A picket fence outlined an attempt at growing grass in the front yard, and a couple of budding rosebushes adorned each side of the porch steps. Sage quickly dismounted and tied the horses and mules, then walked around Storm to help Maggie down, but she'd already dismounted.

"I can't wait to get out of this rain," she declared as she hurried past him and through the fence gate. She bounded onto the front porch to get out of the pounding torrent. Sage took a couple of long strides behind her and leapt onto the porch without using the steps.

They knocked on the front door of the rooming house, and a dark-haired, voluptuous, but aging woman answered. Immediately, her eyes widened with recognition. "Sage Lightfoot! Come on in!"

Sage was dumbfounded. There stood someone from his past, and he couldn't have been more pleased to see her again. "Kate Bassett?"

"You're lookin' at her, honey!" The woman opened her arms, and Sage walked into them. After a long embrace, Sage heard the door close behind them. He realized Maggie must be a bit taken aback by the way he'd greeted the woman who answered the door. Before he could explain anything, Kate captured his attention.

"Where have you been, cowboy?" she asked. "God, you seem even taller than I remembered!" She squeezed him around the middle again, then stepped back and looked him over. "No less handsome, I see," she added with a grin. "You're the best-looking man who ever rode outlaw country!"

Sage laughed. "And you're still a damn good-looking woman, Kate." She was older, but still had the pretty skin he remembered. Although she'd gained several pounds, she still had a hell of a shape. "What are you doing running a rooming house in Lander?"

Kate shrugged. "Don't you remember me telling you once that I was saving my money to open a legitimate business?" she answered with a wink. "I did just that. I've had this place for a year now, and I'm doing pretty good. I heard you settled someplace—built yourself a ranch. I even heard you got married." Her gaze turned to Maggie. "This your wife?"

Sage removed his hat. "Not yet, but as soon as we take care of our business here, that's likely to change. And yes, I was married, but she divorced me and took off for California—didn't like ranch life."

Kate shook her head. "Any woman who'd run off on you has marbles for brains. You should have asked me to settle with you." She laughed lightly and looked at Maggie again. "Don't take me seriously, honey. That big Indian and I go back a ways, but it was a few years ago." She shook her head. "Sweetheart, get that hat off and shrug off that wet jacket. You look like a cold, wet little deer."

"I feel like one," Maggie answered, removing her hat.

Sage saw the wonder in Maggie's eyes, felt her tension and curiosity.

"My, my, look at that pretty red hair!" Kate exclaimed. She reached out and took Maggie's hat from her, then frowned at Sage. "For Pete's sake, Sage, she looks like a kid."

Sage grinned and put an arm around Maggie, who wasn't too fond of the realization that Kate and Sage knew each other intimately. Kate's remark about a "legitimate" business told Maggie all she needed to know. "Believe me, Kate, she's no kid. This is Maggie Tucker, and don't be fooled by her size. She can handle herself like no woman I've ever known up to now. The reason we're here is a long story. I'll tell it to you later over a cup of coffee."

Kate nodded. "Well, you obviously need a room and dry clothes before you come into the kitchen for that coffee." She took Maggie's arm. "I'll take the little lady here to a room and start preparing a bath for her. I have a man who lives out back who can take care of your horses. Take them around back, Sage, and bring your gear into the kitchen after you unload it, so your things can dry out."

"Thanks. Our horses and mules need to be rubbed down and fed some oats."

"Well, my man is called Newell McCabe. He's a damn good friend and sometimes more than that. He'll take care of the animals for you." Kate led Maggie down a hallway.

Maggie glanced at Sage with a rather helpless look. He gave her a reassuring smile. Poor Maggie had come upon yet another rude awakening to the kind of life he'd once led, and she didn't know what to think. One thing was sure. Once they got through all of this, if Maggie Tucker still loved and wanted him, there would be no doubt that her love was real. Any woman who would put up with his past and accept him just the way he was couldn't be more fitting for life at Paradise Valley, but first they both had to make it home alive.

Thirty

Kate poured another bucket of hot water into the tin tub she'd set up for Maggie. "I told Sage to stay in the kitchen and have some coffee with Newell while you take a bath."

"Sage needs a bath too. He's as soaked and tired as I am." Maggie was unsure how she should react to Kate Bassett. It was obvious she'd been special to Sage at one time. He apparently trusted her implicitly because he'd told Kate right off that they weren't married. Up until now, he'd been so adamant that people believe they were husband and wife.

"Don't worry, honey. He'll get his bath." Kate carried the empty bucket to the bedroom door. "I'll bring in one more bucket. I keep plenty of hot water around so I can fix up a bath pretty quick for anybody who needs one. Makes for better business. I keep meaning to put the words *Hot Baths* on my sign, but I haven't got around to it yet. You get undressed and climb in. I'll soap you up and wash your hair for you."

Maggie stood there a bit dumbfounded. "I can do it myself."

Kate waved her off. "Get those clothes off, and let somebody pamper you. If you've been on the trail a long time in this country, you *need* pampering. And believe me, you don't have anything I haven't seen. I used to run a place with ten girls working for me. I know that probably shocks you, but that's the way life is out here for some women. Don't be offended."

"It's not that. I'm just not used to undressing in front of somebody."

Kate laughed, a deep, genuine, good-hearted laugh. "Except for Sage, I'll bet." She left, and Maggie hurriedly undressed and climbed into the tub.

Kate returned with the last bucket and dumped the water into the tub, then walked to a dresser and grabbed a bar of soap. "This is *good* soap, not so harsh, and it smells good too. Nothing but the best for Kate's customers, I say." She walked over and dipped the soap into the water. "Put your feet up, and I'll give you a foot massage," she told Maggie. "Let me do something nice for Sage Lightfoot's future wife."

Maggie wasn't so sure that would turn out to be true, but she said nothing. She put her feet up on the edge of the tub and relished the welcome massage.

"So, you're crazy in love with Sage, I'll bet."

Maggie blushed. "I love him very much." For the next several minutes, Maggie found herself pouring out her story of how she and Sage met, what had happened to her, the unhappiness of her first marriage, why she and Sage were on the trail. Kate had a way of making a person spill out their hearts, a surprising motherly air about her that made her an easy confidante. By the time she finished her story, her bath was over, and her hair was washed.

"You have a beautiful strength and spirit, Maggie. Sage sees that, I'm sure." Kate turned and grabbed a large towel, then held it open. "Come on. Climb out."

Maggie obeyed, wrapping herself into the towel. "I've never been treated so royally," she told Kate. "All the people I meet who once knew Sage are so good to me."

Kate laughed lightly. "That's because they have so much respect for Sage, and they love anybody Sage loves. He needs a woman who's as strong-minded as he is, a woman who's tough. I've just met you, and I already like you, mainly because I can tell you make Sage happy. Sage and me—we go back a long way. He's a man who deserves to be happy—a man who's easy to love. And I have a feeling that even though Sage could throw you across the room, you have a way of hauling in the reins and making him do whatever you want."

"I don't know about that," Maggie answered as Kate wrapped her hair in a smaller towel. "I only know that I love him." She walked to her leather satchel to retrieve a flannel nightgown then moved behind a dressing screen to dry off.

"I met Sage when he was nineteen—an angry, hurt young man with no direction," Kate told her. "It's pretty bad when outlaws and women like me give more food and shelter to an abandoned young man than the supposedly good Christian people who raised him."

Maggie came out from behind the dressing screen, buttoning the gown. "Did you ever travel with him?"

Kate shook her head. "No, I kept a brothel down by Brown's Park. Then I came up to Atlantic City. Sometimes, a few of us would travel the Outlaw Trail for weeks at a time to make extra money. I saw quite a bit of Sage because him and his kind hung out all over the area. Sage seemed to… well… favor my company… I guess you'd say. But I'm about fifteen years older than he is, and I think a tiny part of him was looking for a woman who'd listen to him, comfort his loneliness." She picked up a brush from the dressing table. "God knows, the kind of love I give is a far cry from motherly, but somehow, we ended up good friends who could talk to each other. There were times when that's all we'd do all night—talk—if you can believe that." She let out more rich laughter. "Come on over here, and let me brush that hair."

Maggie sat down in front of the dressing table, and Kate brushed her hair.

"Is Newell your man now?" Kate asked her.

"My man?" Kate shrugged. "Well, I guess you could put it that way. We're good friends, sometimes lovers, when we need that kind of love. Newell keeps an eye out for me, does chores, takes care of the horses—things like that. I pay him with a room to sleep in, meals, and—well—any other needs he has. I know that sounds terrible to somebody like you, but that's how it is with women like me and men like Newell. Neither one of us tries to fool the other that we're anything special."

Maggie frowned. "But you *are* special. You take care of people nobody else cares about."

"Well, now, aren't you sweet?"

Maggie shrugged. "Most of my growing up years I didn't have a mother or any other woman around. You and a lady called Ma Pilger are the nicest women I've ever met."

"Ma?" Kate laughed again. "I don't blame you there. Everybody likes Ma Pilger. She was never a whore like me. She was more of the mother figure I mentioned earlier. There isn't a man in all of outlaw country who'd even consider laying a hand on her wrongly or stealing from her." She pulled the brush through Maggie's hair. "It's a strange sort of character you'll find in country like this. There's the good and the bad, and sometimes, they actually work together to survive."

Maggie thought about Whitey and the men who put them up for a night. "I'm learning that, but some are just plain bad, through and through."

Kate handed her the brush. "Oh, I won't argue that one." She looked at Maggie in the mirror. "I'm going to set up a bath for Sage. I'll make you a tray of food and bring it to you. I make a pretty good beef stew, if I say so myself." She walked to the door. "Get some rest, honey. The other roomers have already eaten, and I have rules here—no visitors or loud noise after supper. They stick to it pretty good. I'll bring you that food and send Sage in later, after he's eaten and had his bath."

Maggie couldn't help but respond in surprise. "Won't he take his bath in here?"

Kate let out another round of deep laughter. "Don't worry. I have a men's bathing room. Soon as the tub is filled with hot water, I'll leave him on his own." She shook her head. "I gotta say, though, it would have been nice if he'd shown up here alone." She laughed again and walked out, closing the door.

Maggie stared after her, a bit bewildered by the characters who lived in this land. She should be offended by someone like Kate—appalled at her past—but she actually liked her. She wondered if she should tell Kate about the baby. She desperately needed to share her predicament with someone, and Kate apparently knew Sage well enough to help her decide what to do. Maybe she could help her tell him… maybe even convince him to accept the child.

Then again, maybe Kate would lose respect for her—be angry that she was deceiving Sage. After all, they were good friends. Maggie decided that from here on, every day she got to spend with Sage was a gift… a gift that would be likely taken away once the truth came out.

Thirty-one

Sage welcomed a chance to talk with Kate, one of the few people from his past he was happy to see again. She was the only woman he knew who smoked cigars. She lit one now as he finished his stew and leaned back to enjoy a cup of coffee. "Sure feels good to be clean and dry and well fed."

"Yeah, well, I miss the times when I *shared* a tub with you," Kate teased.

Sage grinned. "We did have some good times back in the day."

Kate nodded, keeping the cigar in her teeth. "So, tell me about the wife you said you once had."

Sage sobered. "I knew her in San Francisco. You already know what happened to me there. It was Joanna, the one her parents sent away to school and I never saw again, until she found me and Paradise Valley. She came running into my arms like a lost lover." He set down his coffee. "Would you believe I fell for it?" He began rolling a cigarette. "Turns out she was only after my money. When she realized how lonely and remote ranch life is, let alone the fact that

I'm not the type to mix with high society, she left. Simple as that." He licked the cigarette paper and sealed it.

"Oh, I doubt it was all that simple. I see the hurt in your eyes, Sage Lightfoot." Kate set her cigar in an ashtray and drank her own coffee. "Are you sure you're done with her?"

Sage couldn't help the small bit of love left in his heart for the woman who didn't deserve it. "I'm sure. Trouble is—I got a letter from her just before I left on this trip. She claims she wants to come back, but it's a sure bet she's after something again. I don't intend to fall for any more of her bullshit. There isn't an honest bone in her body."

"And what will you do if she's at the ranch when you and Maggie get there?"

Sage got up to pour himself more coffee. "I'll send her packing." He bent down and lit the end of his cigarette from the hot plate on the wood-burning stove. "If she needs money again, I'll probably help her out one last time. But I don't want her back, Kate, not with a woman like Maggie at my side." He came to the table and sat down with his coffee.

"I'm glad to hear that," Kate said with a nod. "Maggie said the same about you."

"So, you approve of her?"

Kate waved him off. "Do you *need* my approval?"

Sage grinned. "You're a damn good judge of character, Kate. Your opinion means a lot to me."

"Of course, I approve. I love seeing you happy." She reached out and touched his arm. "Tell me exactly what it is about her that you love, besides the fact that she's sweet and beautiful, and that it's nice to have a woman to bed while you're on the trail for weeks on end."

Sage ran a finger around the rim of his coffee cup, staring at it reflectively as he spoke. "She's everything a rancher's wife needs to be, Kate, and she understands me because she's been through a lot of the same things I have, as far as never knowing real love." He drew on his cigarette then set it in an ashtray. "She's a fighter, a survivor. There's a lot of punch packed into that tiny body. She grows on you till you wonder how you'd get by without her. She's damn strong and brave as a she-cat protecting her cubs. She can cook and hunt, and she's... well, she's about as opposite from Joanna as she could be, no frills, nothing false about her. She's as honest as the day is long."

Kate nodded. "She sounds like the perfect woman for you, so you'd better make up your mind about your feelings for Joanna. Don't be hurting Maggie even more than she's already been hurt in this life."

He met her eyes. "I don't intend to hurt her, but final decisions can't be made until we settle what we came here for, Kate. I worry about how dangerous that is for Maggie. She almost got herself shot back in Atlantic City." He finished his coffee. "I ran into an old enemy there... John Polk... remember him?"

Kate closed her eyes. "I remember what he did to one of my girls once... and what *you* did to him afterward."

Sage stretched his legs. "He was there at a barn dance in Atlantic City. One of the men I was after showed up, and I shot him. Maggie was involved in the fracas. Things moved so fast I didn't even realize

Polk was watching. I hadn't seen hide nor hair of him since running into him earlier in the day. Just after the shooting, he ran into the dark and rode off. I'm worried he knew the other two, and now, if he knew where they were, he's had time to find them and warn them that I'm on their trail."

"Well, I'm glad you had a chance to explain it to Newell earlier and describe those men to him. Rest assured, he's out on the town tonight to see if he can find out anything. If they're in town, Newell will know it." Kate puffed her cigar one last time before stamping the end in the ashtray. "I've known Newell a long time. He's a good man, Sage. You can trust him."

Sage finished his cigarette. "I figured as much."

Kate rose. "Well, for now, you need some rest yourself. You leave things to Newell tonight, and we'll talk about it over breakfast in the morning." She leaned down and kissed Sage's cheek, then walked to the stove and checked the coffeepot. "I'd better make a little more. I am never without a pot of hot coffee for whenever my customers might want a cup."

"You've always been an obliging woman, Kate," Sage told her with a wink.

Her eyes sparkled with humor, and she laughed lightly. "And you've always had the devil in you, Sage Lightfoot."

"And you, my lady, are an angel."

Kate shook her head, sobering. "I hope Newell can help, Sage. I'd hate to see any more bad things happen to Maggie or to you."

Sage rose from his chair. "Worry about Maggie,

but don't worry about me. You know I can take care of myself."

"Yeah, well, I dug a bullet out of your leg once. Don't forget that."

"And I'm alive and well and will be forever grateful to you." Sage put out his arms, and Kate walked into them.

"A good hug from a man like you does a woman good. I can't help wishing—" She pulled away. "Well, you know." Kate grinned and winked. "Go climb into bed with the lucky woman who *will* get more than a hug. I have a lot to do yet this evening. Boarders mean a lot of work, but it's an honest living—for once."

Sage watched her take some dishes out of a cupboard. "You're still beautiful, Kate. Time hasn't done anything to change that."

Kate laughed robustly at the remark. "And you're a lousy liar, Sage Lightfoot." She pointed toward the hallway. "Third door on your right. All your things are already in there, including a pretty little woman in your bed."

Sage grinned. "See you in the morning." He walked down the hallway and quietly entered the bedroom Kate indicated. He closed the door and undressed by dim lamplight. He quietly moved to the bed, leaning close. "You awake?"

Maggie pulled back the covers. "I decided I'd better stay awake to make sure this is the bed you came to tonight."

Sage smiled and joined her. "Did you actually doubt where I'd sleep tonight?"

Maggie moved her arms around his neck. "No—but

only because I can tell Kate wouldn't take you to her bed as long as I'm here. But if I weren't..."

Sage moved on top of her, pushing up her nightgown. "I know Kate. She's a great lady and loyal friend, but if I'd *wanted* to go to her bed, I have a feeling it wouldn't have mattered if you were here or not."

"Well, I guess we'll never know, will we?"

Sage met her mouth hungrily. He couldn't think of one thing not to love about this spit of a woman.

He moved a hand under her firm bottom, relishing every curve, groaning with the want of her, the feel of sliding into her. Knowing what this had been like for her before they met made this all the more necessary and enjoyable. He wanted her to take pleasure in a man loving her, and he couldn't imagine another man giving her that pleasure. Paradise Valley would be more of a paradise once he shared it with Maggie Tucker. He pushed aside any thoughts about Joanna. Maybe when they got back to the ranch, Joanna wouldn't even be there.

Thirty-two

MAGGIE SIPPED HER SECOND CUP OF COFFEE AS NEWELL McCabe came into the kitchen after morning chores. He hung up his hat and took a chair at the table.

"We've been waiting for you," Kate told him. "Want your breakfast?"

"Sure, Kate." Newell turned his attention to Sage, who was finishing off a plate of scrambled eggs. "Got some information for ya."

Sage waited while Kate poured him another cup of coffee. "Let's hear it," he answered, pushing his plate aside.

"I was out to a saloon called Chet's last night," Newell told him. He rolled himself a cigarette.

Maggie studied the many lines in Newell's face. She could tell he'd been a good-looking man when he was younger. His skin was sun-darkened, which made his eyes look incredibly blue. There was an honesty in those eyes, a hard-living—"this is the kind of person I am—take it or leave it" kind of honesty—the kind she saw in Ma Pilger and Kate, and often in Sage too. Good or bad, none pretended to be anything but their true selves.

"Did some askin' around," Newell continued. "Told those I know that a buffalo hunter named Jasper owed me money for a saddle. I described him the same way you described him to me." He lit his cigarette and took a drag. "A fella I know—Johnny Carpenter—said he saw a man who looked like that a few days ago—big ugly scar over his left eye."

"That's him!" Maggie said, putting a hand to her chest. "He's here in Lander?"

"I don't think so, ma'am." Newell drank some coffee and turned his attention to Sage. "Johnny said as how the man was sittin' in a corner drinkin' with some other fella—bearded man, big… wore a long black coat."

"Polk," Sage grumbled.

"Johnny remembered him ridin' into town the day before. Anyway, him and the fat guy was talkin' alone—like men do when they're plottin' somethin'. Johnny noticed because, well, in places like this, you pay attention when men act like they're up to no good, you know?"

Sage nodded.

Maggie felt a chill at the thought of how close they were to the men they planned to kill. "Well, anyway, the fat man, he got up and walked out," Newel continued. "Johnny—he's kind of the nosy type—he strolled out a minute later and just watched. The big man walked around town lookin' in stores and such, like he was lookin' for somebody. Finally, he met up with a younger fella at a dry goods store. They looked to be arguin' about somethin'. The younger one didn't seem to want to do whatever it was the big one wanted, but finally, they walked off together—went to the livery and got their horses and gear and lit out, headin' north. Johnny figured that whatever they was up to, it wasn't gonna happen in Lander, so he shrugged it off and forgot about it. I asked him if the bearded guy with the black coat was still in town, and he said he's been in Chet's the last two nights—didn't ride out with the other two far as he can tell. He don't know where he's stayin'. Most likely, he's camped outside of town. Johnny said he didn't look the sociable type—comes into Chet's to drink, maybe find a card game, then don't show up during the day."

"He's waiting to see if we *do* show up," Sage grumbled. He turned to Maggie. "It's just like I figured. Polk came here to warn Jimmy Hart and Jasper that I'm hunting for them. The trouble is, he's seen you too. Now, the other two know you're with me. From here on, you've got to stay right here, while I take care of Polk and go after the others."

"No! We've come this far together. I'm not staying behind now. I won't let you go after them alone!"

"Sage is right, Maggie," Newell told her. "I'm bettin' them two are headed for Hole-In-The-Wall, and that ain't no place for no woman, not even whores."

"He's right," Kate added. "I've been all over this country, but I never went to Hole-In-The-Wall." She lit a thin cigar. "Besides, those two might round up some extra men to help them out." She smoked quietly a moment. "You should go back to Paradise Valley, Sage, and leave this alone."

"You know better than to tell me that. They owe me, Kate, and it's not just the money. If I give up now, I'll always wonder when they might come back to Paradise Valley and shoot me in the back, just so they can quit worrying about me coming for them."

Maggie's stomach hurt from a deep foreboding. If Jasper were able to pay others to help him, she and Sage would head into something they couldn't handle alone. Worse, Sage probably meant it when he said he wouldn't take her with him this time. She swallowed at the heavy silence in the kitchen. "What's Hole-In-The-Wall?"

The other three looked at each other as though their days were numbered. "It's not a place for the likes of you, Maggie, that's certain," Sage told her.

Maggie stiffened. "I'm not about to be left behind now, Sage Lightfoot, not after all we've been through to get this far!"

Sage rubbed his forehead as though he had a headache. "Maggie, no one gets into Hole-In-The-Wall unseen. That's why outlaws use the place to hide out. Getting there requires riding single file through a cut in what's called the Great Red Wall—cliffs so high and straight no man can get past them except by one trail, so it's easy to guard."

"There's a wide, beautiful valley that takes you there," Newell added, giving his attention to Maggie. "Trouble is, anybody atop those cliffs can see you comin' for miles. If you think you've seen big country out here, ma'am, wait till you see the valley on the way to Hole-In-The-Wall. Outlaws graze their horses and cattle there. Sometimes, a lot of them camp right there in the valley."

Sage rose and paced. "The damn pathway is so

narrow it only takes one man to guard it. You could send a whole army up that trail, and one man could pick them off, one at a time."

"Sage, you don't know for certain that's where Jasper and the other one went," Kate reminded him. "You need to find John Polk and see what he knows."

"Oh, I'll find him, all right. If the son of a bitch hadn't warned Jasper, he and Jimmy Hart might still be here in town, and we could get this over with. Riding to Hole-In-The-Wall is another matter." He walked to the table and crushed out his cigarette in an ashtray. "Thanks, Newell. Have some breakfast. I'm going outside to get some air. I need to think about this." He grabbed his hat from where he'd left it hanging near the door and walked out.

Newell glanced at Kate. "I'll go talk to him some more. I can eat later," he told her. He drank the rest of his coffee and nodded to Maggie. "Ma'am, Sage is right. Hole-In-The-Wall ain't no place for the likes of you." He rose. "See you later, Kate." He put on his hat and walked out.

Maggie closed her eyes and leaned back. "He'll try to go without me, Kate. I can't let him."

Kate tapped some ashes off the end of her cigar. "Well, honey, it's a rough trip. Getting through the trail that leads up the cliffs is dangerous enough. You need a damn good, sure-footed horse, and then, you have the problem of what you'll face when you get to the top. Even the bravest lawmen won't attempt going there."

Maggie sighed. "There must be some way. Sage will figure it out." She faced Kate. "And I know firsthand what men like that Jasper are like. I want to see their faces when they realize that the woman they raped and left behind to die alone on the plains actually came for revenge. You've got to help me convince Sage to take me with him. If we end up getting killed, then at least we'll die together."

Kate smiled softly, shaking her head. "By God, you are the right woman for Sage." She leaned closer. "Is there anything left that you're afraid of?"

Maggie put a hand to her stomach. "I'm afraid of everything, but not when I'm with Sage. I always know I'm safe when I'm with him." She looked at the skirt of the simple gingham dress she wore, the only dress she'd brought along, except for the fancy one Sage bought for her in Atlantic City. "There is only one thing that truly frightens me, Kate, and that's Sage himself. I'm afraid I'll lose him after all."

Kate frowned. "What makes you say that? The man is crazy about you."

Every day brought her closer to the truth, and she dreaded it. She'd told herself not to trust anyone she'd just met, but instinct told her Kate Bassett was an exception. "I'm carrying, Kate, and Sage doesn't know it. What's worse is that one of the men we're after is the father. It's impossible to know which one."

Kate sucked in her breath and closed her eyes, then let out a deep sigh. "Oh, Maggie, why haven't you told Sage?"

"I'd like nothing more than to tell him, but it's a bastard, Kate. He might not be able to accept how it was conceived. I mean to keep it. When I lost my little girl back in Missouri, I wanted to die. My little

Susan was so sweet and innocent and loving—the best thing that ever came into my life. This baby is just as innocent. I want to make sure he or she is loved. It's not the baby's fault how it came to be."

"You really should tell Sage, Maggie."

"Not yet." Maggie looked at her pleadingly. "Promise me you won't say a word. I only told you because I thought I could trust you."

"But… you can't go riding off to a place like Hole-In-The-Wall with a baby in your belly! You never should have made this trip at all!"

"That's what Sage would say if he knew. He never would have let me leave Paradise Valley. I *had* to come, Kate, and the deeper I got into this, the more important it was that Sage didn't know. Then we fell in love, and now, I'm scared to tell him—not because he wouldn't take me with him to finish this, but because he'd leave me behind for good."

"He'd understand, Maggie. I *know* him. He'd be upset at first that you didn't tell him, but he loves you. He'd come around."

"I wish that was true." Maggie leaned forward and covered her face. "Sage must have told you how his first wife tricked him into marriage to get money. She hurt him really bad, Kate. And when I tell him about this baby, he's going to think I want someone I can pass off as the father of my baby, someone who can provide for me and the child." She faced Kate again. "But I *love* him, Kate. It has nothing to do with my baby—honest."

Kate nodded. "I believe you, honey, but I think you underestimate Sage's ability to accept this. Men like Sage don't judge others the way most ordinary people do."

Maggie shook her head. "I don't know, especially when I realize he still has feelings for Joanna. She'll be at the ranch when we go back. I'm sure of it. And once he sees her, and with me carrying a bastard child..."

The room hung silent.

"There's no chance it's your husband's?" Kate finally asked.

Maggie shook her head. "James hadn't come near me that way since my last time of month. We were too tired from our trip." She couldn't help the tears that filled her eyes. "This baby was bred out of violence, and I can't lie to Sage. It would be easy to say it belongs to James. I could even claim it's Sage's, but he's the type who'd see the lie in my eyes. He knows what happened, and he'd always wonder, so I might as well tell him the truth."

"And soon."

Maggie wiped away a tear. "Please don't tell him. I'll know when the time is right, and it can't be until all this is over. I wanted your opinion on how you think Sage will react."

"Sage loves you. Even if he doesn't accept it at first, he'll never let you go, Maggie."

Maggie glanced at Sage's gun belt hanging near the door. "I'd like to believe that. If it weren't for Joanna... what she did to him... I'd have more hope. But Sage hates being duped by a woman, and I'm scared that's how he'll see this. Even if I wasn't carrying, I think Sage needs to face Joanna again and make sure he's through with her." She met Kate's gaze. "I will tell him the truth, Kate, because I'll have no choice, but he doesn't need this on his mind when he goes after those men."

Kate shook her head in resignation. "If Sage does turn you away, you come to me first Maggie Tucker, understand? You come to Lander, and let me help you. Don't you go running off and try to raise a kid on your own. Promise me that. I know what it's like to be alone against the world, and it's hell for a woman. You've always got a home here, if you need it. And if that does happen, I'll pay a visit to Sage myself and give him a good going over for sending you away!"

Maggie smiled through tears. "Thank you. I feel better knowing there's at least one other woman who understands."

Kate laughed softly. "There aren't many things I *don't* understand. If Sage turns you out, I know damn well he would come looking for you after he had time to think. He'd probably come here first to talk to me. Mark my words, Maggie. That man won't get by without you any more than you'll get by without him." She reached over and squeezed Maggie's hands. "And when you have that kid, I intend to come to Paradise Valley and pay you a visit."

Maggie smiled. "I'd love that."

They heard Sage and Newell outside the door. Maggie quickly wiped away her tears before the two men came inside.

"We're gonna take a little stroll through town—see if we can spot Polk," Newell told them. "Might be we'll have to spend the day at Chet's waitin' for him to show up. No sense ridin' around in the hills tryin' to find his camp when he's likely to walk right into Chet's... where me and Sage will be waitin'."

Sage reached for his gun belt he'd left hanging on the wall. "Don't expect us back any time soon," he told Maggie as he strapped on his gun. "It's not likely Polk knows we're here, so if he shows up at Chet's, he'll walk right into a trap. And I'll, by God, get him to tell us where Jasper and Jimmy went."

Maggie breathed deeply to still her heart. They were closer than ever to finishing what they left Paradise Valley to do. Of all the things they'd been through, she knew deep inside that this was the most dangerous part of their journey. If it meant going to Hole-In-The-Wall, she'd have to do some fast thinking and fast talking to convince Sage to take her along.

First, there was the matter of John Polk. She watched Sage walk out the door, and all she could do was pray she'd see him alive again.

Thirty-three

MAGGIE WALKED TO A FRONT WINDOW IN KATE'S parlor, pressing a lace-trimmed handkerchief to her damp forehead and neck. "I can't believe it's the middle of July already," she commented. "Sage and I left at the end of May. We've ridden so far together. It was cold when we left, and now, it's so hot."

"Maggie, come sit back down, and stop worrying," Kate insisted.

"I can't help it. I don't like this, Kate. Sage and Newell have been gone so long." It did little good to keep staring out the front window. It was dark outside, and she couldn't see beyond the light of a lantern on the front porch. "Sage should have taken me with him."

"To the saloons and brothels? Sure. You'd fit right in." Kate lit a cigar and threw her match into the nearby fireplace, its hearth unlit because of the heat. Maggie wondered at the sounds coming from the streets… distant piano music, occasionally, a woman's shrieking laughter. She couldn't help thinking about Sage once being a part of such wild activity. The sound of yet another gunshot made her flinch. "Every time I hear that I could scream."

"Listen, Maggie, get it through your head that what's going on in town is a life Sage knows well. Most up at this hour are a bunch of drunks being stupid. Sage knows how to watch his back, and he can handle the worst. You should know that by now. If John Polk shows up, by the time Sage is done with him, he and Newell will have all the information they need." Kate leaned back in her rocking chair and picked up a jacket she'd promised to mend for one of her boarders. "There aren't many men who can handle themselves better around that rabble than Sage can." She laid the jacket in her lap and kept the cigar between her lips as she squinted to thread a needle.

Maggie turned from the window. If not for her anxiety, she thought how easy it would be to laugh at the picture of someone like Kate Bassett doing something as domestic as sewing, while at the same time, smoking a cigar. Kate was a wonderful cook—a contrast of character that was so common out here. "Tell me about Newell," she asked Kate. "I need to talk about something besides Sage and what's going on in town."

Kate laid her cigar in an ashtray. She answered Maggie, while she finished threading the needle and searched for the ripped seam in the jacket she was mending. "Newell came here to get away from something, but he's never told me what it is. Could be a woman, or maybe a robbery, or a murder. Out here, everybody comes from someplace else, and usually, it's to hide or to start life over where the law and the government can't do much to stop you." She found the seam and began sewing. "Of course, that's changing now. Lawyers, lawmen, and even the government are trying to make living out here like it is back east, but it will take a long time. Folks here like things the way they are."

Maggie sat across from her, and Kate stopped her needlework for a moment. "Speaking of Newell, though, he's a good man," she told Maggie. "Oh, he likes to drink and gamble, but ninety-nine percent of the men out here do that." She returned to her mending. "He used to visit the brothels, but he's pretty much stopped that. The last couple of years it's just been him and me. And he's a good hired hand. I don't think I could run this place without him."

Maggie sipped hot chocolate Kate had made for her. "Do you think you'll ever marry?"

Kate laughed, shaking her head. "People like us don't marry. I'm too used up for that, and I can't have kids. And Newell—he's fifty. People our age, who've lived the kind of lives we've lived, don't get married and have families. We're comfortable with each other and know that as we get older, we'll need to take care of each other."

Maggie studied her, watched her finish sewing up the torn seam. "I'd call that love, Kate, wouldn't you?"

Kate paused. If Maggie didn't know better, she'd swear the woman was about to cry.

"Well, now, honey, I guess you could call it love." She looked at Maggie and smiled rather sadly. "Love with no strings attached. That's the only kind of love a man like Newell could handle."

"Has he ever *said* he loves you?"

Kate chuckled. "No. And I've never said the word either. It's something that's there. We don't need to say it." She finished sewing the jacket.

"I have a feeling the only man you knew deep in your heart you loved was Sage," Maggie suggested.

Kate gave her a wink. "Sure I did. No sense denying that." She tied off and cut the thread, then studied her finished work. "I loved Sage for the same reasons you love him. He's solid, trustworthy, protective, knows what he wants, and goes after it." She looked straight at Maggie. "And God knows he's easy to look at."

Both women smiled.

"He's flat out the handsomest man I ever set eyes on," Maggie replied.

Kate nodded. "Me too, and I've come across a whole lot more men in my lifetime than you have, honey." She sobered. "Sage has done some bad things, but he was an angry young man with no direction and a broken heart. What those supposed parents of his did back in San Francisco is unforgivable." She set the jacket aside and reached over to pick up her cigar. "And you're wondering about me, aren't you? How I ended up an aging prostitute who will never marry."

Maggie set her cup aside. "That's not my business."

Kate shrugged. "It's natural to wonder. Somebody like you can't understand this life, and I don't blame you." She smiled sadly, puffing on the cigar a couple of times before she continued. "I came out here much the same way you did, Maggie. I was young, stupid, and scared. I had no idea what this land was like before my parents and brother and I left by wagon train from Chicago."

She leaned forward, resting her elbows on her knees.

"That was such a long time ago," she said absently, "but sometimes, it seems like yesterday." She sighed. "We never made it to California. We were attacked by Indians. My whole family was killed. I was taken captive, and a savage claimed me for his wife. When I didn't give him any kids, he passed me off to the single ones who wanted to learn about sex before they took their own young brides."

Maggie closed her eyes against the horrid picture. "How awful."

Kate waved her off, forcing herself to pretend it didn't matter anymore. "Anyway, by the time they deserted me near a gold town, I was already pretty used up. I knew absolutely no one. I walked into that town, and the minute the men knew where I came from, I had no hope of finding a decent man who'd want me. I tried scrubbing clothes to survive, tried sewing, cooking—whatever I could. Then a gambler came along who suggested how rich I could get if I turned to prostitution and opened my own brothel. By then, I didn't have much pride left, figured it wouldn't make much difference what I did... sleeping with men and running a brothel was a whole lot easier than using a scrub board and sweating over a hot stove in the summer to feed a bunch of ungrateful no-accounts. The gambler was good to me, bought me a pretty dress, showed me how beautiful I could be—how I could use that beauty."

She faced Maggie, her eyes misty. "We opened a brothel together. Later my gambler friend got shot over a card game, and I was on my own. My life was pretty well set for me, and I knew by then something was wrong that I'd never get pregnant, so I ended up running one of the fanciest whorehouses in town. That was in the Dakotas." She shook her head at the memories. "Like most gold towns, it fast died when the gold ran out, so I started traveling with my girls. I've been all over the west and ended up here. I ran a brothel here too—saved enough money to try living a decent life for at least a few years before I die. So… here I am, running a boardinghouse."

Maggie shook her head. "I don't think I could have survived what you survived."

Kate sighed. "Sure you could. You already have, from what I've learned about you. The only difference is you found Sage at just the right time. You'll be able to live the life a decent woman is meant to live. And God has blessed you with the ability to have babies. I have a feeling you and Sage will have quite a big family, and I hope I live long enough to see all those kids."

"First, he has to accept the baby I'm carrying."

"Oh, he might stew about it for a while, but he'll accept it."

Someone knocked on the back door. Both women rose and hurried into the kitchen sure it was Sage and Newell. "I hope nothing is wrong," Maggie said, worried as to why they would knock at the back door.

Kate opened the door, and Maggie gasped when two men barged in.

Jasper! She turned to run, but the big man grabbed her from behind and planted a smelly hand over her mouth. He whirled her around in time to see Jimmy

Hart slam the barrel of his gun over Kate's head twice. Kate slumped to the floor. Jasper dragged Maggie out the door. She felt a stunning blow to the back of her head, and everything went black.

Thirty-four

Sage threw in his hand and pulled a watch from his vest pocket to check the time.

Ten o'clock. He and Newell and Johnny Carpenter had searched all day for John Polk, but he was nowhere to be found. They'd checked with most of the businesses, sat on the boardwalk watching people, asked around at brothels and saloons, then stayed here at Chet's Saloon the rest of the day, and now, into the night, hoping Polk would show up at his favorite drinking hole.

Sage feared the man had left the area after all. He might catch up with Jimmy Hart and Jasper and join forces with them. He figured he might as well head for Hole-In-The-Wall in the morning and take the chance he'd find all three men there. He glanced across the table at Newell. "I've about had enough of this card game and enough whiskey."

"You thinkin' of checkin' out some other places again?"

Sage scooted back his chair. "Might as well. I've been sitting at this table so long I'm getting calluses on my elbows." He gathered what money he had left and rose. "I'm out, boys." He picked up his cigarette from an ashtray and took a couple more drags, then snuffed out the stub. Discarded peanut shells crunched under his boots as he walked to the bar where Johnny sat.

Newell got up and collected what was left of his money. "I'm out too, fellas."

"Come back tomorrow night, Newell, and we'll gladly take more of your money." The words came from Rob Fisher, a man Newell had befriended since coming to Lander.

Newell grinned. "You were just lucky tonight."

Rob guffawed as Newell joined Johnny and Sage at the bar. "That Polk fella had better show up before we're too drunk to shoot straight," he told Sage.

Sage rubbed the back of his neck in frustration. "I was thinking the same."

"Why not check the other saloons and the brothels again," Johnny suggested.

"Yeah," Newell put in. "Maybe Polk decided he needed a woman tonight more than he needed whiskey and cards. From what you and Kate have told me about his habit of beatin' up whores, I can't believe he ain't been to see any here in town. And we both know he can get all the whiskey he wants at the brothels. Costs more than in the saloons, but it's generally worth it."

He winked, and all three men chuckled. Sage thought Johnny Carpenter seemed a good sort, more kid than man. He reminded Sage of himself at that age, a homeless young man who'd come to outlaw country at sixteen years old. In Johnny's case, he was seeking safety and protection from his own alcoholic father who'd horribly abused him his whole life. That was two years ago. Johnny found refuge here… and a job with the blacksmith. He'd never gone back home, wherever home was. He never said.

"Sorry I wasn't much help tonight," Johnny told Sage. "I walked out a couple of times to check next door at the Silverheels Saloon. Last time I checked was about twenty minutes ago. Polk wasn't there."

"It's not your fault he chose tonight not to show up," Sage answered.

Johnny shrugged. "Maybe he saw you and decided to leave town after all… maybe join up with them other two."

"That's what I've been thinking," Sage answered, "and it worries me. Something doesn't feel right about this whole thing. Let's go check next door again and then head down the street to Sadie's Saloon. She has whores upstairs. Maybe he's there."

"Fine with me," Newell answered.

The three headed for the swinging entry door when a man stumbled inside with a young blond woman on his arm. Both were obviously drunk, and the woman's low-cut dress hung nearly off the ends of her breasts.

"Shit, it's Polk!" Johnny exclaimed.

Because of the heat, Polk wasn't wearing his trademark black coat. He recognized Sage, but not in time. Before he could go for his gun, Sage grabbed him and flung him through the swinging saloon doors. He landed so hard in the street that it knocked the breath out of him. That gave Sage plenty of time to grab the man's six-gun and fling it aside. In spite of Polk's size, Sage jerked him up by the front of his shirt.

"We have something to discuss!" Sage growled.

"Who the hell are you?" the blond woman screamed. "You let go of him!"

"Shut up, Hilda!"

Sage recognized Newell's voice.

"Go on back to Sadie's place, and stay out of this!"

Hilda's eyes widened with indignation, and she stormed away.

Sage dragged a dazed Polk to a watering trough and dunked him into it, holding him under the water long enough that he'd be disoriented and willing to talk by the time he let him up. He jerked him out of the water and slammed him to the ground, putting a knee in his groin while he held him down with one hand around his throat. Onlookers had gathered to watch. Johnny and Newell forced some back with guns drawn as a warning to stay out of the situation.

"You warned Jimmy Hart and Jasper that I was coming, didn't you?" Sage demanded.

"Get off me," Polk sputtered.

"You knew all of them, didn't you? Cleve, Jasper and Jimmy Hart!"

"You're… cuttin' off… my air! You're… killin' me!"

"I *should* have killed you the last time we met! Now, answer my question!"

Polk squirmed to get away, and Sage backhanded him "Where did they go? Answer me, or I'll gouge out your eyes!"

Blood trickled from the corner of Polk's mouth. "I rode with them three… awhile back… hunted buffalo with them… but whatever reason you're after them… I ain't got nothin' to do with it! I just… knew them once. When I saw you shoot Cleve back in Atlantic City… I figured I should warn the other two!"

Sage jerked him back to his feet, swiftly drawing his forty-five caliber and aiming it directly at Polk's face. "You try to run, and I'll blow your brains out! Did they tell you *why* I was looking for them?"

Polk looked around, guilt in his eyes. "Well, they… they said they took money from you… killed one of your hands."

Sage pressed the revolver to the man's forehead. "That's it? They didn't say anything about attacking a woman out on the plains and murdering her husband?"

Polk swallowed. "They might have, but abusin' a woman ain't somethin' I look at exactly as a crime."

Sage slammed his six-gun across the side of the man's face. Polk spun around and collapsed to the ground. Blood poured from a cut near his temple as he looked at Sage and snarled. "You bastard! All I did was warn them! I didn't have nothin' to do with anything they did!"

"*I'm* the one you should have warned, you worthless son of a bitch! Tell me where they're headed."

Polk wiped at the blood on his face with a shaking hand. "They said somethin' about goin' up to Hole-In-The-Wall, but I don't know if they did or not. You'd better watch your back, Indian," he snarled. "They're itchin' to kill you to get you off their backs, and they talked about havin' a time with that woman you've got with you."

Sage struggled not to pull the trigger. "*You* told them I had a woman with me?"

Polk drew a deep breath. "I might have. Seemed like it might be of interest."

"Yeah, you have a real *big* interest in women, don't you, Polk? Figured maybe you'd join them and have your turn with her once they did me in, right?" Sage walked over and picked up Polk's six-gun, then tossed it at the man's feet. "Pick it up, Polk!"

Polk stiffened. "Now, wait a minute! I ain't as good with a gun as you, and you know it!"

The crowd backed away. Johnny and Newell kept an eye on them, knowing Jimmy and Jasper could be anywhere. Just then a commotion arose across the street. Sage kept a steady aim on Polk as men began shouting.

"Kate! It's Kate Bassett!"

"God damn, look at her!"

Polk's eyes widened, and he backed up.

"What's that all about, Polk?" Sage growled.

"I… I ain't sure."

"Newell, you'd better go see what's happening," Sage told the man, his eyes fixed on Polk.

"I'm already on it," Newell answered, hurrying to three men carrying Kate. Newell recognized them as a couple of Kate's houseguests.

"Where's the doctor's office?" one asked Newell.

"Up there, above the medicine store," Newell told him. "Give her to me!" He took Kate into his arms. "What happened?"

"I found her this way, lying in the kitchen with her head bashed in," the man answered. "That young woman who was staying there… she's gone."

Sage heard every word, and his gut wrenched with agony. Maggie! He had no doubt this was Jasper's doing, and it was all because he'd been warned by the man standing in front of him. He walked closer to Polk, his six-gun only a couple of inches from his face. "You *knew*, didn't you? You knew they were going to take her."

Polk shook his head. "I swear, I didn't!"

"You're *lying*, Polk! Pick up your gun!"

"No!"

"Pick it up!" Sage roared. He put his own gun back in its holster. Polk hesitated, glanced at his six-gun on the ground. Then he made a dive for it. Sage waited until the gun was in his hand and cocked. Before the man could pull the trigger, Sage drew his own revolver and shot him between the eyes.

People gasped as Polk crumpled to the ground.

A saloon girl screamed and ran inside Chet's Saloon.

Several followed her inside wary of the mood Sage was in.

Trembling with rage and dread, Sage turned to see Newell heading up the stairs to the doctor's office with Kate in his arms. Sage felt responsible. He never should have got Kate involved in this mess, never should have left her and Maggie alone. Jasper or Jimmy must have watched Sage's movements earlier today, figured out where he was staying—maybe even caught sight of Maggie. How in hell either man went unnoticed, Sage couldn't be sure, but he had no doubt Polk had helped in this, and now, they were damn well headed for Hole-In-The-Wall… with Maggie! They meant to lead Sage right into a death trap. Poor Maggie could already be dead… or wishing she were. He walked to Polk's dead body. "Her name was Maggie," he groaned through gritted teeth, "and she's the best woman who ever stepped foot in Wyoming!"

Thirty-five

For untold miles over the last three days, Maggie survived a hellish journey that followed a wall of red-rock cliffs meandering alongside a vast, yellow-grass valley. She knew without a doubt that Jimmy and Jasper were headed for the famed Hole-In-The-Wall. The huge valley and rock walls that guarded it stretched for mile after endless mile. She felt swallowed up by the landscape of grass and shale and rippling hillsides that graduated to the intimidating cliffs.

It was impossible to guess how many miles a person could see in any direction. It was as though this place had no beginning and no end, and she imagined that from the top of that bastion of a wall that bordered the valley, one could see for even more miles. How was Sage going to find her in this maze of sand, grassland, hills, plateaus, caves, and mesas? In some places, huge boulders lay scattered as though God himself had been playing marbles and just tossed them wherever He chose. There was no explanation for them lying in the middle of miles and miles of flatland, too far from the cliffs to have rolled there on their own.

She told herself not to lose faith in Sage's ability to track men in this godforsaken country. If any man could find her, it was Sage Lightfoot. This thought was all that kept her going through a constant pounding headache that sometimes caused her to vomit. She tried to concentrate on the landscape to help keep from thinking what might happen to her next.

Jimmy and Jasper had ridden from dawn to dusk the past three days to get here as fast as possible, changing horses twice—once by dickering with a rancher, and once by trading with men they met along the trail who were herding several mustangs they'd broken. In both cases, Jasper kept Maggie at a distance with Jimmy, so the men he dealt with couldn't see her up close and realize she was a captive.

Maggie suspected both men knew that even out here, there were men who wouldn't abide abusing a decent woman. She hung on to the realization that part of the reason the men traveled so fast was fear. Jimmy Hart and the ugly Jasper were afraid of not only some of the men they met on this journey, but also afraid that Sage Lightfoot was no doubt, hot on their heels. That's exactly what they wanted, yet she could feel their uncertainty, read the anxiety in their eyes. Once they reached their outlaw fortress, they would have their supreme vantage point, where they could lie in wait for their prey, and they were in a damn big hurry to get there. What they might do with her while they waited, Maggie didn't want to think about.

She wasn't sure how much longer she could hang on to a desire to live. She'd been treated like baggage, tossed to the ground at night with nothing but one light blanket to stave off the cold. By contrast, the days were hot and dusty and windy. She was afforded little water and even less food. She'd hardened herself against the humiliation of relieving herself in front of the filthy men she hoped she'd never have to see alive again. She told herself that lifting her skirts in front of them was better than wetting herself and smelling like urine.

She'd refused to cry, refused to scream, refused to beg, and she continued to believe there were good men out here who might help her. Through all the hard miles of riding, Jasper kept her in front of him on his horse, taking privileges with his hands on her body. She was glad that her head wound made her vomit, glad for the heat that made her perspire, and glad to add how bad she must smell by now. All of it kept both men at bay, along with the fact that they were too tired from the hard ride to force themselves on a sick woman who was a mess to boot. They kept her hands tied behind her back most of the time, and at night they tied her ankles. Escape was impossible. Even if she found a way out of this, where would she go in country like this? She'd die from exposure and the elements. How she'd kept from losing her baby she would never know, but one thing was certain. The life inside her belly was one strong little being.

Her misery was made worse by the memory of hearing Kate's skull crack and seeing the woman slump to the floor. Her own head injury caused her to black out at first, but she'd come around quick enough to realize she was being loaded onto Jasper's horse. She was too dazed and weak to fight or scream, and for the rest of that night and part of the next morning, she'd moved in and out of consciousness.

Was poor Kate dead? Sage would blame himself for this. Her worst fear was that for all she knew, Sage could be dead too. Maybe he'd found John Polk. Maybe Polk had shot him in the back. She'd heard Jimmy mention Polk a time or two. With every breath, she begged God to protect Sage, pleaded that he was still alive and coming for her. All that kept her from wanting to die was that hope. More than anything, she wanted to live just to see these two men die a horrible death at Sage's hands. Any form of suffering on her part would be worth hearing Jasper and Jimmy Hart scream with pain and beg for their lives.

She'd decided that until that time, she'd not speak one word. Keeping quiet seemed to make both men nervous, and the more nervous they were, the more likely they might get careless and let their guard down. She enjoyed their frustration over the fact that she wasn't begging and pleading with them to let her go. She tried to think like Sage would think—studied the land, watched, listened, and avoided insanity by considering ways she could either escape or find a way to help Sage once he caught up. She took hope. Because of what these two did to Kate, Newell would come with Sage to find them.

Newell wouldn't be able to let this go any more than Sage would. That meant Sage would have help.

She watched the landscape ahead and saw what looked like horses and cattle grazing—stolen stock grazed by outlaws, no doubt. Outlaws… many of who, oddly enough, had scruples when it came to how men like Jasper treated women. Jasper knew it, which was why he made sure she had no opportunity to speak to anyone. Some men out here might have known Kate. They wouldn't like knowing what Jimmy did to her.

She told herself that this was not the time to crumple under terror and sickening memories, or to allow her bone-deep aches and weariness to cause her to lie down and never get up. She would not let her constant misery make her fold. She'd heard Sage brag about how strong she was, and that's what she'd be, no matter what lay ahead.

Jasper halted his horse and studied the camp in the distance. "Better keep avoiding others for now," he told Jimmy. He gave Maggie a painful jerk that hurt her ribs. "If we do run into somebody with you close by, you'd better keep your mouth shut. You're my woman. Got that?"

Maggie continued her silence.

Jasper squeezed again. "Answer me! I'm tired of you not talking! Answer me, or I'll cut out your tongue so you'll never talk again!"

Maggie didn't doubt he'd do it. "I'm your woman," she said with obvious disgust.

Jasper's hand moved to her throat with a threatening squeeze. "That's right. And your only chance of getting out of this is keepin' quiet around others. Once we're rid of Sage Lightfoot once and for all, we'll turn you over to anybody here who wants you."

"Why didn't you wait at Kate's house and kill Sage when he got there?" Maggie decided that perhaps now was a good time to work on their nerves in another way—make them wonder if taking her was the worst mistake they'd ever made.

Jasper chuckled. "That would be too easy. Lightfoot's been doggin' me for weeks. You think I didn't know? I'm tired of it, and I'm pissed that he shot Cleve. Cleve was my cousin, and I want Lightfoot to suffer. I want him to come to me on a silver platter. Back in Lander he could have got help. Out here, it's just him and me."

Maggie studied the men in the distance. "Is it? Sage has friends out here too, you know. You might not be as safe as you think you are. He used to ride this country—lived here. Kate Bassett was one of his best friends. He's going to be furious, and you don't want to deal with a furious Sage Lightfoot."

Jasper grasped her jaw so hard she feared he'd break it. "I'll be safe enough when we get to the top of Hole-In-The-Wall. The men who go there are the worst of the lot, so don't be expectin' help from them. And some might take a shine to you, little lady. A lot of them ain't been with a woman in a while, let alone one as little and perty as you. Once this is over, I'll get you cleaned up and offer you up like a Christmas present." He looked at Jimmy. "Go talk to them men up ahead, and see if you can trade for some fresh horses. I'll stay behind with the woman this time."

Jimmy rode off, and Maggie watched. *Help me!* she screamed on the inside, but out here in this vast valley, she knew a scream would be lost in the wind. The men up ahead would never hear it.

Thirty-six

Sage stared at the flickering fire as he leaned against a rock, quietly smoking. He was bone tired, yet he couldn't sleep for worrying what kind of hell Maggie was suffering. He knew it was the same for Newell, who sat on his bedroll nearby. Both of them felt sick at Kate's condition. When they left Lander, she was barely clinging to life, and the doctor feared she might be paralyzed or have permanent mental problems if she lived.

They had ridden so hard to get this far that Storm went lame. Sage hated abusing horses, especially a good steed like Storm, but time was of the essence. He'd left the horse with a rancher several miles back, and he and Newell bought three more horses from the man, who told them that someone who fit Jasper's description had bought horses the day before.

Didn't have no woman with him, but looked like a fella way in the distance was standin' with a woman—thought I could make out a dress. I figured it was just a companion, probably a whore.

Sage felt crazy with the need to find Maggie. At

least he knew she was still alive… although she was probably wishing she were dead. Realizing that Jasper and Jimmy were still ahead only meant that they, too, were riding harder and for longer hours than they should, which would be miserable for Maggie, especially if they were abusing her in other ways.

"They're scared as shit, Sage," Newell spoke up, as though to read Sage's mind. He took a slug of whiskey from a small flask. "They know we're right behind them."

"And every time they stop for horses or any other reason, they risk being found out," Sage answered. "That's why they kept Maggie at a distance when they bought those horses. They didn't want that rancher to see her up close."

Newell rolled himself a cigarette. "We know there's a lot of no-goods out here, but this here is a case of attempted murder on a woman some of those no-goods knew well. Kate was popular. The men in these parts ain't gonna like knowin' somebody bashed her head in. And they ain't gonna' like knowin' they stole a man's wife—least ways, that's what we'll let them believe."

Sage finished his own cigarette and tossed what was left into the fire. "Which means we might be able to rustle up some help."

"Could be. Most men in these parts figure a man's fight is personal—none of their business. But them men brought Kate Bassett into this. The mood I'm in, I probably don't need no help, cuz I'm lookin' to cut their balls off and stuff 'em down their throats."

Sage felt sick with rage. "That would be a start. You do that, and then I'll finish the job… Indian style."

'll be at the base of Hole-In-The-Wall by the er tomorrow," he said aloud to Newell. "If we make it any faster than that, we'll lose these s too, and that will cost us even more time. We t be sure we'll come across another rancher with ses to sell." He had to think positive now. They ere close. They would find Maggie.

"I expect we'll find more men who've seen Jasper," Newell put in. "A face like that sticks in a man's mind, you know? I mean, I ain't never seen him, but the way you described him, I'm just figurin' he'll be easily spotted and remembered, what with that scar over his eye and all."

Sage lay back on his bedroll, resting his head on his saddle. He had to at least try to sleep. "I'm figuring the same. And I'm thinking there are men out here who'll help us get to the top of the cliffs without Jimmy and Jasper knowing it."

"Won't be easy." Newell also stretched out on his bedroll. "How clever is that woman of yours?"

"What do you mean?"

"Well, in this country, if a woman is clever enough, she can find ways of gettin' out of the fixes she's in."

Sage ached to hold her. "I'd say she's more strong and stubborn than clever. Takes a lot to break a woman like Maggie."

The air hung silent for several minutes before Newell pulled a blanket over himself and settled in for the night.

"She'll be all right, Sage," he spoke up. "From what little I seen of her, she'll be all right, long as she knows you're comin' for her… and she damn well knows that."

Both took pleasure at the
men who'd battered Kate.

"Do you think Kate will mak
Newell sighed, shaking his hea
I'm fearful that if she does, she wo
same." He took a drag on his cigarett
woman, Sage, and I ain't never loved
whole life. Didn't even love my own m
mean to me, ran off when I was six or seve
weren't no better—taught me to steal, so he
have drinkin' money. I met Kate when she wa
runnin' a whorehouse, but even then, she seem
like the most decent person I ever knew. Oh, I kno
there's good people who live in that world, outside of
drinkin' and smokin' and gamblin' and leadin' the life of an outlaw and hangin' with no-goods, but my kind would never fit in with good, Christian folks. Kate, she's my kind, and if she needs takin' care of the rest of her life, I'll do it. She's as good and decent as them other kind of folks, if you know what I mean."

Sage watched an ember float upward into the darkness. "I know what you mean." He thought how Maggie was one of those outsiders Newell talked about, but she'd been molded into a woman who fit both worlds he'd known. She'd experienced enough of the rough side of life to understand him and put up with him.

Still, a woman could take only so much. If Jimmy and Jasper raped her again… or if they handed her off to other men for the same reason… it could break her spirit. And if he and Newell couldn't reach them in time, or if they were killed while trying, God help Maggie Tucker.

Sage closed his eyes. "Yeah. All we have to do is ride into a trap at Hole-In-The-Wall and take on two well-armed men who can pick us off like jackrabbits, and who by now, probably have even more help—and do it all without taking any lead in our guts and without Maggie getting hurt."

Newell chuckled. "That's right encouragin', Sage. Should help me sleep real good."

"Glad to help out." Coyotes yipped and howled somewhere in the distant red cliffs. Sage thought about the night Maggie helped him stave off wolves back at Wolf Canyon… a lifetime ago… how she'd saved him from being mauled to death by that grizzly—what a strong, uncomplaining woman she'd been during all these weeks of hard riding through rugged country. She didn't deserve to have it end like this.

With a deep sigh, he pulled a blanket over himself and closed his eyes.

Hang on, Maggie.

For the life of him, he couldn't remember coming so close to crying—not when his father ran off, not when his mother was slaughtered by soldiers, not when his adoptive parents kicked him out—not even when Joanna left. But the thought of losing Maggie… that brought tears to his eyes.

Thirty-seven

Maggie's hope of Sage being able to get to her and live through it was dwindling. Two more men rode with them now. Jasper came across their camp last night and soon figured them to be the type of men who'd do anything for money… and they were. He promised to pay them well… and throw Maggie in on the bargain… if they helped him and Jimmy kill Sage Lightfoot.

One man, named Walt Sloan, was tall, and actually could be considered handsome, if he weren't so mean-spirited. He wore two guns, one on each hip, and he didn't care about anything but getting paid to kill a man. Jasper asked Walt straight out if he knew Kate Bassett.

"Slept with the bitch once, a year or so ago," the man had replied with a shrug. It didn't bother him that Jasper and Jimmy had left Kate for dead. He needed money for drinking, whoring, and gambling.

Walt's partner, Arny Clay, was an ornery little man with long, dirty blond hair. Arny didn't talk much. Mostly, he catered to Walt and obeyed anything the man told him to do. It was obvious that these two men were the "worst of the worst" Sage had told Maggie about, and Maggie feared she'd soon see Sage shot down in cold blood.

Jasper roused her early, giving her one swallow of coffee and one bite of dried beef, then let her relieve herself before he plopped her on his horse again. Every bone and muscle in her body hurt, and her lips were cracked from lack of water.

"We're headin' up today," Jasper told her.

Maggie soon learned what "headin' up" meant. Within an hour they were climbing over accumulated talus at the base of a searing cliff, on to a steeper incline riddled with loose rock and shale, making the trek so slippery and dangerous that the men dismounted to lead their horses by the bridle. Jasper tied Maggie's wrists to his horse's tail, leaving about three feet of leeway, then took the roan gelding and continued the climb.

In her weak condition, it was close to impossible for Maggie to stay on her feet, let alone keep her balance with so much loose rock. The horse balked several times, and she realized that if the horse slipped, it would land on her and take her all the way down the slope. Every move sent rocks and gravel tumbling past her, creating dust that stung her eyes.

She wondered how in God's name Sage would make it up here without getting shot. She knew now why desperate men came here to hide from the law. What lawman in his right mind would come to this place where he would have to climb this miserable pathway to get to the top, then face murderers and thieves once he got there, if he even made it that far without being shot?

A piece of shale gave way under her foot, and she went down. Jasper kept going, letting the horse drag her for several yards, before he and his men finally stopped long enough for Jasper to walk back and jerk her to her feet. "Keep up, or I'll let this nag drag you all the way to the top," he snarled.

Maggie wanted to spit on him, but her mouth was so dry she couldn't. Her arms stung from bleeding scrapes that were coated with dust. She looked down to see that the front of her dress was filthy and in shreds. She grunted when the horse jerked to a start again, and she determined she'd keep up just to spite Jasper, who would probably enjoy seeing her fall again.

She glanced behind her at the sweeping panorama below. Sage was right. A man could see half of Wyoming up here. It would be an indescribably beautiful view, if not for her current situation. Far across the endless sea of yellow grass below, she spotted a lone rider moving at an unhurried gate. She daydreamed it might be Sage, riding easy, so as not to draw attention.

She looked ahead again, seeing that they were headed into a pathway so narrow that they had to go through single file. Red walls on both sides made it impossible to go anywhere but up.

So, this was Hole-In-The-Wall. They climbed and climbed. The air cooled—Maggie's only relief. Still, the struggle of climbing and fighting to stay on her feet made Maggie sweat. She couldn't imagine what she must look like by now—let alone what she must smell like. She knew instinctively that the men didn't care. Once they reached the top and could finally rest, all eyes would turn to her as the only woman. She would no longer be able to depend on their own haste and weariness to keep them at bay.

After a good hour of climbing, they reached a mesa, where at last the ground flattened out. Jasper came back and untied the rope from the horse's tail, then plopped Maggie on the mare and climbed behind her. "We're home, honey," he said sarcastically.

Maggie studied her surroundings. This place was something from another world. People in cities, even on farms and ranches elsewhere, surely had no idea anything like this existed. She vaguely remembered someone saying that she'd not seen "big" country, until she traveled through the valley to Hole-In-The-Wall and ascended the towering cliff that bordered it.

Who'd said it? Sage? Kate? Newell? She couldn't remember, but now, she knew what they meant. It seemed impossible she could get help or survive, even if she managed to escape. Flashes of her incredibly changed life since the night these men killed James left her feeling removed from her weary body. She remembered the ugly terror of men groping her, the hopelessness, the crimson welts on her hands from digging James's grave. She remembered the first time she saw Sage Lightfoot, sitting tall on his horse, offering to help. She remembered shooting the grizzly, remembered Sage's wonderfully warm, solid home at Paradise Valley… thought about how nice it would be to live there, sleep in Sage's arms every night. She thought about that old cabin where she and Sage first made love.

He would come for her. She had to think positive and not allow herself to give in to lost hope. Jasper moved a hand over her stomach and breasts, rousing her anger and her desire to fight these men in any way possible. She saw one rather large and two smaller cabins ahead, which surprised her. She couldn't imagine anyone living here, but then she chided herself for forgetting how different life was here. Anyone who came here to avoid the law would, of course, need shelter.

Walt Sloan and Jimmy Hart dug spurs into their horses' sides and charged toward the cabins, whooping and hollering. They were finally "home," as Jasper had put it. Maggie knew it was no home at all. For her, it would be hell.

Thirty-eight

Sage and Newell cautiously approached a cabin nestled amid boulders and wildflowers, surrounded by outbuildings, all located a half-mile from the gravelly escarpment that led to Hole-In-The-Wall.

"Stay alert," he told Newell.

"You bet. The men we're after, or even Maggie, could be here, for all we know."

More than ever, Sage hoped to find Maggie without traveling to the top of the grand mesa in the distance. It would be a lot easier here, but he doubted they would get that lucky.

The sun was settling behind the western mountain range as they came closer to the structures, after spotting them from miles away. For the last hour, they'd watched the buildings turn from dark dots on the horizon to a well-kept ranch, that for all a tenderfoot would think, was a peaceful, picturesque home for a law-abiding family.

Several men were gathered around a campfire. He counted six, but knew there were likely more in the outbuildings, or in the cabin.

"Recognize any of them?" he asked Newell.

"No, but it's gettin' pretty dark. The sun will be set pretty quick."

The men turned at their approach, two of them stepping closer with rifles in hand. Sage and Newell halted their horses.

"Speak your names," one demanded.

"Sage Lightfoot," Sage answered. "This here is Newell McCabe, good friend of Kate Bassett back in Lander. Any of you know her?"

The man instantly relaxed. He looked at Newell and grinned. "How's Kate?"

"Not good," Newell answered. "She might even be dead by now. We're after the men who beat her head in and stole this man's wife."

The man frowned, turning his attention to Sage again. "That a fact?"

"It's a fact," Sage answered. Several others came closer, concerned looks on their faces. "We're heading up the wall tomorrow," Sage told them. "We're pretty sure that's where they are. We need fresh horses for the trip—hoping you can oblige—maybe help us find a way to the top without getting our heads blown off."

"Well, hell, if this is because of Kate, we'll see what we can do," the first man told Sage. He shoved his hat more tightly onto his head to keep it from blowing off in the wind as he walked around Sage's horse, studying the sturdy gelding. "Looks like a good piece of horseflesh."

"He is, but he's worn out. He's a good strong gelding, and he'll be fine in a day or two. If you don't want to trade permanent, I can bring your horse back when we're through. We just need fresh mounts for the climb."

The man stepped back. "My name is Bob Yates."

Sage nodded. Yates was perhaps thirty-five, built solid. Sage saw honesty in his eyes as Yates studied him a moment longer before he spoke again. "Seems like I've heard your name."

"I've ridden this area and camped here more than once. That was a few years ago. I have my own ranch now, south of here—Paradise Valley."

Yates nodded. "I think I've heard talk of you a time or two." He folded his arms in front of him, while the men around the campfire watched and listened. "Who was it that hurt Kate and took your wife?"

"One is a fat, filthy man with a scar over his left eye. He's called Jasper. He's riding with a younger man called Jimmy Hart. There was a third man, but I killed him back in Atlantic City. The other two might have picked up more men by now, figuring they'll need help when I come for them."

"The bastards doubled back on us at Lander," Newell added, "took this man's wife, and left Kate for dead. Lightfoot's been trackin' 'em for weeks on account of they killed one of his ranch hands, raped the man's wife, and stole money from Lightfoot."

Yates scratched the stubble on his chin. "Nobody like what you described stopped by here, but in a valley this big, you can ride for days—see men in the distance, but never meet them. You know how it is out here."

"I know all too well," Sage answered.

Yates looked at the surrounding cliffs. "When we

see men riding off in the distance, we don't pay much attention, unless they head our way. Out here everybody minds his own business. I did see some men head up the cliffs late yesterday—far enough away that it's impossible to say who they was, or even if there was a woman along. That area down there where we spotted them is where the narrow trail through the wall leads to the top."

"I know the spot." A sudden gust of dust-filled wind stung Sage's face.

Yates studied him a moment longer. "Mister, if I was the marrying kind, and it was my wife up there, I'd be doggin' those men too. Get on down off your horse, and I'll show you what's in the corral." He turned to the other men. "Get these two some coffee. They're okay," he shouted. He looked at Newell. "Were you close to Kate?"

"Close as you can get without a weddin' ring," Newell answered.

Again, Yates tugged on his hat. "Well, now, me and a couple of others over there know Kate real good—and she's a gem. They ain't gonna like the fact that some bastard broke her skull. I don't like it either. Could be I can get you some help in this." He nodded toward the other men. "This bunch here—they're all no-goods—but they ain't the kind to beat on no woman, not even a whore. And they wouldn't go riding off with some other man's wife neither."

Newell nodded. "I've met this man's wife. She's a good woman."

"Come on then. Get yourselves some coffee, and I'll go with you to pick out a couple of horses."

Newell glanced at Sage. "You thinkin' what I'm thinkin'?"

Sage grinned. "I'm thinking we might have found ourselves some help."

Newell studied the red cliffs nearby. "Up there, though, they might have pulled five or six more men to their side. If we manage to get up there, it's gonna be a real gun battle."

Sage dismounted. "Then we'll just have to be ready, help or no help."

Newell followed suit, climbing down from his horse and shaking his head. "I reckon' so," he muttered. "All I know is, I ain't goin' back to Kate without bein' able to tell her that the men who hurt her so bad are dead."

Sage put out his hand. "And I'm not going back to Paradise Valley without Maggie."

Newell smiled sadly and shook his hand. "Agreed. We both came to finish what them men started, and it ain't gonna be pretty."

Sage squeezed his hand. "Thanks for coming along, Newell."

Newell turned to follow Bob Yates to the corral. "Wild horses couldn't have kept me away," he answered. "And speaking of horses, let's go find us some good horseflesh to get us up that little hill over there."

Sage walked beside him. He'd been up that "little hill" before, and he didn't relish going up there again.

Thirty-nine

Maggie felt like a trapped animal, waiting for a hunter to come along and torture or kill it. After arriving at this cabin at the top of Hole-In-The-Wall yesterday, Walt Sloan shot two men inside and declared the cabin would now be used by him and those who accompanied him. In some ways, Walt seemed to be taking over as boss of the four men rather than Jasper, who was afraid of the man and probably regretted asking him to join him and Jimmy.

After the shooting, several men in a nearby cabin shrugged it off, all but one who challenged Walt using the code of the gun. He, too, was shot down, and that was the end of the argument over cabin occupancy.

Animals. They were all animals, like the wolves that tried to occupy the cave she and Sage claimed that night at Wolf Canyon. Survival of the fittest, or the smartest—or in this case—whoever was fastest with a gun.

In spite of her miserable, aching, filthy, tired condition, she'd been ordered to make coffee and a meal for her abductors, who after filling their bellies, started drinking and playing cards. By some miracle, they left her alone after that, probably too worn out to pay her any sexual attention. She knew that couldn't last, not when she felt their eyes on her constantly and heard their crude remarks. She could only thank God that last night they'd left her alone, but while they used the beds, she was forced to sleep on the wood floor with only two blankets, her wrists tied behind her. She'd used her teeth to pull the blankets over herself and laid awake most of the night, imagining Sage coming for her, but so far today, no help arrived.

She'd hauled wood, hauled water, cooked breakfast on an old iron stove, scrubbed pans and dishes, and cooked a rabbit. Jasper kicked her in the rear more than once when she didn't move fast enough to suit him. She was not allowed to bathe, and she'd never been so achingly tired on this whole journey as she was now. Her stomach lurched at how filthy and stained the blankets and mattresses were. She was actually glad to have slept on the floor last night.

From what she'd seen, she figured there were at least six men living in the cabin next door, all thieves and murderers, no doubt. Apparently, these cabins were used by any number of men at different times, with blankets and utensils left there for whoever might use them next. And as one would expect of such men, no one cared if anything was washed or organized.

Maggie knew better than to expect any of those next door to have a change of heart and try to rescue her. Jasper had ordered them to stay away from her, told them she was his woman. They probably figured that if Jasper wanted to abuse her that was his business as long as she really belonged to him. A few of them had stared at her curiously, probably wondering if they might be able to trade a couple of horses for her. One man looked as though he was wondering if Jasper was telling the truth. Maggie suspected he at least gave some thought to helping her, but he'd seen Walt Sloan in action and was not about to go up against the man.

Today, Walt and Arny took turns watching the trail to the top, lying in wait for Sage. Maggie felt sick with dread at what would likely happen, if and when Sage did come for her. *No, not "if."* She must not think that way. *When.* On one hand, she was relieved that their attention and conversation centered around Sage's arrival rather than on her, but the fact remained Sage would be a sitting duck. Once it was over, if Sage were killed, she would have no reason to live. She'd find a way to kill herself before she allowed these hideous men to have their way with her and then hand her over to the filthy cowards in the next cabin.

Her only hope for Sage was Jasper's comments that he could "take that sonofabitch down in a fair gunfight any day." He'd actually commented that rather than pick Sage off on his way up, he might let Sage reach the top and face him squarely. Walt Sloan relished the idea, and the two men argued earlier over which one would have the pleasure of shooting it out with Sage. They decided that whoever won at cards tonight would get to face Sage—and would "win" Maggie. Maggie figured that even if it came to a one-on-one gunfight, it would not likely be "fair" at all. Someone would end up shooting Sage in the back, even if he did beat whomever he faced.

Tonight she slept on the floor again, more fearful of what she dreaded most. Jasper and the others had taken baths earlier, if one considered jumping into a watering trough in their long johns a real bath. They were rested. Walt had even shaved. Their bellies were full, and now, while she lay trying to sleep they played cards… and talked about needing a woman.

"We've got one right here," Walt Sloan said.

Maggie wanted to vomit. Apparently, it didn't matter that she needed a bath. It didn't matter that she was tired to the point of collapse, that she was covered with scrapes and bruises and dirt—her hands raw from scrubbing so much wash all day. She was their slave, there to be used however they pleased. It had only been a matter of time… and the time had come.

She lay waiting, like a rabbit hiding in the bushes, trying to decide when to flee, yet knowing that once it tried, it would be caught and killed. Finally, the inevitable happened. Walt Sloan rose and walked to where she lay. He removed his gun belts.

"I won," he told her. "And since Jasper is out of money, you were the payoff." He reached down and grabbed her wrist.

Forty

MAGGIE WINCED WHEN SLOAN JERKED HER INTO ONE of the other two rooms in the cabin. He shoved her onto a bed, while in the outer room, the three men laughed and made more crude remarks.

"You gonna cooperate, or do I have to tie your wrists and ankles?" Walt asked. "I ain't aimin' to hurt you long as you don't make it necessary." He loosened his belt and started unbuttoning his pants.

Maggie scrambled to think. She'd rather die than let another stranger touch her. "Do you really think Jasper is out of money?" she asked, hoping to get him to think about something else.

He hesitated. "What are you talking about?"

"He stole a lot of money off Sage Lightfoot," Maggie answered, "more than what he told you. He only told you he's broke and offered me up, so you couldn't get more of his loot. He's made a fool of you."

Walt stiffened. "You're lying."

"Am I? Why do you think Sage Lightfoot is so bent on finding Jimmy and Jasper? Jasper told you Sage would come here for me, but it's *not* for me.

You already know Jimmy and Jasper raped me once. Sage knows it too. He happened to come along and help me afterward, and together we started looking for those two. But do you really think Sage Lightfoot would risk coming here for a raped, pregnant woman he's known only a couple of months? It's the *money* he's after!"

When she spoke the words, they sounded too sickeningly true. Maybe once this was over, and Sage had most of his money back, she would learn that the money was the real reason he'd come this far.

"Pregnant?" Walt asked.

It was only then that Maggie realized she'd mentioned her condition. In her addled, desperate state, she'd blurted it out. She got off the bed and faced him. "Would Sage Lightfoot care about a woman who's carrying an outlaw's child, especially when it belongs to one of those two wretched men out there—men who *stole* from him?"

Sloan stood there looking befuddled, and Maggie took hope in his confusion and hesitation.

"Yes, I'm carrying a baby fathered by Jimmy or Jasper—or maybe, by their third partner—the one Sage Lightfoot killed! The baby is a bastard! Why would Sage Lightfoot care about me when he knows that?" she reiterated, hating to refer to her baby as a bastard. Right now, she would do anything to discourage Walt Sloan from what he wanted to do. She walked closer, facing the tall, intimidating man as though she were just as tall and intimidating. "I'm telling you it's the *money*! Go ahead. Ask Jasper where the *rest* of the money is."

Sloan squinted, studying her closely. "You telling me the *truth*, woman?"

"I sure as hell am!"

Walt took a deep breath, then buttoned his pants and stormed into the next room.

"What the hell!" Maggie heard Jasper yell. His exclamation was followed by the sound of a man's fist landing into someone. There came a crash. Maggie walked to the curtained doorway and looked to see Walt jerking Jasper to his feet.

"You didn't tell me and Arny that she was carryin'!" he roared. He threw Jasper against a wall. Jasper grunted and stood there with the breath knocked out of him. Walt walked over and strapped his guns back on. "I might stick myself in anything with a skirt on," he growled, "married or not, willin' or not—but I'm not pokin' a woman with a kid in her belly!" He pulled out one of his revolvers and charged back to Jasper, shoving the barrel of the six-gun under the man's chin. "Where's the *money*, Jasper?"

Jimmy and Arny sat staring, neither reaching for a gun.

Jasper swallowed. "*What* money?"

"The rest of the money you stole from Lightfoot! The money you didn't tell me about!"

"I paid you plenty to come along and help us," Jasper told him, his face covered in perspiration. "I gave most of what I stole to you. You won the rest tonight."

Walt cocked his gun. "I don't believe you." He finally backed away. "You lied, Jasper." He holstered his gun and grabbed his hat and jacket. "I ain't helpin' a liar! Out here you gotta be straight about what you're doin'. I'll sleep at the other cabin. Be back for my gear in the morning—*after* I kill Sage Lightfoot. Then you and me are gonna have a little showdown of our own! If you don't come forth about the rest of the money, you're a *dead* man! I'll let you think about it tonight." He walked out, slamming the door.

Jasper stood there looking dazed. Jimmy and Arny exchanged glances. "She's *carryin'*?" Arny asked.

Jimmy shrugged. "I don't know."

"You should know," Maggie said, moving into the main room. "You could be the father." She moved her gaze to Jasper. "Or you!"

Jasper stared as though she was some strange creature he'd never seen before. "You're lyin'," he growled.

"I don't think she's the type to make up somethin' like that," Jimmy spoke up. "And as long as we ain't sure, we gotta leave her be. Jesus, Jasper, let her go. We can still lay in wait for Lightfoot and kill the son of a bitch, but let the woman go. We still have a lot of money left."

"How *much* money?" Arny asked.

Jimmy rolled his eyes. "Look, we'll pay you more, if that's what it takes. Just stay with us. By this time tomorrow, I'm figurin' it will all be over. Lightfoot will be dead. We can hand the woman to that bunch in the next cabin, and they can decide what to do. You can come with us back to Lander. The rest of the money is in a bank there."

"Shut up, Jimmy!" Jasper warned.

"What the hell, Jasper? The cat's out of the bag. I'm tired of runnin'. We've been high tailin' it for nearly two months now. We've made the woman suffer, and if she's really carryin' a kid we put in her, that's good punishment for givin' us such a headache ever since we had our fun with her. She'll be carryin' a bastard kid. It's like Walt said. He's comin' for the money, and he won't get it. Killin' him and leavin' the woman to fend for herself from here on is good enough for me."

Jasper glowered at Maggie. "I ain't so sure about that."

Jimmy turned back to his cards. "If you want to go pokin' a pregnant woman, go ahead. I ain't got no desire for it."

Maggie folded her arms, glaring at Jasper. She felt a sudden resurgence of strength. God had put exactly the right words into her mouth to get rid of Walt Sloan and give the other three second thoughts. "Go ahead," she sneered at Jasper. "I already know you don't have a brave bone in your body! Prove it again!"

He came for her, but rather than push her into the bedroom, he jerked her back over to the fireplace. He shoved her to the floor and threw a blanket at her. "You'll sleep out here on the floor again tonight," he huffed. "I ain't wastin' my time with a used-up piece of woman carryin' a bastard kid."

He returned to the table and took a long slug of whiskey. "Deal me in," he told the other two. "Now that Walt is out of the game, I'll keep playin'. He was a little too lucky tonight for my likin'."

"What are you gonna do about Walt tomorrow?" Arny asked. "He meant it about facin' you down, if you don't tell him where the rest of the money is."

"I ain't worried about that bastard. I'll shoot him on sight and not give him the chance to pull his gun on me."

Arny chuckled. "Tomorrow's gonna be a real interestin' day."

Maggie curled up on the floor, miserable physically, but exultant mentally. She'd found a way to stave off her abductors for another night, and that's all she needed. She prayed that tomorrow Jasper and Jimmy would regret messing with the likes of Sage Lightfoot, that tomorrow Sage would finally catch up. The only trouble was that he was up against incredible odds.

Worse than that was her worry that she'd been right in saying Sage Lightfoot wouldn't care about a woman carrying a bastard child spawned by the likes of the men he was after. Once this was over, if Sage lived, she'd be forced to tell him the truth.

Forty-one

Someone pounded on the door. Maggie jerked awake, then squinted against a shaft of sunlight that glared through the one and only front window of the cabin. She groaned with pain-filled bones and muscles as she managed to get to her feet, realizing the last few hours were the first time she'd truly slept in days, mainly because she no longer felt the threat of rape from Jasper and Jimmy. If it weren't for the rude awakening from the banging on the door, she might have been able to get a little more rest.

A hungover Jasper stalked grumpily out of the bedroom wearing only his long johns. "Who the hell is it?" he demanded.

"I don't know," Maggie replied. "In a place like this, I'm not about to open the door to strangers."

"Well, heat some coffee, woman!" Jasper pulled his handgun from its holster where it hung on the wall. There came more pounding.

"Who is it?" Jasper shouted.

"Name's Skeeter," came the shouted reply. "I was the watchman last night for the men next door."

Jasper finally opened the door, covering his bloodshot eyes against the bright sun. "What the hell do you want?"

"Just lettin' you know that some men are comin' up the wall." Skeeter was tall and lanky, and Maggie noticed his eyes were huge with excitement. "I know the one in front. Name's Bob Yates. He's from a ranch below, and he's bringin' up supplies. He does that sometimes. Me and the others are anxious to have fresh food and tobacco. I reckon' he's carryin' whiskey too. You might want to do some tradin' with him."

Jasper squinted and ran a hand through his matted hair. "Do you know a man named Sage Lightfoot?" he asked Skeeter. "Anybody in their party look Indian?"

Skeeter shook his head. "I ain't never heard of the man, and ain't none of them looks Indian."

Maggie's heart fell. She busied herself with lighting a fire in the stove to heat the coffee and start breakfast.

"You sure it ain't the law comin'?"

"Shoot no. Ain't no lawman ever comes up here. Like I said, it's just Yates comin' to do some tradin'. I rode part way down to be sure. He even brung along a travois he says is packed with potatoes, beans, and such. I rode hard back here to tell everybody, so's you can be ready to trade. They're just now makin' it to the top and will have to rest their horses a bit before they get here."

The man left, and Jasper turned to Maggie. "Fry up what's left of the bacon and eggs from yesterday," he ordered. He shoved his gun into its holster and headed for the bedroom to pull on his pants. "If your man ain't in the bunch who's comin' today, looks like maybe he won't come for you at all," he goaded.

Maggie hurt so bad that she wondered if she might have broken bones. It was all she could do to lift the cast iron fry pan to the stove. She turned to the bacon barrel and glanced at Jasper's gun hanging nearby.

"Don't be thinkin' to use that gun." The words came from the corner where Arny Clay lay on a cot watching her. "I'll shoot you down, pregnant or not. Fix that coffee and bacon like Jasper told you to do. And don't be thinkin' them men that's comin' are gonna help you. They're here to trade. Best you can hope for is they'll try tradin' somethin' for you. If they do, your fate ain't gonna' be any better with them than with us."

Sage. He should be here by now. How disappointing to learn he was not among those coming to trade. Maggie stoked the fire in the cookstove, poked the dying embers to get flames started as she added wood. She wondered how on earth men got such a heavy stove up here, but she supposed where there was a will, there was a way. She prayed the same was true for Sage.

She set a coffee kettle on one of the burner plates, deciding to heat the coffee left from the day before rather than make fresh. She lifted the lid and added water to ease the thick bitterness yesterday's brew was bound to carry. She turned to the bacon barrel and lifted the lid, using a fork to dig what was left of their supply of bacon from the lard in which it was packed. She threw the bacon and extra lard into the cast iron fry pan then replaced the lid on the wooden barrel.

The lard heated quickly, while Maggie's thoughts raced with possibilities for escape, if Sage didn't make it after all. She had to face the reality that any number of situations could arise out here that would prevent him from getting to her. He could be wounded, or maybe his horse went lame, and had slowed him down by a day or two. She had to believe there was a good reason he'd not come yet.

The bacon sizzled. Maggie went outside to get the eggs she'd left there to keep cool. She looked out to see two men riding across the mesa toward the cabin. They dragged a travois built narrow enough to get it through the path that led here. It was loaded with supplies and covered with canvas. Behind them, a third man led six good-looking horses tied together with a string of rope. He kept his hat pulled down over his eyes as though nearly asleep in the saddle.

"Get in here!" Jasper growled from the doorway.

"I was getting the eggs," she answered, turning back inside with the basket in her hands. "The men coming look to have a lot of supplies, even some horses."

"I don't want them men seein' you," Jasper ordered. "We'll see what they want first and make sure they're on the up and up. Might be I'll trade you for one of their horses. Now that I know you're carryin' a baby, and Lightfoot apparently ain't comin' for you, I'd just as soon trade you off and get rid of you. That would twist Lightfoot's gut right good, which is all the better."

Fine. I'd rather take my chances with strangers than spend another minute with you, Maggie thought. She walked to the stove and took the coffeepot from a hot plate, pouring some into three tin cups on the table. She replaced the pot and broke eggs into the fry pan along with the bacon. Jasper left the door open, so he could keep an eye on the new arrivals while sitting at the table. He and Jimmy and Arny sat down and slurped their coffee.

"Hurry it up," Jasper told Maggie. "Them men out there is gonna be ready to trade, and I don't want to miss out."

"Then you should go there to greet them first instead of feeding your face," Maggie answered. She no longer cared about Jasper's threats or how he might treat her. She moved away from the table and walked to the open doorway again. The traders were close now, approaching the men next door. She noticed Walt Sloan amble out of the other cabin. He was not wearing his guns.

Maggie glanced at the traders again, and it was then she saw him.

Sage! He moved from under the canvas that covered the travois. Maggie realized then that the man who'd been riding with his hat pulled down was Newell! She forced herself to show no reaction as she tried to think straight, her heart pounding. She decided the best thing to do was act quickly to help Sage without giving anything away to the men inside.

She walked casually back to the stove, glad Walt was not armed, and realizing that he wouldn't know Sage anyway, unless someone pointed him out. With shaking hands, she took Jasper's tin plate from the table and used a spatula to put eggs and bacon on it. She did the same for the other two men, setting their food in front of them, then picked up the pan of hot grease as though to remove it from the fire.

It was now or never. Difficult as it was to hang on to the heavy pan, Maggie swung it around, slamming the open pan with its hot grease against the side of Jasper's face. She heard a sizzling sound, and Jasper screamed and jumped up. Maggie ran to the door and yelled Sage's name. "In here!" she screamed. "There are three of them!"

Everything happened so fast then that Maggie wasn't sure what took place first. Jimmy was suddenly there. He slammed a fist into her face and sent her sprawling onto the porch. Maggie rolled away from the doorway. She heard gunfire, saw Sage ducking and rolling, fire spitting from his six-gun. In near unconsciousness, she scrambled farther away, heard Jasper still screaming and cursing inside the cabin. She took satisfaction in causing him pain.

Newell rushed past her and flattened himself against the outside of the cabin wall. Maggie managed to sit up. She forced herself to concentrate. Now she saw Sage at the far corner of the cabin. He motioned for her to stay down. Maggie obeyed. She glanced at the supply train. One man was on his knees near the travois, apparently ready to help. The other man with him ran behind a watering trough, his gun ready. But the men in the nearby cabin all stayed inside, none of them willing to help. Maggie was not surprised. It worried her that she didn't see Walt Sloan anywhere. Had he gone for his guns?

"Come on out, Jasper!" Sage yelled.

"You come get me, you son of a bitch!"

A barrage of gunfire came from the doorway and the one window of the cabin. Maggie wasn't sure if anyone inside was hurt, other than Jasper's burns. Pain throbbed at her cheek where Jimmy had hit her. She could tell it was already swelling.

"Step in the doorway, and I'll blow our head off!" Jasper added. "Then I'll take care of that goddamn bitch you're after. I'll give her to the rest of them men out there, if any of them wants a whore carryin' a bastard kid!"

Maggie gasped. This was not the way she wanted Sage to find out about the baby! She met his gaze and saw surprise in his eyes. What was he thinking? She couldn't tell, and the matter at hand was too pressing to give it much thought. Sage looked at Newell and made a gesture toward the roof. Newell nodded. He shoved his six-gun into its holster and made a mad dash for a pole that supported an overhang of the sagging front porch. He shimmied up the post and onto the roof.

Realizing what was happening, Arny came running out, guns blazing. Sage stepped out and shot him down, then darted around the corner. Walt Sloan came charging out of the other cabin then, both guns blazing. Newell flattened himself on the roof, and Sage cried out, apparently hit.

"Sage!" Maggie screamed. She barely got his name out before he fired several shots at Sloan. The man's chest seemed to explode, and he crumpled to the ground.

Sage ducked back again, and Maggie hoped he'd have time to reload before more shooting started. How badly was he injured? To her great relief, the rest of the men stayed barricaded inside the other cabin.

According to the code of conduct among such men, this was not their business.

Jasper mouthed off a string of curses, daring Sage to step inside, while Newell removed his vest and laid it over the top of the stovepipe that stuck up through the roof of the cabin. In just seconds, smoke came pouring out of the cabin door and windows. Jimmy stumbled outside, coughing and gagging, shooting randomly at nothing.

Sage charged onto the porch and shot Jimmy as he ducked and rolled to get to Maggie before Jimmy's wild shooting could send a bullet into her. A bullet spit across Sage's face, opening a cut across his cheek. He spun around, landing beside Maggie.

"Sage!"

He didn't answer. Stunned but awake, he quickly grabbed her and dragged her off the porch. Maggie noticed his upper arm was also bleeding.

Smoke finally forced Jasper outside. He fired wildly, striking a horse. The animal whinnied and reared, and Sage stepped up and shot Jasper twice. The man screamed and collapsed with a bullet in each knee. Maggie realized Sage had deliberately avoided hitting Jasper in any vital places. He wanted him alive... for a while.

More curses poured from Jasper's mouth in ugly screams. Once he was down, Sage left Maggie and stormed to where Jasper lay. He took his hunting knife from its sheath near his ankle and dragged Jasper around the side of the house. Jasper's screams grew so loud that even Maggie almost felt sorry for him.

"Where's my money!" Sage raged.

"Lander!" Jasper screamed. "In the bank! I swear—most of it is still there!"

There came a couple of seconds of quiet, and in that brief moment, Maggie found herself wondering if Sage really did come just for his money.

She wouldn't believe it. She couldn't believe it.

Jasper began begging then. "No! No! No!" His protests sounded desperate, like a man being tortured. Maggie wasn't sure what Sage was doing to him… nor did she want to know. She put a hand to her stomach, her emotions roiling in her gut at the realization that the last two men who might have fathered her child were dead… or soon to be dead, when Sage was finished with Jasper.

Suddenly, Newell was beside her. He helped her to her feet. "You need to get farther away," he told her. He hurried her behind an abandoned buckboard wagon.

"Newell! Are you all right?"

"I'm okay. Is Jasper the last man who was inside?"

"Yes, but Sage is wounded."

"Don't worry about Sage. He's too pissed off to go down."

"I can't believe both of you made it up here."

"Had some help. Men in these parts won't help the law, but they'll help each other if they think it's necessary. They don't like other men takin' a man's wife—and the men who helped us knew Kate. They wasn't happy to hear Jasper and Jimmy beat up on her."

"How is Kate? Is she alive?" Maggie saw the pain in Newell's eyes.

"She was when we left Lander. I'm not sure she'll still be alive when we get back."

"Oh, Newell, I'm so sorry!" Maggie couldn't help her tears—a mixture of relief Sage and Newell had found her, and sorrow over Kate.

"You couldn't help it," Newell answered, watching both cabins. "Me and Sage are the ones who are sorry. We never should have left you and Kate alone."

Sage walked around the corner of the cabin and into view. Jasper was still screaming, calling Sage every name in the book, and begging him to kill him.

"Maggie!" Sage shouted.

Maggie stepped from behind the buckboard. There was a wild look in Sage's eyes that made her hesitate.

"She's carryin', Lightfoot!" Jasper screamed, deliberately baiting Sage, apparently in an effort to get Sage to shoot him and put him out of his misery. "It's my kid! Maybe it's Jimmy's... or Cleve's! Your woman is carryin' a bastard!"

Maggie watched Sage's eyes. She could not read them. At the moment, she was the one who wanted to die, realizing the other men were listening, that they all heard Jasper's ugly words. Newell walked up beside Maggie.

"You gonna kill him?" Newell asked Sage. "Or do you want me to do it?"

"Let him suffer," Sage answered, his eyes still on Maggie. "He'll die soon enough."

Maggie realized then that Sage's hands were bloody, and he still held his knife. Blood poured down the side of his face from the bullet wound, and his shirtsleeve was soaked with blood. "Sage," she said softly, not sure what he wanted or needed.

"Is he telling the truth?" Sage asked.

Maggie swallowed. She was losing him. "Yes."

He looked her over. "How long have you known?"

"Since before we left."

He closed his eyes and struggled with emotion. "Not your husband's?"

"No."

He turned away, bracing himself against a porch post. "How do you know?"

"How do you think?"

Sage walked off the porch and went to a barrel that held water. He dipped his hands and the knife into the water and washed off the blood, then shoved his knife into its sheath. He washed some of the blood from his face, but more poured forth. He stood bent over for a moment, looking broken. Finally, he walked to the men with the pack train. He reached into his pocket, handed them money. One of them helped him take two saddles and gear off the travois.

"You'd better sit down," Newell told Maggie. "Give Sage a few minutes. Takes awhile for a man to settle down after bein' so angry, especially after he's killed somebody. He has some dickerin' to do with them men over there. They did a right good job of helpin' us out."

Maggie sank to the edge of the porch. Smoke poured from the cabin's front door. She waited while one of the men who'd helped ripped open Sage's shirtsleeve and doused his wound with whiskey, then wrapped gauze around the wound to slow the bleeding. She heard the man say something about the bullet going all the way through. He asked Sage about the deep scar already on his arm.

"Grizzly," Sage answered.

To Maggie, it seemed a lifetime ago that she'd shot that grizzly.

Newell climbed back onto the cabin roof and retrieved his vest from the top of the chimney, then jumped down and tossed it aside. "All smoked up," he commented. "Ain't no good now." He walked over to help Sage saddle two horses. The men in the other cabin slowly came out and talked with the traders. They all proceeded to go about their business as though what just happened was a daily occurrence. Jasper's curses weakened and turned into the ugly groans of a man slowly dying.

Maggie felt dazed. Silly as it seemed at the moment, she worried how she must look. She was filthy. She didn't need a mirror to know her hair was a mess, her cheek swollen, her lips cracked, her hands blistered, her dress in shreds, and her arms covered with dirt and scabbing scrapes. On top of that, she figured she must smell horrid. If Sage had seen her at her best back in Atlantic City, he was now seeing her at her worst.

Sage finally walked closer and pulled her into his arms. "Thank God, you're alive," he groaned.

Maggie wilted against him. "I'm so sorry, Sage, about the ugly way you heard about… the baby." She felt him stiffen.

"Why didn't you tell me?"

Maggie pulled away and looked at him. "Because you would have left me behind. When I fell in love with you, I not only feared you'd leave me, but that I'd lose your love and respect. I meant to tell you when all this was over, and we were both safe. I thought maybe… if I picked the right time and place…"

"Just tell me you didn't intend to pass the baby off as mine."

"No!" Maggie felt sick with regret. She turned away. "You should know me better by now."

He closed his eyes. "I'm familiar with a woman's deceit, Maggie."

"You're too worked up right now to deal with this." She faced him again. "And I'm so… so worn out, and…" She couldn't finish, too emotionally and physically drained to argue or explain. A hint of softness moved into Sage's dark eyes… the eyes of a man who could be as savage as the wildest Indian… and perhaps, as unforgiving. She saw doubt in those eyes, and it devastated her. Yet, in the next moment, in spite of his injuries, Sage scooped her into his arms and carried her to one of the saddled horses. He set her on it.

"We have two more horses below the wall," he told her. "When we get to the pathway, you can sit on the horse while I lead it down. The descent can be more dangerous than coming up." He paused, settling into the saddle behind her and wrapping both arms around her. "Maggie," he groaned her name. "What have they done to you?"

Maggie grasped his strong forearms and let the tears come—deep, wrenching sobs of relief… and sorrow. He'd come for her… found her… but in a different way, they'd likely lose each other again.

Forty-two

Sage held Maggie in his arms until they reached the edge of the massive red-rock wall and began their descent. In spite of its beauty, Maggie hoped to never see this place again. Sage remained quiet, and Maggie was grateful. She was too weary and hurting too much to talk about anything that touched on raw emotions. It was enough that their journey was finally over—at least the part that kept them searching for the men who'd caused so much havoc in their lives. She could sense the rage that still seethed in Sage's blood. Even Newell remained tense and quiet.

The trip down was the most harrowing of any other part of their journey, but the horses remained sure-footed and stable. Sage put Maggie on one of two more horses held for them at the bottom of the trail.

"Looks like you had a bit of a battle," said one of the two men waiting with the horses.

"You might say that." Sage packed supplies they'd left with the men. Maggie realized any one of them could have ridden off with all of it.

The man helping Sage glanced at Maggie and nodded. "Ma'am."

Maggie nodded in return. "Thank you for watching the horses."

"Well, ma'am, I don't cotton to anybody stealin' a man's wife. Looks like you've been sore-treated. Sorry about that." He turned his attention to Sage again. "Yates still up there?"

Sage tightened the cinch on one of the extra horses. "He stayed to do some trading. He and the others didn't get hurt. I'm glad of that."

"The men you went after... are they dead?"

Sage nodded. "The one I wanted most should have bled to death by now." He turned to the man beside him and put out his hand. "Thanks."

The man shook his hand. "Anybody gives you trouble on the way back, just mention Bob Yates, and tell them what happened to Kate. They'll leave you be." He grinned. "Not that you can't handle yourself. I've got no doubt that you can."

Sage mounted up, and the three rode off, Newell leading the fourth horse. Sage rode beside Maggie. "Can you make about five miles?" he asked her.

"I think so."

"It's a bit out of the way of the regular trail through the valley, but I know a place not far from here where you can hole up, while I go on to Lander with Newell to check on Kate and get my money out of that bank."

Maggie felt panic rising. Did he intend to leave her? Had he already made up his mind? "I don't want you to leave me again—not out here. And I want to see Kate too."

"In Kate's condition, it won't matter if you're there or not. And time is of the essence. If Kate's dying, I want to get there quick as I can, and the condition you're in—you'd just slow us down. If Kate is alive, she'll understand why I left you behind."

"But you're hurt too."

"Don't argue, Maggie. You've been to hell and back, and you're carrying. There is no way I'd make you ride all the way back to Lander yet."

"Where are you taking me?"

"To a place where an older couple run a rooming house and supply store. They have six grown kids, most of them married now and moved away. The woman, Sarah Becker, is a crusty, seasoned old woman who knows that out here you don't ask questions, so she won't press you about the bruises and all. She'll understand what you need, and she'll make sure you get a hot bath and a decent bed. You need to sleep—not for a couple of hours, but for a couple of days, maybe longer." Maggie was too tired to think straight. "You're going to leave me there and not come back." She felt the tears coming again.

Sage halted his horse, and Maggie followed suit. "I'm doing this so you'll be rested for the ride home, Maggie."

Home. Maggie wondered if she dared think of Paradise Valley as home. Newell interrupted her thoughts when he told them he'd head on into Lander.

"Got to get back to Kate. You go on to the Becker place, Sage. That little gal there is in need of female attention."

"I'll catch up soon as I can," Sage told him.

"Newell," Maggie spoke up. "I can't thank you enough for what you did, helping Sage and all. You risked your life, and you hardly know either of us."

"Don't need to know you long to realize you're worth helpin'. Besides, Kate would want me to help, and I wanted those sons of bitches as bad as Sage did after what they did to her."

Maggie felt sick at the memory. "I pray she's alive and will be okay," Maggie told him. His eyes looked so sad. He gave Sage a nod, pulled his hat farther down on his forehead, and headed south.

"I feel so sorry for him," Maggie said softly. She turned her gaze to Sage, who watched Newell for a moment. "Sage, look me in the eyes, and promise you'll come back and get me."

When his dark eyes met hers, she could see not all the rage had left him. She ached for him, his wounds, all the blood—his guilt over what happened to Kate... and to her. "I just risked my life to come for you on top of that mesa," he told her. "Why wouldn't I come for you this time?"

Maggie looked away. "When you came for me up there, you didn't know I was carrying the child of one of those awful men."

"Maggie, I can't talk about that right now, but I'm not going to leave you over it. I need time to let this settle in my head. The important thing is to get you some help and some rest." He sighed, removed his hat, running a hand through his hair. "Jesus," he muttered. "Maggie, what did Jasper do to you? And I'm not talking about the obvious... the injuries I can see."

She knew he felt he'd failed her. She wiped at tears

with a shaking hand. "They didn't touch me that way. They rode so hard to get there that they were too tired for anything else, even these last couple of days."

"That the truth?"

"Yes. I'm just sorry about how you found out about… the baby. I intended to tell you privately once this was all over with. I didn't say anything because I knew you'd leave me behind, and I wanted to stay with you till we found those men. The only reason Jasper knew was because… last night that extra man they picked up won me in a card game. I was desperate to figure out a way to keep him from… you know." She sniffed and struggled to stay in control of her emotions. "I told him I was carrying… that it was the bastard child of Jasper or Jimmy and…" More tears came. "And that you'd never come for me because of it. I told him the only reason Jasper figured you were after him was because he stole your money… that Jasper lied and had more money than he let on. That angered the man, and he left me alone—clobbered Jasper and walked out." Her body jerked in a sob as she met Sage's gaze. "I'm keeping this baby, Sage, even if it means losing you. I called him a bastard to make things look as bad as I could to that man. I don't intend to think of my baby as a bastard. It's all I've got after losing my little girl."

Sage put his hat back on. "I'm so goddamn sorry, Maggie" he told her. "This should never have happened in the first place. I thought I'd go out of my mind knowing you were with that son of a bitch again."

"You couldn't have known." Maggie breathed deeply to fight her crying. "The only thing that kept me going was knowing you'd come and get me. And you did. It's over now. We've done what we came to do."

Sage rubbed the back of his neck. "I know what you're thinking," he told her, "that I won't want anything to do with you now. Get those thoughts out of your head, Maggie. I need time to think. The first thing we need to do is for you to get some rest and me to go see what's happened with Kate. Believe that I *will* come back for you. Will you do that?"

Maggie nodded, more tears streaking through the dirt on her face.

Sage sidled his horse closer, reaching out to wipe at her tears with his fingers. "I was scared to death over how I might find you. You're some scrapper, Maggie Tucker." He gave her a smile. "Jasper's face was burned pretty bad. Did you do that?"

Maggie felt better at his touch… his smile. "I sure did. I had to find a way to warn you and keep Jasper from getting to his gun too soon. My only weapon was a frying pan of hot grease."

Sage nodded. "I told Newell you were a hard woman to break."

She held his gaze. "Sometimes, it's the little things that break us, Sage."

He moved an arm down and around her waist, pulling her off her horse and onto his. "Right now, you look ready to fall off your horse. Hang on to me."

She wrapped her arms around him. "I'd like to hang on to you forever." She rested her head against his chest, deciding that for now, she could deal with life an hour at a time, a day at a time, for however long it took Sage Lightfoot to decide if his love was strong enough to accept her condition... and to believe she'd not intended to betray him by claiming he was the father.

Sage took the reins to her horse and headed east. Maggie watched Newell in the distance, already far enough to be a mere dot on the immense landscape, a man alone with an unknown past, like so many men out here... and so many women too.

Forty-three

Eight days later

MAGGIE WATCHED LITTLE WHIRLS OF DUST DRIFT upward far off in the yellow-grass valley beyond the Becker home. *Men on horses*, she thought… *going somewhere… going nowhere.* Maybe it was Sage, finally coming for her.

Today was a rare day of no wind. The heat felt heavy, and the dust swirls hung lazily in the air for several minutes. She wondered how many riders were out there, how far away they were… five, maybe six miles? Distance seemed to have little relevance in this country. She couldn't tell if the riders were headed toward the ranch, or maybe, just riding past it.

She sat in a rocker on the wide veranda that stretched across the front of the Becker's two-story frame home. It was lovely here, peaceful. Large pine trees encircled the house and barns, and today they were filled with colorful, chirping birds. On the north side of the trees was a combination store and restaurant, run by Sarah Becker, a thin but tough old woman with a heart as big as the valley that stretched into forever beyond the homestead.

Maggie leaned against the wide wooden slats of the rocker and closed her eyes. It was July twenty-first, and she'd been here over a full week… waiting. When Sage first dropped her off, Sarah prepared a wonderful, warm bath and washed her hair. After that she ate… then she slept… and slept… almost constantly, for nearly three full days. Sage was right. Sleep was what she'd needed. She was grateful that Sarah had indeed asked no questions. After living out here for years, nothing shocked or surprised the old woman.

Maggie put a hand to her belly, which was growing a little. Her waist was a bit thicker, but nothing the unknowing person would notice. Sarah gave her a lovely blue gingham dress to wear today. It belonged to one of the woman's grown daughters who left clothes at the house for the times she visited.

My Jessie has four children now—lives down in Cheyenne. Her husband owns a dry goods store there, Sarah said. She was proud of her children.

Maggie had decided she, too, would raise children of whom she could be proud, starting with the life that fluttered in her abdomen. Yes, this baby was indeed alive, and he or she was strong—a fighter. This baby could bring her the happiness she'd never known… fill the void in her heart left there when her pretty little Susan died.

She shook away the awful memory and concentrated on the approaching rider. Could it be Sage? The spirals of dust indeed seemed to be drawing closer now, and she was sure there was only one man coming, one man leading two horses. Her heart raced a little faster. Had he made any decisions? Was Kate all right?

And what about Joanna? She'd had time to think about the fact that Joanna would likely be at Paradise Valley when they arrived. The woman was yet another obstacle to be faced when they reached home… if Sage even took her back with him.

"Rider comin'… looks like he's got a couple of packhorses with him." Joe Becker came to stand beside Maggie on the veranda.

"I've been watching the dust," Maggie answered. "I thought, at first, there were only two horses, but now, I see three. How far away do you think he is?"

Joe stretched and rubbed the back of his sunburned neck, then sat in a wooden chair next to Maggie's rocker. "I figure about four miles. He's ridin' easy, most likely to save the horses cuz of the heat."

Joe was old and thin like his wife, but there was nothing weak or soft about him in spite of the man's wrinkles and age. Maggie could tell he was tough as nails, probably a lot stronger than he looked. She wondered how he and Sarah ended up running a restaurant and boardinghouse in outlaw country, but just as they'd asked no questions, Maggie obliged the same courtesy.

"I'll bet you're used to watching the horizon," she told Joe.

"In this country? You bet." He licked at dry, cracked lips. "Been watchin' for newcomers for years. Always have my guns ready—and a couple of men to back me up—just in case, but most are respectful in spite of their backgrounds or their reasons for being out here. There's kind of a code in this country."

"I figured that out not long after I met Sage and his men."

Joe nodded. "Ain't many men out here who'd abuse you like them men did up yonder at Hole-In-The-Wall. Sage, he did right by killin' them." He scratched at stubble on his chin. "Sage is a good man. I've knowed him for years—since he wasn't much more than a kid."

Maggie continued watching the little clouds of dust as Joe talked.

"I could tell he was different from them men he ran with. All men have good and bad in them, Miss Maggie, and most of them wrestle with which one is gonna take over. Sage mentioned once over a meal that he'd like a ranch of his own someday, said he'd have a family too. Not many men who come to these parts care much about either one. I reckon most had a bad childhood that made them like they are, so they don't much care about nothin'."

Maggie thought about Kate and Newell and how hurt Sage must have been when the people he thought loved him kicked him out at an age when he needed guidance. She figured Sage's biggest fear was rejection. His father rejected him, the people who raised him rejected him… and Joanna rejected him.

I would never do that to you, Sage. Sage must figure she'd betrayed his trust, which was yet another rejection in his mind. He liked honesty, and she'd not been honest. It might be impossible to get back the love and trust they'd shared for such a short time.

The hardest part was trying to imagine living without Sage Lightfoot.

Joe rambled on a little longer about the kind of men in these parts, then rose and said he was going inside to get his shotgun, "Just in case." The rider in the distance finally began to take shape… three horses… one man who sat tall in the saddle. After another half hour, he came close enough for Maggie to recognize him.

It was Sage.

Forty-four

Joe Becker walked out to greet Sage as he dismounted.

"Just in time for supper," Joe said. "I'll have somebody take care of the horses for you."

"Thanks, Joe. Maggie and I will be leaving right away early morning." Sage took a leather supply bag from his horse. "This is all I need for tonight. After supper I'll wash up and get some sleep. Thanks for all you've done."

"No problem. You go on inside, and Sarah will set a place for you and Maggie at the table."

Sage walked to the porch, and Maggie rose. He wore a red shirt and looked so handsome, but Maggie's heart fell at the fact that his eyes were unreadable. "How is Kate?"

Sage leaned against a support post and took a drag on a thin cigar he'd been smoking when he arrived. "She'll be okay. Believe it or not, she was up and walking when we got to Lander. One leg is partially paralyzed, but she gets around pretty good with a cane. By the time I left, she was harping on Newell to quit hovering over her and get back to work." He smiled sadly. "Those two were nagging each other like an old married couple."

Maggie breathed a sigh of relief. "Thank God." She folded her arms. "Maybe they *will* get married someday."

Sage shook his head. "That's something I'd have to see to believe." He studied her a moment. "You look rested."

So stiff… all the comfortable closeness gone. "I'm much better."

"Good." Sage tossed his cigar to the ground and opened the screen door, following Maggie inside.

"Did you get your money back?" she asked.

She heard the screen door close behind her.

"Only about a third—not nearly enough, after all we went through."

They walked into the dining room—the only two there at the moment. Maggie faced Sage. "You said we'd leave in the morning. I'm grateful that you're at least taking me back to the ranch." She studied his dark eyes, still full of doubt. "That *is* where we're going, right?"

Sage removed his hat and hung it on a hook by the door. "That's where we're going."

"I don't suppose you've made any decisions beyond that?"

He faced her. "No, Maggie. It's all too fresh. I feel… raw. That's the only word I can think of. It must be the same for you."

"I guess you could describe it that way. I slept a lot… nearly three days. I still hurt in a lot of places, but overall, like I said, I feel much better."

He looked her over. "You look nice in that blue dress."

A compliment. Small as it was, Maggie welcomed it. "Thank you. And I've never seen you wear red. It's a good color on you."

Sarah came in with a porcelain bowl full of mashed potatoes. "Well, you made it!" she told Sage. "Good to see you, Sage! You two sit down. I was just putting supper on."

Sage nodded. "Thanks, Sarah."

He sat down, and Maggie took a chair across from him. "Did you get that shirt in Lander?"

Sage took up his cloth napkin and laid it over his knee. "Figured I'd get some new shirts. After all that traveling, what I had was getting pretty well used up. I got you a couple of dresses."

Maggie was surprised he'd thought to do something like that. "You did?"

He shrugged. "Figured it was the same for you... clothes worn out and all. And I supposed you wouldn't want to wear pants again when we leave. It's time you dressed and felt like a woman."

Maggie wished she knew what his thoughtfulness meant. Was it because he still loved her, or was he helping her stock up for when he sent her away?

"I hope they fit," he continued. "I don't know how much you've gained by now. I expect your waistline will be growing pretty quick. I don't know much about those things, but from what I see, you don't look much different yet."

There it was. He was hinting at her condition, bringing it up in a roundabout way. She felt a flush come to her cheeks. "I haven't changed much yet, but yes, my waist has grown a little." She put a hand to her stomach, suddenly too aware of the awkward situation.

For the next several minutes, there was no more talk between them. Joe came inside, and Sarah brought more food. Talk turned to Lander and Kate and Sage's money—how Sage was doing now—if Kate might be able to walk without a cane someday. They talked about the weather and ranching… small talk… anything to avoid what really needed discussing.

The next thing Maggie knew, Sage excused himself to wash up. He asked where he should sleep giving no indication he had any intention of sleeping with Maggie. He looked tired, and Maggie had a feeling he was more worn out from emotions than from what he'd been through, then the long ride to get back here. He retired without another word.

Maggie made herself busy helping Sarah clean up and took food to the bunkhouse for the men there. Her mind raced with all kinds of scenarios of what Sage intended to do, how he felt, what would happen when they reached Paradise Valley. Did he still love her, or did he have no feelings at all? Did he see her differently now? It surely had been difficult enough loving her after knowing how the outlaws abused her, but he'd accepted that and understood… loved her anyway.

Now that he knew she was carrying a baby that belonged to one of them, this was something altogether different. And to have kept it a secret was, to someone like Sage, probably unforgivable. She'd been dishonest, which was the worst choice she could have made, after what he went through with Joanna.

When she finished helping Sarah, she decided she'd

try to sleep. Knowing Sage, he'd want to leave the minute the sun was up enough to see the way. She'd better get some rest. She went to her bedroom, which was right across the hall from Sage's. How she wished he'd sneak into her room later, come to her bed, and profess how much he still loved her, then take her into his arms and make love to her, promise to keep her with him forever once they reached Paradise Valley.

She went to bed, tossed and turned and waited... but he didn't come. The next thing she knew the sun was up, and it was time to leave.

Forty-five

THREE DAYS OF RIDING HELPED CALM TWO HEARTS. Hole-In-The-Wall was only a few days from Paradise Valley, so the worst of their journey over the long summer was nearly finished. Maggie thought how they'd actually made a huge circle as they chased Jasper and the others, heading south, then west and north, now south again.

Sage remained caring and attentive, but he'd made no effort to discuss the baby or any final decisions he'd made. Maggie felt his quiet, unspoken love, but she knew the stubborn, confused side of Sage Lightfoot was bent on making sure he never allowed himself to be hurt or used again. He'd made no move toward anything physical, and she knew part of the reason was his indecision about her condition… let alone the fact that a woman he'd once loved fiercely was likely waiting at the end of their journey.

They'd ridden in relative silence, except for small talk, mostly about Sage being anxious over how things were at the ranch. He'd never been gone this long, and the ranch meant everything to him. At night he slept beside her protectively, his rifle close by. He let her lie against him because she felt safe there, and she loved him for it. But he'd gone no farther than a solid hug. When Maggie removed her dress at night to sleep in her slips and camisole, she felt Sage watching her. She could only hope he still wanted her. She knew that if danger presented itself, he'd die for her. The deep scar across his left cheek where Jasper's bullet had come close to killing him proved that. There would always be that scar on that handsome face to show the courage and skill it had taken for him to come after her, but she would never forget the look on his face when Jasper shouted the words… "She's carryin', Lightfoot! It's my kid or maybe Jimmy's—or Cleve's!" Maggie understood the burden that had thrown on Sage's heart. Accepting her meant accepting a child spawned by one of the men he'd hated and killed. That might always come between them.

Mid-morning of the fourth day found them riding through yellow grass that was belly-high to the horses. The air hung too quiet, today's wind soft and gentle. The only sound was the occasional snort from one of the horses. They crested a hill that led down into a sprawling valley of deep green grass splattered with wildflowers of white and gold, red and purple.

Maggie drank in the explosion of color. She felt as though she and Sage were riding into a grand painting only the likes of God could create. As the stronger wind in the valley moved across the blades of grass, the prairie undulated rhythmically in waves of dark and light green.

"Sage, it's beautiful!" Maggie commented, halting

her horse to look. She glanced at him as he lit a thin cigar and studied the valley below. She thought how handsome he looked today, how strong and fitting he was for this land, how well he sat on a horse, how brave he could be when necessary. He was more man than she'd ever known… and it broke her heart to think she still might lose him.

"That scene is why I call this place Paradise Valley," he answered. "It's so fitting. It feels good to finally be…"

Did she dare say it? "Home," she finished.

Sage smoked quietly for a moment then faced her. "It sure does. It will be another day before we reach the house, but this is part of the ranch… the north section." He turned to scan the horizon. "I guess the boys decided to let the grass in this area get plenty tall before they bring the cattle here. You need to save certain areas in case of drought." He faced her again. "There's a lot to running a ranch, Maggie."

What did he mean? Did he want her to learn? Did he mean to keep her here? "I figured that out in the short time I was here before." She turned away, fighting an urge to cry. "Sage, we need to talk before we get to the ranch house."

Sage kept watching the horizon. "I know," he answered with a deep sigh.

"Whatever you've decided, I love you, no matter if you turn me out or not. If you do, I guess I'll understand, but I intend to have this baby… and love it. It's a tiny, innocent being who will never know how he or she was conceived because I'll never tell. I'd hoped—"

"You hoped you could marry me and let the child

think I'm the father," Sage finished for her. He met her gaze. "Maybe you wanted me to think I *am* the father."

She closed her eyes with a sigh and shook her head. "Never! My God, Sage, you should know me better than that by now."

"Yeah, well, I thought I knew Joanna pretty well too."

Maggie stiffened. "I am not Joanna and never will be. I already told you that I never intended to mislead you. I was scared to tell you, not simply because I was afraid you'd leave me behind, but more because you might react exactly the way you are now. You'd think I meant to trick you, but that's never been the reason I said I loved you. I love you for the man you are, and I've grown to love this land in a way I never thought possible. It's like you—wild and dangerous, but there's something about it that ropes you in like a wild horse and makes you love it. It makes you want to stay here and tame it and prove to yourself that you can survive out here. And I think I *have* proven that."

Maggie was unable to hide her tears then. She quickly wiped them and took a deep breath to keep from breaking down. "I don't want to live without you, but I'll give it a try, if it means staying with any man who can't accept the child I'm carrying. I won't let him or her grow up feeling unloved and unwanted."

Sage swung a leg around his saddle horn and sat nearly sideways, facing her. "You should have told me straight out, Maggie. I feel like a fool, worrying about not using protection because I was afraid of getting you pregnant—and there you were, already carrying."

Maggie closed her eyes. "You wouldn't have taken me with you if you knew. And then, we never would have fallen in love. I never would have known what it's like to want the man who's making love to me."

For a few tense seconds, the only sound was the soft rushing of the rippling grass as the wind brushed it.

"Maggie, I still love you," Sage finally told her.

Her heart raced at the words, but she was afraid of what would follow.

"But this whole thing about the baby—a man needs to think, that's all," he continued. "It makes no difference in my love for you, but it's like you said—you don't want to be with a man who can't love and accept that baby. When we talked about marrying awhile back, we decided we wanted to make sure it was for all the right reasons. Remember that?"

"I remember."

"Well, now that's more important than ever. I want you to be real sure you aren't just wanting a man that baby can call a father, and I want to make sure I can be a good father. Hell, even if it were mine, I'd be doubting myself. Of all the things I've been through, this is the first that really scares me."

The remark surprised Maggie. "Scares you?"

"Hell, yes. I'd rather face that grizzly again. How do I know I could do right by the kid when I'm so full of resentment for my own father—for the way the people I thought of as parents kicked me out? And with the life I've led, how can I be a good example to *any* kid, even my own?"

Maggie could hardly believe what she was hearing. Doubts about himself were bothering him more than doubts about her. "Sage, you'd make a wonderful father. You already told me you wanted to have a family. And it's *because* of your own disappointments that you'd make a good father. You'd never want a child to suffer what you suffered."

He looked over the valley again. "Maggie, I've robbed and killed and whored around, and I come from two different worlds. I don't belong in either. What kind of an example would I be for that kid?"

Did that mean he really could care for this child once it was born? "You can teach a child about honesty and bravery and how to be strong and survive. And because you've seen and done so much, you're wiser than most men, able to show a child all the right ways to live his or her life. You, of all men, can teach a child about love and loyalty… and how to be proud no matter what his heritage or background. This baby is *innocent*, Sage—just like *you* were innocent when those missionaries took you in."

Sage smashed out his smoke against his canteen. "You're right in a lot of ways, but that life in your belly brings out all the natural, motherly love and instinct in you. But me… it's hard for a man to understand that kind of feeling, especially for some other man's child. Maggie, if I take in you and that baby, it would only be right to fully adopt the child as mine, which means the kid would one day inherit some of this. That's like giving a piece of everything I've worked for to the men who put us through all that hell and stole from me. I need to get it straight in my head. Can you understand?"

Maggie nodded. "Of course, I can. But I have a feeling that once this little girl or boy walks up and calls you daddy, you'll turn into a bowl of pudding."

Sage smiled sadly. It was good to see him smile, even though not with great joy.

"I can only promise that I'd never be mean to the child. I'm a man who goes all out in whatever he does, so if I take in that baby, I'll be a real father. I know how it feels to be unloved and abandoned. I wouldn't wish that on any kid."

Maggie still wasn't sure how much to hope for. "Are you saying I can stay? That we can be together?"

"I'm saying I have a lot of things to consider, and that I love you. I need to know I love you enough to accept your child." He faced her. "Let's get down to the ranch and spend time living like normal folks again before we make up our minds. For that baby's sake, and yours too, we have to make the right decision."

He wants to see Joanna first, Maggie thought, pain stabbing her heart. After all they'd been through, Joanna Hawkins Lightfoot was the last big test, perhaps something harder to face than a gang of outlaws, or the fact that the woman he loved was carrying another man's child.

"Fine," Maggie told him. "I can accept that."

"And you have to consider, Maggie, that I can be pretty violent. This land is unsettled, and there could be more trouble like what happened with Jasper and them. Men like me tend to make enemies… dangerous enemies. Life isn't easy out here. Staying with me means signing up for possibly more trouble."

"I've already seen some of the worst, Sage. It doesn't frighten me."

He looked her over thoughtfully. "I guess it wouldn't, would it? When I first left this place to find those men, I never expected to come across the likes of you. You're not like any woman I've known, but I was fresh off the hurt Joanna caused me. You were so different… the strongest, most honest and outspoken woman I've ever met." His smile faded. "Can you understand why it hurt so much to find out you were pregnant and never told me—why the first thing I thought of was that you pretended to love me, so you could claim the kid was mine?"

"Of course, I understand. I wanted to savor every moment before I *had* to tell you."

Sage moved his leg over the saddle. "Let's get to the ranch house and settle other matters. We have a lot to think about and talk about."

"I already know what I want, Sage. I want to be with you forever, but more than that, I want you to be happy."

He adjusted his hat against the sun. "You deserve to be happy too." He headed into the valley.

Maggie tried to picture him riding out of her life. The pain in her chest was almost unbearable. She took a deep breath and let the wind and sun bathe her in their warmth before she adjusted and retied her bonnet, following Sage into the valley… toward what she hoped to someday call home.

Forty-six

Hank Toller came riding out to meet Maggie and Sage as they made their way carefully through a huge herd of steer. The ranch house was in sight now, a lazy wisp of smoke meandering from its stone chimney. Maggie breathed deeply of cattle and horses, ranch smells that some might find offensive. To her, they meant security, love, brave men, and a big, solid home nestled in a spectacular green valley surrounded by purple mountains.

"Boss!" Toller rode closer, looking the same as when they'd left—bristly beard, sweat-stained Stetson, checkered shirt and denim pants, guns on hips.

Another man from nowhere, with no background, probably an outlaw's past no one knows about. Maggie thought how there was probably nothing left to learn about someone that would surprise her.

"You've got company," Hank told Sage.

Maggie's heartbeat quickened. She could tell by the tone of Hank's voice that he didn't like the "company" he spoke of.

Sage adjusted his hat. "Damn," he muttered. "I figured we might. How long has she been here?"

"Must be six weeks now, boss. She's been cleanin' and she sewed and put up curtains and settled herself in like you two was still—" He hesitated, glancing at Maggie. "Ma'am." He nodded. "Glad to see you made it back okay."

"Thank you, Hank."

"Good to see the two of you," Hank answered. "For as long as you've been gone, and from the looks of that bruise on your face, Maggie, and the scabbed-up scar on Sage's, you two have been through hell." He turned his attention to Sage again. "Did you get 'em?"

"I got them, all right."

Three other ranch hands trotted their horses among the cattle several yards away. One of them whistled for attention and waved his hat at Sage. "Good to see you back, boss!"

It was Julio. Maggie truly felt as though she'd come home, and it infuriated her to know Joanna was here, keeping house as though she and Sage were still married. She had no doubt that's what Hank started to say, before he realized maybe he shouldn't.

Sage took a cigarette Hank offered him and lit it. The two men sat there for a while, smoking, talking about the roundup, the condition of the cattle, how soon they'd make the drive south to meet the cattle cars headed for Omaha, what the price of beef might be.

Julio and Joe Cable rode closer then, greeted Sage, shook his hand, and nodded to Maggie. She could tell both men were anxious to know how things went, and they were probably wondering about Maggie and Sage, what they'd been through, if anything romantic had taken place.

"You got somebody waitin' for ya," Joe told Sage.

"I'm aware of that," Sage answered. Maggie couldn't tell if he was glad or angry.

"Bill rode down to let her know you're back."

Two more men rode up then, all happy to see Sage back home. Sage got his horse into motion, and the five men ambled their horses through the valley toward the house, while Sage answered a barrage of questions.

Joe turned his horse and came back to ride beside Maggie. "You doin' okay, ma'am?"

"It was a pretty rough journey, Joe," Maggie answered. "Thanks for asking."

"You must be some woman, sticking out that whole trip with Sage. From that bruise on your face—things wasn't easy on you."

"It wasn't easy for either of us."

"Did you get your money back?" Hank asked Sage.

Sage kept the cigarette at the corner of his mouth. "It's a long story, Hank. I'll tell you sometime over coffee, but not now." He watched the house. "I apparently have some important things to take care of first."

Apparently, Maggie thought. She wished she'd been able to clean up before meeting the infamous Joanna Hawkins Lightfoot. Here she was wearing a plain blue dress that was dirty around the hemline. Her hair was twisted into a simple bun, upon which sat a floppy straw hat to keep her face shaded, so she wouldn't get even more freckles. She needed a bath, needed to feel cream on her skin. She wished she could look as nice as she'd looked the night of that dance back in Atlantic City.

She drank in the scene before her as though this might be the last time she saw it… the wide, green valley… grazing cattle scattered as far as the eye could see… the sun lighting up the surrounding purple mountains… the feel of a gentle summer wind. Right now, it all smelled wonderful. She thought about how Sage smelled—tobacco and leather and sunshine and prairie wind.

How could she ever say good-bye to him or this land?

"Shit," Joe commented under his breath.

Maggie saw someone riding toward them from the house and instantly knew the reason Joe had cursed. Even from this distance, she could see it was a woman.

"Let's go, boys!" Joe spoke louder. He glanced at Maggie. "Right glad to see you came back with Sage."

"I'm glad to be back."

"We're lookin' forward to more of that chicken stew."

Maggie smiled and nodded as all the men rode off. *I hope I'm here long enough to cook for all of you*, she thought. She rode up beside Sage then, and her heart nearly stopped beating as she watched the woman ride closer. She'd never considered that anyone could actually look elegant bouncing up and down on a horse, but this woman did. She rode sidesaddle, like a proper lady should. Maggie didn't even know how to ride sidesaddle.

The woman's dress was finer than any Maggie had seen, a green that matched the grass. It was made out of beautiful, crisp cotton material, and it perfectly accentuated the woman's voluptuous figure.

She didn't need to dismount for Maggie to tell

she was tall, a head taller than Maggie, which meant, she probably had long lovely legs. Her blond hair was piled into perfect curls, upon which sat a lovely bonnet of green velvet and darker green ribbon, with a touch of silk flowers. She wore gloves that matched her dress. Everything about her spoke of money and schooling and beauty, and Maggie couldn't figure out how in the world she was able to quickly groom herself to such perfection. Did she dress like that for household chores?

"Sage!" the woman called as she drew close. "Thank God, you're finally back!" Her lightly painted, perfect full lips opened into a lovely smile that in turn showed perfect teeth.

Sage kept the cigarette between his lips. "Hello, Joanna."

Forty-seven

JOANNA URGED HER HORSE CLOSER AND REACHED OUT to touch the still-scabbed scar on Sage's face. "My God, Sage, what happened to you? I've been so worried! When I heard about the reason you left, the kind of men you were after—"

Sage grabbed her wrist and pushed her hand away. "What are you doing here, Joanna?"

Her smile faded. "Now what kind of a greeting is that?"

"The kind a man gives a woman who divorced him and took off with his money." Sage spoke the words matter-of-factly.

Joanna's cheeks flushed. "You don't need to be so mean, Sage."

Sage's horse tossed its head and snorted, as though it too, disapproved of Joanna's presence.

"Look, Joanna, Maggie and I have been to hell and back," he said. "I'm in a pretty foul mood, so coming home to find the woman who once tried to cut my heart out living in my house and pretending nothing ever happened doesn't set well. And you might show a little concern for the woman beside me. Her name is Maggie Tucker, and she's been through things you never would have survived."

Joanna glanced at Maggie. "Well, of course. I'm sorry for what happened to you, Maggie. You must come to the house, and I'll help you clean up."

"No, thank you," Maggie answered, devastated at the condition she was in compared to the stunning Joanna. "I'll be fine on my own. You and Sage have things to talk about."

Joanna turned her attention to Sage again. "My gosh, Sage, she's a child."

"She's by God no child, I guarantee that. And I asked you what you're doing here."

Joanna stiffened. "Well, I..." Her eyes filled with more tears. She seemed hurt by Sage's abruptness. "I guess I've gone about this all wrong."

"I guess you have," Sage grumbled.

Joanna maneuvered her horse closer. "I'm sorry for the surprise at such a bad time, Sage, but how was I to know? I wanted to get here before you left on a cattle drive. And I'm here because I missed you. I've come to realize you're my only true friend." She reached out and touched his leg, leaning in close to talk directly to Sage as though Maggie weren't there. "I still love you, Sage. I did a stupid thing, and I want a second chance. I've waited here alone nearly six weeks. That should tell you how sincere I am, but we don't need to talk about it right now. I can see you need to clean up and rest first."

Sage snickered. "Jesus, Joanna, did you honestly think it would be this easy? You just show up, and we go on as though nothing happened? You hate it here—remember? So what's the real reason you came back? Are you broke again?"

Joanna jerked her arm away, a tear running down her cheek. "How can you be so insulting to the woman you always loved? I came back to ask your forgiveness, Sage. I'm so sorry for all that happened."

Sage took the cigarette from his mouth. "You're one hell of a good liar, Joanna, I'll say that. And truth or not, this isn't the time to profess your love and talk about forgiveness. I'm not much good at it." He took up the reins of his packhorse. "Let's get to the house, Maggie."

Maggie rode beside him, saying nothing. She could feel Sage's tension. The air hung thick with it, and she feared it came more from Sage wanting Joanna, than from being angry. When they reached the house and prepared to dismount, Maggie could see Joanna was still quietly crying.

Maggie's heart fell. The woman honestly did seem to love Sage and want him back. She had, after all, waited six weeks by herself. If Sage decided to believe she was sincere…

"Sage," Maggie spoke up as he climbed off his horse. He tied the horse and came to help her down, but Maggie waved him off. "You and Joanna go inside and talk things out," Maggie told him. "I'm just in the way right now." She struggled not to show her own tears.

Sage removed his hat and rubbed his eyes. "Where in hell would you go? You need to get inside and clean up and get some rest. God knows, we both need a lot more sleep."

Maggie knew by his words that he agreed with

her. She felt sorry for his awkward predicament, and she hated Joanna for putting him in such a situation at probably the worst time she could have chosen.

"Is that little cabin still empty?" she asked Sage. "The one where Standing Wolf lived with his wife?"

Sage looked beyond the house to the tiny log cabin several hundred yards to the south. "Far as I know. I don't know what kind of shape it's in, Maggie. It's just one room with a woodstove and—"

"Sage, after everything I've been through, that cabin will seem like heaven, no matter what shape it's in. And it's bound to be better than that rambling old shack we stayed in when I was hurt."

He met her eyes. That shack was the first place they'd made love, and Maggie was damn determined to remind him. "You do what you have to do, Sage Lightfoot. Do what you want to do in order to be happy. I'll be just fine."

Sage took hold of her hand. "I'm sorry for this mess, Maggie."

"So am I." Maggie glanced at Joanna, who was watching and listening. Joanna covered her face and cried even harder. Maggie actually felt a little sorry for the way Sage had talked to her. If she wasn't sincere, then she was indeed a wonderful actress.

Maggie backed up her horse. "I'll take my satchel and go to the cabin. I can have one of the men bring me whatever I might need."

"Maggie—" Sage caught hold of her horse.

"Take Joanna inside. This isn't something you can put off, Sage. You have decisions to make." She turned her horse. "Even if it takes all night," she added, anger rising deep inside now. This was certainly not the homecoming she'd imagined. Joanna had ruined it. She told herself the woman couldn't possibly understand what she and Sage had been through, so she couldn't be totally to blame for the awkward position they faced.

She rode off, wanting to cry and scream. She couldn't hold a candle to the beautiful, sophisticated Joanna, and she knew the woman would do everything in her power to entice Sage into taking her back. Maybe she'd even talk him into sleeping with her tonight. Sage was tired and vulnerable.

She slowed her horse and looked back. Joanna was crying in Sage's arms. Maggie felt like someone had stuck a knife in her heart. They were home now… back to reality. The journey was over… in more ways than one.

Forty-eight

MAGGIE CLEANED UP THE CABIN AS BEST SHE COULD, her heart aching to realize two people in love had lived here once.

She pulled blankets from the wood-frame bed, wanting to keep busy… busy… busy. What was happening at the house? She hated Joanna for jerking Sage's feelings one way and another, toying with his emotions. She folded the blankets and laid them on a trunk in the corner. She ached with a need to sleep, but she knew sleep wouldn't come, and she needed clean blankets.

She built a fire in the woodstove. Even though the air outside was warm, the cabin was chilly and damp from not being used. She took a kettle from the top of the stove and made ready to take it outside to a nearby well, so she could heat water and wash. Someone knocked on the door before she reached it. She opened it to see Joe and Hank standing there, one man holding an armful of blankets and towels, the other carrying a loaf of bread and a kettle of hot water.

"Sage said we should bring this stuff over here, ma'am," Hank told her.

Maggie felt relief that Sage had thought to do that much. "Oh, thank you. Come on in," she told the two men, with whom she felt completely relaxed now. She remembered meeting the plump, balding Joe Cable at the line shack where she'd taken Sage after the bear attack.

Hank turned and spit tobacco juice on the ground before coming inside with the hot water. "I've got a jar of jam too," he told her. He set the kettle on the stove and put the bread on a small wooden table in the corner, then pulled a small jar of dark jam from where he'd stuck it into his waist. He set it on the table, while Joe put the blankets on the thin mattress supported by rope springs. Both men stood there for a moment then, awkward and uncomfortable, glancing at each other as though they had something to say.

Maggie folded her arms and frowned. "What is it?"

Hank cleared his throat and scratched at his proverbial stubble of a beard. "Ma'am, we want you to know we greatly admire what a strong woman you are. Me and Joe—we know what it's like out there in the places you and Sage went. We figured you'd never make it back, and we want you to know that we're glad you did… and that we hope you'll stay."

Maggie wanted to hug them, but she knew that would only embarrass them and make them feel more uncomfortable. "You have no idea how much that means to me," she told them. "But whether I stay depends on Sage."

Joe removed his hat. "Pardon us bein' so bold, ma'am, but we're all hopin' it's you who stays. Ain't no woman ought to be forgiven for what that one at the house did to Sage. If Sage don't see your worth compared to that woman, it's gonna be hard for us men not to take him out to the barn and make him regret it."

Maggie couldn't help a smile, even a light laugh. "Well, I'd like to watch, and maybe, get in a punch of my own."

Hank grinned, his teeth brown from too much chewing tobacco. "We're hopin' that means… well… all of us was hopin' by the time you two got back, there'd be somethin' more between you than goin' after those men, if you know what I mean."

Maggie felt her cheeks growing hot. "I know what you mean… but there are complications." *I'm carrying the child of one of the men Sage killed.* She reached out and touched Hank's arm. "Thank you for the kind words. Whatever happens, I'll never forget any of you or the things I've learned over the past couple of months."

She put on a brave front until the two men walked out. She couldn't help the tears then. It wasn't just from the possibility of losing Sage. It was a culmination of all that had taken place. She even wept for James, lying alone out there on the plains. She wept for the little girl she'd never hold again, buried a thousand miles away. She'd never again visit either grave. She wept for the life growing now in her belly. If she ended up heading out on her own, she had to start thinking about how she was going to support and protect her child. She had to think about where she would go, what she could do to earn a living, without compromising her pride and morals like Kate ended up doing. She even wept over how much she'd miss the men on this ranch.

After several minutes, she straightened and vowed to stop feeling sorry for herself. She'd fallen in love, and she'd made the decision to sleep with Sage Lightfoot because it was so wonderful to love and be loved properly by a man. She'd made the decision to keep her baby, and she was the one who'd decided not to tell Sage. It wasn't his fault he was blindsided by the news. He thought he could trust her implicitly, and trusting was a delicate matter for a man who'd been hurt so deeply by his own wife.

She busied herself again, put clean blankets on the bed, locked the door, and stripped down to wash. She took her time, letting the hot water calm her. She dried off and put on a clean flannel nightgown rather than dress again, figuring she'd spend the rest of the night in this cabin.

How will Sage and Joanna spend the night?

She couldn't wash her hair with a basin of hot water, so she simply unpinned the bun and brushed it out. Frustration, anger, jealousy, and a determination to hold her head up caused her to brush harder than normal. All she could see was Joanna—beautiful, poised, perfect. She could see her crying in Sage's arms, begging his forgiveness. Sage would be craving a woman by now. It would be easy for him to cave in to the voluptuous woman he'd loved for years and who'd once been his wife.

Maggie stood and looked at herself in a broken, spotted mirror. There she stood, all hundred and ten pounds—or whatever she weighed—her waistline growing, her face bruised and plain, her freckles showing, her feet bare, her fingernails needing a good filing. She was a used and abused woman carrying a bastard child. How could what she saw in the mirror compare to someone like Joanna? It was a lost cause.

Even though it was still light out, she walked to the bed and got under the blankets, then cried herself to sleep.

Forty-nine

Sage sat down in one of his big stuffed chairs near an unlit fireplace, watching Joanna clean off the table at the kitchen end of the great room. She'd cried in his arms and seemed truly repentant, sincere about wanting to try their marriage again. She'd cooked a roast and baked a pie yesterday, and she'd warmed both for him this evening, carrying on about how every day for the last week she'd watched for his return, sure it had to be soon. That was why she made sure there was a good meal ready every night.

"The men and I were getting worried because you were gone so long," she'd explained over their meal. "We were really beginning to wonder if you'd make it back at all, and all I could think of was how awful it would be if I never saw you again."

Sage ate a little, but only enough to be polite. His appetite was gone. He had too much to think about. The last thing he wanted was to come back and find Joanna here, nesting in the house. She had no right.

One thing he'd learned their first time around was not to fall for her pathetic crying and pleading. She was damn good at it. He thought how, after all the things Maggie went through, he couldn't remember her carrying on like that even once. Still, what was unusual this time was that Joanna had waited several weeks by herself. Apparently, she'd even cooked a time or two for the men, or so she claimed. That was something she never did the first time around. All she did was complain about their raw, unkempt condition.

It would be easier to concentrate on Joanna, whatever it was she wanted, if he could stop the memory of watching Maggie ride off alone to that cabin. It tore at his heart to imagine her riding away from Paradise Valley forever. After knowing Maggie, everything he'd admired about Joanna didn't seem important anymore. Yes, she was beautiful, and her curves felt good in a man's arms. But she couldn't shoot an old Sharps rifle, wouldn't dream of wearing pants or riding a horse like a man. She would never consider killing a chicken and plucking it, or spending weeks on the trail sleeping on the cold ground. She hated the smell of cattle dung and never did want to learn anything about ranching and the chores involved.

So far, all she'd talked about after he let her cry in his arms was how much she still loved him, how once she was away from him she realized how much she needed him, his friendship, and his strength. She talked about her trip here, all the things she'd done to the house while waiting, and how worried she'd been when she learned the reason for his trip.

He rolled and lit a cigarette. "Joanna, quit busying yourself, and come sit down," he told her, wanting to get to the truth and get it over. He didn't believe a word that came out of her mouth. How could he consider getting back together with a woman who'd used him the way Joanna had?

Then again, Maggie had lied to him too. But that was different. It wasn't a lie to get money, and he honestly believed Maggie's love for him was unchanged—it was her love that made her afraid to tell him about the baby.

He watched Joanna walk across the room, and he could not help being struck by her physical perfection. What man wouldn't notice? As he watched Joanna sit down, he thought how attracted he'd become to a wisp of a woman with small breasts and freckles and red hair that was never in place like Joanna's. He'd grown to love looking into green eyes that matched the prairie grass, and he liked the thought of a wife who would often ride beside him on roundups, probably even cattle drives. Joanna could never do those things and wouldn't even try if he asked.

The sun was beginning to settle behind the western range, and Joanna took a moment to light a lantern on the small table next to her chair. She turned and smiled a fetching smile, came closer, and started to sit on Sage's lap.

"Sage, I want so much to feel your arms around me again."

Sage grasped her about the waist and lifted her away. "Sit in the other chair. It's time to talk, Joanna… *really* talk."

She looked surprised, and her eyes teared again. She moved to the other stuffed chair and sat on the edge, as though she might soil something, or mess up her hair, if she sat all the way into it and leaned back. She waited quietly as Sage studied her intently, thinking how stiff and defensive she looked.

"Let's have the truth, Joanna. Why are you here?"

She blinked. "I told you." She wiped at a tear. "I love you, and I want to be your wife again."

"Are you out of money?"

She straightened even more, raising her chin. "N—no. I have some left. Money has nothing to do with this." Her tears disappeared, and she frowned. "Why are you being so mean? Surely this doesn't have anything to do with that woman… *girl*—I should say… you've been traveling with. I mean—she's a mess! And from what the men told me about you two going after those outlaws… well, I deduced what must have happened. I know it's a terrible thing, but what man would want her now?"

So, the *real* Joanna was beginning to peek through. "*This* man," he answered. "I'm in love with her, Joanna. She's ten times the woman you'll ever be—perfect for ranch life—out on that trail, she saved my ass more than once. She can ride and shoot and cook, and she loves this ranch and this land. She's been through things I can't even tell you about because it would horrify you. And she goddamn well knows how to love a man in every way possible."

Joanna sucked in her breath, her blue eyes turning from a look of pleading repentance to pools of jealousy and hatred. "Sage, this is me, Joanna, the woman you've loved since you were seventeen! How could you possibly choose that used-up farm girl over someone who can bring respectability to you and this ranch? I can go out in society and erase all the rumors about your heritage and your background and how you started this ranch."

Now Sage felt his anger rising. "Respectability?" He struggled to keep his urge to choke her in check. Here was the old Joanna, still talking about propriety and mingling with high society. Nothing had changed at all. He took another drag on his cigarette. "Maggie Tucker is a woman to be respected more than any woman I've ever known, including you. And if you raise one more insult about her, I'll have a hard time not hitting a woman for the first time in my life. You can stop right now when it comes to saying anything about Maggie. She loves me just the way I am. I don't need to put on airs for her, or change my life. And you should know by now that I don't care what other people think of me. I don't run in those circles, and I never will, Joanna. You know that about me, so I'll ask you again. Why are you really here?"

Joanna stiffened even more.

"Tell me the truth, Joanna. You know what honesty means to me."

She rose and walked to a window. "I'd *like* to tell you the truth, but I'm scared of you, Sage… scared because of how angry you were the last time we parted. Promise me you won't yell at me… or hit me."

Sage smashed out his cigarette in an ashtray and leaned back. "Jesus, Joanna, you know better than that."

She continued staring out the window. "I suppose I do. It's just that… men like you can be pushed only so far before the stubborn wildness comes out."

Sage thought how Maggie understood that part of

him, knew how to handle it, knew when to back off, and when to fold him into her arms. More and more, as he watched and listened to the beautiful Joanna, he realized which woman had won his heart, baby or no baby. He rubbed his eyes, worried about what Maggie was going through right now, alone in that cabin. He knew it must have taken all the courage and fortitude she had to ride away from him and Joanna, letting them be alone.

"Joanna, tell me why you're here. You might as well know that Maggie is carrying, and I should be with her right now. We have a lot to talk about."

Joanna whirled. "Carrying!" She shook her head. "Good Lord, Sage. *You?*"

Sage didn't feel like explaining. Joanna could never understand what Maggie had been through. "Yeah, *me*," he lied. "The kid is mine, and I mean to do right by it." For Maggie's sake, he didn't want anyone knowing any different. It was then it struck him that he could love Maggie's baby, because *Maggie* loved it. He came even closer and trapped Joanna against the wall. "Now, for the last time, tell me the truth. Are you here because you're broke again?"

She looked at him, wide-eyed. "Please don't be angry."

He leaned down and kissed her roughly, and in that moment, he knew the magic was gone. He pulled away, grasping her arms. "Out with it. How much do you need?"

She hung her head and sighed. "When I went back to San Francisco, I… I met someone. He was from a wealthy family, and he owned businesses, or so I thought. I… married him. He turned out to be a gambler… and he used up all my money, and then left me. Now I'm twice divorced."

Sage turned away with a groan, realizing she couldn't help how she was raised any more than he could do anything about his own background. Joanna needed "things," a fancy life. She'd do anything to get them. She was who she was, and they couldn't be more different.

"I need enough to start a finishing school." She sobbed. "I know I could do well at something like that. I promise to use the money well, Sage, put it to good use so I'll never be broke again." She looked at him pleadingly. "I'm sorry. I honestly wanted to try again when I first came here. I mean, I was out of money and needed a place to live, but I wanted to do it the right way—be your wife again. You're my only real friend. But after a couple of weeks out here, I knew nothing had changed, and that I just can't live this life. I stayed on, hoping once you got back I'd fall into your arms, and that would help me want to stay. When I saw that woman… the way you looked at each other… I knew there was something strong between you… something you and I never had. I knew it was truly over between us. I thought maybe after being alone together for a while that would change, but I can see in your eyes that it won't. I'm not meant for a man like you, and you aren't meant for a woman like me."

She took a handkerchief from the waist of her skirt and wiped her eyes. "So yes, I need money. I'm sorry, Sage. I didn't know where else to turn. I thought about bringing a lawyer with me, so that if you wouldn't give me the money, I'd threaten to somehow get you in trouble for the lawless, underhanded way you built this ranch. But then, I figured that if I brought a lawyer along, you might have slit his throat and thrown him over a cliff or something."

Sage grinned, remembering Cutter. "That's a real possibility. I don't know one man out here who welcomes the sight of a lawyer. But considering that threat, maybe *you're* the one I should throw over a cliff."

Joanna raised her chin defiantly. "Sage Lightfoot, you are so bad." She looked him over appreciatively. "And yet so good." She sauntered past him to the fireplace. "You're a lot more man than I could ever handle." She studied the bobcat head mounted over the fireplace mantel. "I'm amazed that that little bit of a woman you've only known for two months is able to take you on and win you over like she has." She sighed and faced him. "I don't suppose you could spare two thousand dollars?"

Sage shook his head in wonder. The woman would never change. He wondered now how he could have loved her so much—even considered allowing her back into his life. He supposed the young Sage would always love her, but not the man he'd become. "I came back with fifteen hundred, all that was left of what those outlaws stole. That will have to do. And that will have to be the end, Joanna. I don't want to see you back here again. I intend to start a family, so I won't be handing out money like candy anymore. I'll need it to keep building this ranch. Handle the money right, and you'll be fine."

Joanna nodded. "I know." She stepped closer. "Thank you, Sage."

Sage sighed deeply, thinking how superficial her beauty was. "I'd say you're welcome, but that wouldn't really be true." He turned and headed for the door. Thunder rolled in the distance. A storm was coming... the only thing that frightened Maggie. He should be with her.

"Where are you going?" Joanna asked.

"Where do you think?"

Their gazes held. "If you came to my bed tonight, Sage, I wouldn't turn you away."

"A thank-you gift?"

She smiled. "I guess you could call it that."

He grinned, shaking his head. "Sleep well, Joanna. Be ready to leave in the morning. Joe or Bill can take you where you can catch a train. While you're in town, see about sending a preacher back to Paradise Valley, will you? Maggie and I are going to need one."

"But, Sage... can't we talk some more... for old times' sake?"

More thunder... a flash of lightning. "These are new times, Joanna, and someone in that little cabin out there needs me." He walked out and shut the door.

Fifty

A clap of thunder caused Maggie to jump awake. Other than a faint glow through the grate of the woodstove, the room was dark. It took her a moment to gather her thoughts.

She wasn't sure of the time, but it was dark, and Sage was still at the house with Joanna. Was he in her bed? Had she truly lost him?

Lightning flashed, and a louder clap of thunder caused her to pull a quilt closer around her neck. She thought about that night in the cabin with Sage, when she woke to a storm and was afraid. He'd held her in his strong arms and said he'd protect her. That's when she asked him to make love to her.

What a glorious, magical night that was. She became Sage Lightfoot's woman, and she didn't regret it, even if she'd lost him now.

Rain poured down. She heard footsteps on the stoop outside then. Someone banged on the door. "Maggie, it's me. Let me in."

Sage! Maggie climbed off the rope-spring bed and hurried to unbolt the door. Sage stepped inside and shut the door, then stood there a moment, studying her by the glow of the embers.

"I love you, Maggie Tucker."

His words were like heaven to Maggie.

"I couldn't stand the thought of you being alone in a storm," he continued. "When I watched you ride away this morning, I imagined how it would feel watching you ride out of my life, leaving Paradise Valley. I knew I could never let that happen, or let you be alone out there in the world."

"Sage..."

He swept her into his arms. "I'll never be an easy man to live with, Maggie, but I hope you'll still have me."

"You know I will!" Maggie wrapped her arms around his neck.

"I'll always come for you, Maggie," he told her, his voice gruff with emotion, "just like I've been doing since we met. I'll always be here for you... you and that baby you're carrying."

"Sage, I love you so much!"

Hungry kisses. Breathless wanting.

Sage lifted her and carried her to the bed.

"Sage, what happened with Joanna?"

"It was just like I thought. She needed money. You might have fallen for her tears, but I knew they weren't sincere." He undressed, then moved under the quilt and pulled her into his strong, sure arms. "I'm afraid that the money we recovered will be in Joanna's purse when she leaves in the morning."

"Leaves? For good?"

"For good."

"You mean, after all we went through to get that

money back, you handed it over to Joanna?" Maggie saw by the dim light that he was grinning.

"Would you rather I came over here to tell you Joanna and I were getting back together?"

Maggie wondered if she was dreaming. "Of course not. I wouldn't care if you gave her the whole ranch, and we lived in a tent, if it means we can always be together."

"And that's what I love about you, Maggie Tucker."

Another loud clap of thunder nearly made the cabin shake. Maggie jumped, and Sage wrapped her tightly against him. "I can't live without you, Maggie. You're no ordinary woman, and I'm sure as hell no ordinary man. I guess that means we belong together."

Maggie was afraid to believe any of this. She'd prayed so hard that she wouldn't lose this man. "What about the baby?"

More kisses. "It's mine, and no man or woman is ever going to know any different—ever. Neither will the baby. He or she will grow old never knowing I'm not the father."

A tear slipped down Maggie's cheek. "You're *sure* you can love the baby?"

"I can love anything you love. The old life is gone, Maggie. We'll start a new one together—right here in Paradise Valley." He kissed her again, kissed away her tears.

"You'll never regret this, Sage. I'll make the best ranch wife you—"

He cut her off with another hungry kiss, moving his hands under her hips. Mating with this man seemed as natural as breathing. He was beautiful in soul, wild in spirit, and achingly handsome from head to toe.

They were sealing a pact. Sage made up his mind and had chosen Maggie Tucker. They'd known each other a little over two months, but the time they'd spent together, the things they'd been through, made it seem like a lifetime.

For Maggie, this place wasn't called Paradise just because of the incredible beauty of the land. Her own paradise was right here in Sage Lightfoot's arms, and she was never going to let go, no matter what hardships might lie in the future. They'd face them together.

A fierce storm raged outside the little cabin, but this time Maggie was not afraid.

Acknowledgments

A good deal of Rosanne's research for *Paradise Valley* is based on her own travels as well as a book titled *The Outlaw Trail (A Journey Through Time)* by Robert Redford (Grosset & Dunlap Publishers, 1976).

Are You In Love With Love Stories?

Here's an online romance readers club that's just for YOU!

Where you can:

- **Meet** great *authors*
- **Party** with new *friends*
- **Get** new *books* before everyone else
- **Discover** great ***new reads***

All at incredibly BIG savings!

Join the party at DiscoveraNewLove.com!

Thunder on the Plains

by Rosanne Bittner

In a land of opportunity

Sunny Landers wanted a big life—as big and free as the untamed land that stretched before her. Land she would help her father conquer to achieve his dream of a transcontinental railroad. She wouldn't let a cold, creaky wagon, murderous bandits, or stampeding buffalo stand in her way. She wanted it all—including Colt Travis.

All the odds were against them

Like the land of his birth, half-Cherokee Colt Travis was wild, hard, and dangerous. He was a drifter, a wilderness scout with no land and no prospects hired to guide the Landers' wagon train. He knew Sunny was out of his league and her father would never approve, but beneath the endless starlit sky, anything seemed possible…

"Bittner has a knack for writing strong, believable characters who truly seem to jump off the pages."—Historical Novel Review

"I hated having to put it down for even one second."—Romancing the Book

For more Rosanne Bittner, visit:

www.sourcebooks.com

Wildest Dreams

by Rosanne Bittner

With more than 7 million books in print, RT Book Reviews Career Achievement Award–winning author Rosanne Bittner is beloved by fans for her powerful, epic historical romances.

Lettie McBride knew that joining a wagon train heading West was her chance to begin anew, far from the devastating memories of the night that had changed her forever. She didn't believe she could escape the pain of innocence lost, or feel desire for any man...until she meets Luke Fontaine.

Haunted by his own secrets, Luke could never blame Lettie for what had happened in the past. One glance at the pretty red-haired lass was enough to fill the handsome, hard-driving pioneer with a savage hunger.

Against relentless snows, murderous desperadoes, and raiding Sioux, Luke and Lettie will face a heart-rending choice: abandon a lawless land before it destroys them, or fight for their...Wildest Dreams.

"Extraordinary for the depth of emotion."*—Publishers Weekly*

www.sourcebooks.com

Heart of a Texan

by Leigh Greenwood

In the wrong place...

Roberta didn't mean to hurt anyone. But the night that masked bandits raided her ranch, it was hard to tell friend from foe. She didn't know Nate Dolan was only trying to help when she shot him in the chest. And when he offers to help her catch the culprits, she only feels guiltier. The absolute least she can do is nurse the rugged cowboy back to health...

with all the right moves

Nate has been on the vengeance trail so long, he nearly forgot what a real home looked like. And Roberta is mighty fine incentive to stay put for a while—even if she has a stubborn streak as wide as the great state of Texas. She might be convinced she's healing the wound in his chest, but neither of them know she's also soothing the hurt in his heart.

"Readers will enjoy the battle of wits between these two stubborn protagonists."—RT Book Reviews, *4 Stars*

"Strap yourself in for a wild ride with this cowboy and the stubborn love of his life."—Fresh Fiction

For more Leigh Greenwood, visit:

www.sourcebooks.com

Texas Pride

by Leigh Greenwood

A Prince Among Men

Carla Reece had never met anyone more infuriating in her life. The blond giant who swaggered up to her door had no right to take over half her ranch—no matter how stupid her brother had been gambling it away in a high-stakes poker game. Her new foreman claimed to be some foreign royalty who promised to leave in a year. Still, a year was way too long to spend with a man who made her madder than a wet hen and weak in the knees all at the same time.

A Hellion Among Women

Ivan may have charmed everyone in town into thinking he was the perfect gentleman, but Carla knew better. There had to be a chink in his armor—a red-hot passion under that calm, cool gaze. But once she finds it, she may be in for more than she ever bargained for…

Praise for Leigh Greenwood:

"For a fast-paced story of the Wild West, Leigh Greenwood is one of the best."—RT Book Reviews

For more Leigh Greenwood, visit:

www.sourcebooks.com

About the Author

Award-winning novelist Rosanne Bittner is highly acclaimed for her thrilling love stories and historical authenticity. Her epic romances span the West—from Canada to Mexico, Missouri to California—and are often based on personal visits to each setting. She lives in Michigan with her husband and two sons. You can learn much more about Rosanne and her books through her website at www.rosannebittner.com and her blog at www.rosannebittner.blogspot.com. Be sure to visit Rosanne on Facebook and Twitter!